Mafia Property

Dark Mafia Romance

Boston Irish Mafia Romance
Book 2

Jamila Jasper

Edited by
Haley O.

www.jamilajasperromance.com

ISBN: 979-8-3303-6251-6

Ingram Spark.

Thank you to my Patreon subscribers for your support with this book.

❀ Created with Vellum

Boston Irish Mafia Romance Series

Mafia Playmate

Mafia Property

Mafia Surrogate

Mafia Possession

Mafia Stalker

Click here for the complete collection:

www.jamilajasperromance.com/catalog

Description

Years ago, Darragh Murray broke her heart.
They hooked up after a drunken, awkward night.
He used her.
He took her v-card.
He told her he never wanted to see her again.

Darragh left Kamari heartbroken.

He's back after all this time and wants only one thing.
Her. Her body. Her womb.

Kamari doesn't know why he chose her after all this time.
She wants nothing to do with Darragh Murray.

The mob boss wants his second chance.
His baby.
The family he should have had.

He'll never let Kamari go again.

Thank you to all my patrons for your support with this story.
www.patreon.com/jamilajasper

Thank you to my most supportive readers:

Gwendolyn, King Turtle 22, Jessica Lawrence, Nic, JustChill, Dashauna, Atira, TheeLastHokage, Yvonne K., Chrissy, Janelle, Rian, LaRonda, Deanna, Dlawson382, Jasmine, Haley, Belinda, Sercee, Yvonne, Jadclock, Farah, Tumiya, Quin, J.Payton, Geek Girl, Ashley, Rubi, Pilar, Sandra, June, Anni, Shannet, Joneesa, GlitzyHydra, Amanda, Barbara, Brianna, Jamica, Lyons, Mary Ann, Marketia, SarahD, LoverofHawaiiHearts, Cortney, Yolanda, Monagirl, Dianna, Mary, Amna, Nysta, Fayola, Ty, Shyra, Andi-Mariee, Keisha, Jennett, Fredericka, Candece, Lydia, Sabrina, JM, Jackie, Mo, Ashaunte, Tolu, Lori, Dionne, ZLB, Nicol, Elbert, Jesi, Brenda, Desiree, LaShan, Only1ToniD, Debbie, Tiffanie, Shawnte, Lisema, Christine, Trinity, Monica, Juliette, Letetia, Margaret, Dash, Maxine, Sheron, Javonda, Pearl, Kiana, Shyan, Jacklyn, Amy, Julia, Colleen, Natasha, Yvonne, Brittany, June, Ashleigh, Nene, Nene, Deborah, Nikki, DeShaunda, Latoya, Shelite, Arlene, Judith, Mary, Shanida, Rachel,Damzel, Ahnjala, Kenya, Momo, BJ, Akeshia, Melissa, Tiffany, Sherbear, Nini, Curtresa, Regina, Ashley, Mia, Sydney, Sharon, Charlotte, Assiatu, Regina, Romanda, Catherine, Gaynor, BF, Tasha, Henri, Sara, skkent, Rosalyn, Danielle, Deborah, Kirsten, Ana, Taylor, Charlene Louanna, Michelle, Tamika, Lauren, RoHyde, Natasha, Shekynah, Cassie, Dreama, Nick, Gennifer, Rayna, Jaleda, Anton, Kimvodkna, Jatonn, Anoushka, Audrey, Valeria, Courtney, Donna, Jenetha, Ayana, Kristy, FreyaJo, Grace, Kisha, Stephanie E., Amber, Denice, Marty, LaKisha, Latoya, Natasha, Monifa, Alisa, Daveena,

Desiree, Gerry, Kimberly, Stephanie M., Tarah, Yolanda, Kristy, Gary, Janet, Kathy, Phyllis, Susan

Thank you to my Patrons *for allowing me to use your names to name some supporting characters after you!*

I offer this fun little option for patrons who are at the $10+ tiers behind the scenes.
Thank you also to everyone who helped name the other characters in this book.
🖤

Content Awareness

Read this passage if you require content warnings for sensitive material. I do not give detailed content warnings that will spoil the plot, but be aware of this note.

This is a mafia romance story with dark themes including potentially triggering content of **all** varieties, violence, frank discussions and language surrounding bedroom scenes and race.
All characters in this story are 18+
Sensitive readers, be cautioned about some of the detailed romantic material in this dark but *extremely hot romance novel.*

Part One

Chapter One
Darragh Murray

Darragh \d(a)-rra-gh\ an Irish name meaning oak.

Then

It's my twenty-fourth birthday party. Rian just got out of jail for assaulting that officer. We have an impressive fucking boat in the Boston harbor. Pa and I both love boats – it's the one thing only the two of us share, and this yacht is fucking stunning. The Dreamline 34 double-decker has been a dream for a while. With an over $8 million price tag, I'd rather rent this one for my birthday weekend than go through the headache of owning it, but man this boat is fucking beautiful.

My dad would *love* to get his hands on one of these. He just wouldn't like what we've done with it. I have a DJ on both decks and the boat is fucking *packed* for my party tonight. It's Rian's first night out since getting out of jail and he needs this just as much as I do. He needs *women*. Real women. That's the part dad wouldn't approve of – the diverse women from Boston wearing barely anything strutting around the decks.

I've got Michelle, so I can't do anything, but it doesn't hurt to look right? I'm doing the right thing by sticking with an Irish girl.

What dad doesn't know won't hurt him anyway. My mob boss father is away in Dublin, my older brother Aiden, the stick in the mud, is doing business out of state, and I just won my last boxing match ever. I'm officially retired. Everything's perfect tonight. I throw back a shot of Fireball Whiskey with my training partner, Tavarius. I'm too drunk for the shot to burn on the way down. Tavarius doesn't even flinch as he chases his shot with another shot. *That man is fucking crazy.*

"Have you seen my sister?" Tavarius asks once he polishes off the shots, glancing around the deck. I shade my eyes from the sunset with a flat palm and search for Kamari on the deck above. Keeping track of Kamari is Tavarius' full-time job.

"Nope. She's probably moping around somewhere. She hates parties," I say to him, trying to comfort him with the truth. His dorky little sister who just got back to Boston from her first semester at college can't be far, and I haven't seen her all night. She's not the type of girl to go crazy at parties.

"Yeah, you haven't met the new Kamari," Tavarius responds. "She's gone ape shit since college, man. She could be anywhere getting up to all types of shit."

"She's eighteen and she's stuck on a boat. What type of trouble could she really get into, huh?"

"Whatever, man. I gotta find her. You have another shot. Enjoy the party. Try not to screw around with anyone."

I ignore him and let him wander off to search for his sister. I don't want to talk to anyone else here. I'd rather be in the boxing ring or talking about boxing than getting smashed, but I have a black eye, I'm fucked up everywhere, and if I don't get black out drunk, I won't be able to stay asleep through the night because of the pain that comes with healing all these injuries.

It's been months since I've seen Kamari. I didn't see her get on the boat at the docks and I haven't seen her wandering around either of the decks. I bet Tavarius' kid sister is the same little girl I remember – buck teeth, glasses, skinny as a stick. That's the teenager I remember when I hauled her ass off to college last August.

Tavarius goes downstairs to search for his sister and I go upstairs to burn off some of the liquor in me on the dancefloor. He can handle tracking his sister down in a confined space like this. Kamari. Probably for the best if I didn't see her.

She's always had a crush on me and I've always ignored it. Kamari just isn't the type of woman I can ever date seriously. It's not allowed and it's not my preference to make more trouble for myself than women are worth.

She's a sweet girl, but Kamari isn't fit to be a Murray for several reasons. She's too dark. Yes, she's several shades lighter than Tavarius, and she has this pale coppery complexion but very dark features otherwise. She has a large ass, boobs, curves that make guys stare. And then lips. Fuck, she has big full lips.

Inappropriately dark features, all of them.

You can be friends with them, but you can't screw them or marry them or involve them in our business. Dad's wise words, and he's right. I don't want to end up like Rian, stuck with a Hispanic toddler – I think my niece's name is Tegan – that he can barely take care of because he's spent so much time in court and jail.

As I ascend to the top deck with the rowdier partiers like my brother Callum, I hear a woman's voice shrieking with excitement and an excited cheer from the crowd. What the fuck is going on up here? I steady myself against the railing when I spot Tavarius' missing sister.

This is *not* the Kamari that I remember. Holy shit. She shrieks again and pours another shot of vodka down her throat. Evie's brother-in-law, Seamus, grinds up behind her and Kamari positions her hands on her thighs, arches her back and shakes her ass all over him.

Instant outrage surges through me. *What the fuck is she doing?* She's only eighteen and she's taking shots plus grinding on a guy old enough to be her fucking dad. Kamari looks different too. She's clearly lost the glasses, fixed her charming bunny rabbit front teeth, grew a couple inches and she isn't stick thin anymore. Kamari has curves. An *ass.* She's still short as fuck, but her body looks more grown up and fluffy.

Her ass bounces against Seamus and he puts his hands on her waist. I can't fucking take it anymore. Without thinking, I push through the crowd of my party guests, mostly guys from the gym, their girlfriends, family, and far too many business associates.

I wrap my hand forcefully around her forearm. *No.* She can't be doing this.

"Darragh! What the hell are you doing?" she shrieks. It crosses my mind for a second that I'm too drunk to handle this right now, but I don't care. I have to get her away from him. Several guests start laughing. The DJ keeps playing a popular rap song that awakens the crowd. Bodies gyrate around us with enthusiasm, but as far as I'm concerned, there's only one woman on my boat. I'm able to drag her outside of the crowd before she really starts to lose it.

Kamari shrieks and pushes my chest with her free hand, struggling to get away from me. I don't want her to succeed so I clamp down harder. A possessive urge demolishes all my common sense as I grab her like she's my property. It's too possessive. *I have a girlfriend. Michelle is Irish. She's right for me.*

This is the first time I've seen her since she went off to college, so it's been months since our last interaction. I don't expect to meet fierce Kamari tonight, but she's livid that I've dared to touch her and drag her away from shaking her ass all over an Irish gangster.

My body's reaction to her squirming nearly causes me to let go. I can't help but notice how her skin doesn't change color as I squeeze her. She remains a pale cinnamon shade with only slight reddening where I grip her tightly.

That doesn't stop her from thrashing like I've broken her flesh open.

Kamari yells at me, "Let go of me!"

She's eighteen now, so it shouldn't surprise me that she's even more stubborn and independent than I remember. Her pouty face doesn't make me want to give into her at all. She doesn't know what sort of trouble she could get in with my family. I obey the laws of my family and blood purity will always be my priority, but that doesn't mean I hurt people for their skin color.

I'm not like my older brother Aiden, and I'm definitely not like Rian. Any anger, any loathing I have towards anyone else, I eliminate in the boxing ring. None of the men in my family are above hurting her because of her skin color. My friends tend to be more open minded, but I can't account for the other Murray folks. Kamari isn't like the other girls on this yacht. She's too naive to notice evil in people.

"No fucking way, kid," I grunt, fighting back against her. It's effortless, but I let her feel like she has a chance against me for a few seconds before taking control.

I wrap my arms around her waist and despite her protests, I throw Kamari over my shoulder and carry her downstairs to the deck of the party boat with all the bedrooms. She fights and screams at me the entire way. Her insults are quite colorful. The last time I held her at all, she was a little girl. I gave her a piggyback ride at Tavarius' last boxing match in high school. She must be heavier since she's older and she looks thicker in the thighs, but to me she still feels weightless, like it's nothing to carry her.

It's my birthday, so when I planned the rental, I called the biggest room. Rian's room is next to mine, Callum gets the one down the hall, and Tavarius has the room across from Callum.

She's lucky I'm the one who found her and not her brother. He would've beaten the shit out of Seamus and probably tossed his ass in the fucking harbor.

"Let me go you fucking caveman!" Kamari shrieks, her fists beating into my raw, sore back muscles. Even if it hurts like hell, I can't let her go. My heart pounds as I drag her to my bedroom.

"Put me down!" she shrieks again. I grunt and keep carrying her towards my room. I just need to get her out of sight and out of trouble. There's no way I'm putting her down just so she can run off.

She smells like vodka even though she's underage. She shouldn't be drinking. I push the bedroom door open, walk through the doorway, and kick the door shut behind me. Using one hand, I swipe away Michelle's hair curler and bag of makeup from the bed.

I throw Kamari onto the pile of white sheets and she lands with a thump. I can't believe she's acting like this. She's nearly naked, dancing on some older guy and she's *drunk*. I try to calm down and tell myself that she's only eighteen, she's doing what college kids do.

That doesn't fucking work and I don't sound calm at all when I open my mouth.

"What the hell were you doing out there? Tavarius is looking everywhere for you."

She refuses to talk to me and glares at me like I'm the bad guy in this situation. She's drunk and messing with shit she doesn't understand – shit that could really mess with her. I'm just trying to protect her. Why the hell is she so mad? I definitely remember her being fierce, but not like this. Her brother was right, she's different since she went off to college.

"Let me out of here, Darragh. It's none of your business and it's none of my brother's business what I'm doing. I just want to get drunk and have a good time."

"You're eighteen. You shouldn't be drinking. Let me go get your brother…"

I start for the door, even if I know I'll have to lock her in to keep her from escaping. That should make her scream like a wildcat. Kamari lunges forward and grabs my forearm instead.

"Wait, Darragh, don't get Tavarius."

"Kamari, let go of me," I say calmly, trying to peel her off me as she drags my arm and attempts to pull me away from the door with all the force she can muster. What the hell is her problem now?

"You can't go get him."

"What the hell do you want then?" I grunt, trying to pry Kamari's hands off me. She ups the ante by slumping to the ground and wrapping her arms around my leg. *Christ.*

"Kamari, get off me," I say sternly as I try to unwrap her from my leg. I drag my body towards the door, but I can't move without hurting her.

"You can't tell him I've been drinking again. You can't…"

"I won't go to him but you have to stop touching me. Get off. Now."

My stern voice causes her to scramble away and gaze up at me with large brown eyes, set far apart on her golden-honey face. I suppress the flash of emotion I experience when she gazes at me. I bite my tongue to avoid my mind wandering anywhere it shouldn't and try to focus on getting Kamari on her feet and sober within the next thirty minutes.

If we're lucky, her brother will get too drunk to look for her.

"I promised Tavarius I wouldn't drink tonight. You can't tell him," she says, slurring her words. She can barely string a sentence together but she was upstairs grinding her hips all over one of the most dangerous men in the city. I swear, I could sock the shit out of him just for looking at her.

"He'll find you eventually even if I don't bring him down here. What the hell were you thinking, Kamari?"

She swallows and scrambles backward so she's sitting on the bed. She buries her head in her hands and sits there for so long I think she's trying to hold back getting sick all over the boat. I put my hand on her back and she groans.

"No," she says. "Don't touch me, that'll make it worse."

"You gonna throw up, kid?"

"No," she whimpers. "No... But Darragh, I love you. I can't take it anymore, I love you."

Fuck. Not this again...

"My girlfriend is gonna have a problem with that, just like I have a problem with it. Kamari, we've talked about this. You're my best friend's little sister, I have a girlfriend, I'm way too fucking old for you and–

Before I can finish my sentence, my girlfriend bursts through the door. Michelle struts in, towering over Kamari in black high-heels. She has legs for days and she's skinny as a stick.

"Darragh," she says. "I've been looking everywhere for you? What the hell are you doing back here?"

She stumbles as the boat moves and leans against the wall. She's even more drunk than I am. Kamari groans and holds her head in her hands. She really is going to be sick.

"Kamari had a little too much to drink. Can you go get her brother? He's above deck."

"I don't want to talk to him, D. Molly's here. She'll tell my dad if she sees me talking to a black guy and he'll kick my ass."

I've fucking had it with Michelle.

"Then get his attention some other way, Michelle. The kid's gonna be sick, can you hurry?"

Kamari groans again and retches on the floor by the bed. Michelle wrinkles her nose and disappears to avoid the vomit. I push Kamari's waist-length curls away from her face and hold them back in a large handful behind her head.

"What were you thinking?"

"I just wanted to talk to you."

"We don't have anything to talk about, Kamari. You and I are never going to happen."

"You can't deny our connection, Darragh."

She's so drunk, she doesn't have a clue what she's saying. The kid is eighteen and she's clearly not experienced enough to hold her liquor if she's acting like this. What the hell was Kamari thinking? Anything could happen to her when she's drunk like this.

"Michelle will be back with your brother before you know it. I'll get you some water. You lie down and settle your stomach, okay?"

"No," she moans. "I'm not doing that until you admit that... admit that on some level you have feelings for me, Darragh..."

I don't have feelings for her. Even if I did, it wouldn't matter. She's black. I'm white. In Boston, that means you live in different worlds that hardly intersect outside of the world of sports. Her brother gets it, I get it, Michelle gets it. Kamari lives in a dream world where she can dance with white boys and get away with it.

I WON'T ADMIT to anything, especially not something like caring about Kamari, like wishing we could have been together – something which could get both of us killed because of my family and who we are...

I'm drunk, but I'm not that drunk.

Chapter Two
Kamari Roberts

Now

I have to quit my job.

Go to Cornell, they said. Your life will be easy once you go to an Ivy League school. Yeah, that was a lie. After graduating with $218,272 in student loan debt for my fancy degree, I got a job at a prestigious consulting firm where I currently work eighty hours a week, my boss refers to me as Jamal (a boy's name) despite having interacted with me on several occasions, and I only make $5,000 after taxes.

That sounds like good money, right? Except out of that $5,000, I spend $2,279 on my student loan and $1,700 a month on the four bedroom apartment I share with a couple of my coworkers, who are other recent college graduates. Our place at least has a *great* view and even if it's hard living with strangers, we get along just fine.

We pay our rent to our "house mom", Maggie Plyman, who keeps our chore chart organized, the compost heap empty, and the kitchen sink smelling like Mrs. Meyer's lemon soap.

The apartment is expensive, but it's in the city, and it's easier to commute to work on foot than bother with the traffic around here. I don't see the point in having a car in Boston. If I need one in an emergency, there's always Tavarius, who would be happy to drive down from Shirley, even if he would act like it's the biggest deal in the world. He doesn't box anymore, so he left the high rents for the suburbs.

The only reason I'd need a car would be to get to parts of the city I have no business being in anymore.

This city is *expensive* and once I get my big expenses out of the way, and put a tiny amount of savings, I have nothing left. Tavarius thinks I should move to a cheaper neighborhood, but if I give up more of my time to commuting, I'll lose more of myself than I already have.

I have savings to last two months, which should be plenty of time to find another job and get on my feet. It's hard to explain what my job *is* exactly, but I can ask Maggie for help with the resume stuff. She's good with that and she would totally understand how soul-crushing these consulting jobs can get.

I hear Holly coming up the stairs to the apartment door. I can tell it's Holly from the heavy footsteps and because she always leaves in the morning to go for a run. The apartment door creaks open and Holly carefully shuts it. She's the only one who shuts the door care-fully, so it's definitely her.

I can hear her panting in the kitchen as I round the corner. She's dressed in a peach-colored skin-tight work out set and her ponytail swishes as she slams an envelope on the table.

"Have you seen Maggie this morning?" she says. "Look at this."

"Past due." I read the envelope out loud. "What's that about?"

"Doesn't have a name on it, just our unit number. There's another one."

She moves the envelope to reveal another equally scary looking envelope with bright orange text and an "open immediately" sticker across the front.

"I've never seen one of these in the mail box before," I say to her. "I'll check Maggie's room to see if she's up."

"Get Seth up, too," she calls to me as I head towards Maggie's room. Seth's room is the first door down the hall so I go to him first. I rap gently on his door. I can hear Seth grunting his way through his morning push ups on the other side of the door.

"Seth, get up. We've got a nastygram." The grunting stops, and a couple seconds later he opens the door.

"What?" Seth asks.

"Hate mail. Go out to the kitchen. Holly found something weird in the mailbox. I'm waking Maggie up."

"I do *not* want to see Holly right now," Seth groans. "I'll come with you to get Maggie."

What happened with him and Holly? I don't bother asking because we have an important task ahead. I let Seth towel off the gross sweat in his hair and all over his upper body. He's in really good shape and I don't know how he stays motivated to maintain his physique like this. Since I turned eighteen, all I've done is put on weight.

Seth leads the way to Maggie's door and knocks. It's quiet on the other side.

"She's normally awake right now," Seth says before knocking again and calling Maggie's name out loud. There's still no response from the other side of the door.

"Did she go for a run or something?" I suggest, even if it's a ridiculous suggestion. Seth rolls his eyes dramatically and makes a tutting noise, confirming the suggestion is ridiculous. Maggie prefers hanging out at home, cooking and crafting, to anything athletic. Holly and Seth are the house athletes.

"Guys!" Holly yells. "Guys, where are you?!"

"That's it," Seth says, holding Maggie's door handle. "I'm opening the door."

He pushes the door open and there's nothing inside Maggie's bedroom.

"What the fuck," Seth says out loud. The room seems to spin. There are no sheets. No shoes. There isn't a laptop on the desk. Her prayer flags and Himalayan salt lamp are gone. The deck of tarot cards we used to predict the future of my love life are nowhere to be found. There's no sign that Maggie Plyman ever lived in this room.

Seth flicks the light on as if that will make Maggie's stuff reappear.

"Holy fuck," he says. "Holly's gonna lose her fucking mind."

We walk quickly back to the kitchen. Holly's pale as she grips an opened envelope in one hand and a pink sheet of paper in the other.

"She's gone," Seth says, avoiding eye contact with Holly as he strides across the room and grabs the paper out of her hands. He scans it and then swears loudly. Several times.

"What's going on?"

"I don't even want to tell you," Holly says. "This is bad, Seth."

"Yes, Holly. It's very fucking bad. Where's the other envelope? That bitch…"

He hands me the sheet of paper so I can see for myself. My throat knots and it feels like there's a heavy stone sinking to the bottom of my stomach. *No. This isn't possible.*

The letter demands that we pay $33,600 in rent, approximately 6 months of back pay *and* we face immediate eviction. We each paid depending on the size of our rooms, except Maggie who paid $500 because she took on the role of property manager. Holly shreds open the other bills. My palms instantly glisten with sweat as I set the paper down on the kitchen counter.

"I don't understand," I whisper, although of course I understand. I just can't fucking believe this is happening.

"That bitch pocketed our rent money and took off," Seth says. "I'm calling my dad. My uncle's a small town lawyer out in Deerfield, but he has connections in the city. She's not going to get away with this."

Holly lets out a panicked yelp as she reads through the contents of the other envelopes. I take each piece of paper once she's done with it. Three months of unpaid electricity bills. Two quarters of unpaid water bills. A threatened fine over trash disposal.

"We have 24 hours to come up with the money and get out of here."

"That's easy," Seth says pompously. "We split it three ways. I'll call my dad to get my share. Holly, Kamari, you can handle this, right?"

"Yeah," Holly says. "I'll get my half from my savings and call my mom to see if she'll unlock the summer home in Newport. I'll stay there until I can find a new place."

My roommates both have rich parents helping them out. I don't have that. If I called Tavarius and asked him for over $50, he would laugh and hang up the phone. I have a savings account, but this plus everything in my checking account would leave me with $34 to get through the rest of the month.

Chapter Two

It's like someone hit me in the chest. I answer in a strangely numb fury.

"Yeah. I got this."

"We need to pack our things and get our lawyers," Seth says firmly, as if everyone just has lawyers on retainer.

"Should we go to the police?" Holly says. "I mean, where is she? I'm calling my therapist and then I'm crafting a strongly worded text message."

"We don't have time for that, Holly," Seth says. "We need to get our shit, get out of here, and then we can handle that stuff. If these people find us in here… they could repossess our stuff or something. We have to move."

I don't bother texting Tavarius until I have everything I can fit in three suitcases packed. I have to leave almost everything else behind. Seth promises to contact the rental agency and let them know to expect our payments via eCheck online. I'll have to drag my things to Tavarius' house and he won't want me there for long. Not just him. Caitlin won't want me there either. My brother's girlfriend hates my guts.

Sucking up to her will be my worst nightmare come to life.

Chapter Three
Darragh

Then

She passes out after a glass of water and I wait, like a fucking idiot, for over forty-five minutes for Michelle. Where the fuck is she? I text her. Then I call Michelle, but she doesn't answer. The boat isn't that fucking big. I text my girlfriend again, my annoyance growing as my slow crawl towards sobriety heightens my awareness of my boxing injury.

Ugh. My eye feels like shit. My face feels like shit. A tiny snort from the bed takes my eyes off my phone for a second. This girl Kamari scares the crap out of me. The things she says, the way she acts like there are no consequences for anything...

Her brother is right to be so damn protective of her. Without someone looking after her, Kamari's the type of woman to keep diving headfirst into trouble. She's always in way over her head, especially tonight. I glance over at Kamari sleeping on the bed, sprawled out like a toddler napping on the couch at a family barbecue.

It's weird that I miss her dorky glasses and even her buck teeth, but the college girl I found shaking her ass on a mobster looks beautiful. Her brother should hire spies to keep an eye on her at college because she's... *something*.

I don't have feelings for Kamari, don't get me wrong. She's black, so it's not like I think she compares to Michelle. I believe what I've been taught. Irish women first. Always. But Kamari has her own charms despite her skin color. It's a pale copper color that can seem dark and bronzed in the summer, but brighter than a new penny in the winter.

She's always had thick, long curls that she dyes a dark maroon color. The hair matches the red undertones in her skin and right now she has *so* much of that skin exposed. Heat prickles around my neck, so I attempt to turn my attention back to my phone without success.

"Kamari," I call out to her, hoping my voice will wake her up. It doesn't. I'd better find Michelle and then find Tavarius to take care of this.

There's no way I can win tonight. I push the door open and look back at her to see if she's stirred at all before I lock her in. She's unconscious and utterly vulnerable with her top pulled up over her navel to expose that smooth light copper skin. Her breasts bulged from her chest with hard nipples sticking out visible for anyone who walked into that room to see. Somewhat reluctantly, I close the door and lock it.

There would be a war if anything happened to her. The blacks around here might not get into mob business, but their families run deep and they protect their own when necessary, especially from the likes of us. You fuck with the wrong family, and you could lose all your teeth.

We're not the only predators out here, and her brother has been in the boxing world for so long that he's a danger to any asshole who decides to touch her. No one will get the chance tonight.

I stop by the bar to grab a bottle of Wild Turkey whiskey from the bartender. I live for whiskey, and the pain in my head is getting too extreme to handle without some more alcohol. There's loud dancing above deck and everyone seems to be enjoying the party. I don't think Michelle would be there looking for Tavarius. She would have already found him.

I step up to the top deck and search around. There aren't so many people that I wouldn't be able to easily pick out a black guy and a very blond white girl with eyes like the summer sky. Neither of them are there. They could be in the living quarter's downstairs.

Once we dock, my closest friends are staying on the boat overnight for another day of partying and getting away from the bullshit back in the city. We have money, champagne, music, drugs and women. Everything you need for a good time. I'm officially retired which means I get to stop treating my body like a fucking experiment. I'm living the fucking life.

I wander downstairs, still drunk enough to stumble into the walls for support, when I hear loud moaning from a bedroom at the end of the hallway, one floor down from the room where Kamari lies passed out from her foolish drunken escapades. The moaning gets louder as I approach the furthest room at the end of the hall and the moans sound familiar. That must be why I move closer to the door. *Is that her…?* I don't want to fucking believe it.

And it's the craziest fucking reaction, but I have to know if it's even possible. Sorry to the sad motherfuckers I walk in on if I misplaced the sound.

I push open the first door and my stomach drops. There's my girlfriend, on her back, with Seamus on his knees between her legs.

Her pale thighs are spread wide and she doesn't notice me at first. She doesn't hear the door clicking open. Neither of them hear a fucking thing until after I've reached for my gun, taken it out of my pants, and rack the slide of the pistol. It's a Murray party, of course I'm armed. Michelle hears the gun click and looks up from her position on the bed. Everyone in her family is in this life, so she recognizes the noise.

She shrieks once she sees me, but I already have the gun leveled at the bastard's head. I try not to look at her, but I fail of course. She has his spit on her thighs. That perfect, blonde hair is in a scraggly mess. Her eyes are terrified.

"D, don't shoot him! It's not what it looks like!"

It looks like Seamus Doyle had his tongue in her cunt. *I can handle this. I won't be reckless.*

If I fire a gunshot, everyone on this ship will know. There will be witnesses, Michelle will be a witness, and then there's Kamari upstairs. Who knows what will happen to her if I fire a gun and cause pandemonium. I'm angry. So fucking angry, I could just pull the trigger. My chest heaves as I try to keep my hand off the trigger with all my morals. All my training. I was born without Aiden's self-control so they put me in the boxing ring so I could have a place for my rage. I don't need a gun to do what I need to do. I point it at Michelle.

"Get in the fucking closet, Michelle."

Seamus is too smart or maybe too fucking stupid to do anything. He kneels there frozen, his cheeks red. He exchanges a worried glance with Michelle which only pisses me the fuck off. There's something going on between them and it's either happened tonight for the first time, or it's been happening right under my fucking nose. I can't take it.

"I said get in the fucking closet!" I scream at her. Michelle's face crinkles and reddens with the tension building in her. I put my hand on the trigger and she yelps loudly.

"I'm going!" she yells. "Fuck, D, don't kill him. Please…"

"Quiet," I scream at her. "Shut the fuck up and go into the closet before I blow both of your brains out."

My finger trembles on the trigger and I'm very fucking tempted to make my threats a reality. The room smells like sex. Michelle's familiar scent makes me ill now.

I could shoot him. I could shoot him right now and who would give a fuck about him? I'm Darragh Murray and this humiliation is more than I fucking need right now.

I take the bottle of Wild Turkey and throw it at the wall as Michelle screams and crawls into the closet with her bare cunt and ass exposed. I'm so fucking mad I could hit her. Obviously I don't, but I can barely get a grip on my anger right now.

The boat sloshes and Michelle nearly loses her balance as she shuts the closet door and continues whimpering loudly.

She has a tattoo above her ass of my name. *Darragh.* Seeing it bare turns my stomach completely. I can't even fucking look at her. Once she's in the closet, Seamus balls up his fists like he's going to fight me. Like he could. I've won every boxing match I've ever entered. But boxing matches have rules about going too far. There's nothing holding me back from splitting his jaw open. Or killing him.

I put my gun in my pocket and take a swing at that motherfucker's ugly fucking face. Michelle shrieks as the noise from my fist connecting with his face fills the room. He falls to the bed unconscious from one hit. I don't want him to live.

I hear Michelle scream.

"Don't hurt him!"

I tune her voice out and I punch the guy's face in until he stops moving and his blood soaks the bed. My fists are covered in blood. I know I've gone too far. The guy could be dead.

"Michelle, get out of the closet."

She heaves and sobs loudly. "No," she says. "I'm not coming out there for you to kill me. I'm not."

I can hear her breathing. I want to drag her out of the fucking closet and punish her, but I can't hurt a woman. This... What Seamus did violates every rule of the Irish mob. He may not be a part of our literal family, but he's a part of the mob. *The family.*

You never touch another person's woman unless you want to die. For him to do this to one of our own means I automatically have my father's permission to kill him.

"I'm not gonna kill you. Now get out here."

I can hear her sobbing. I don't care. I grab the handle of the tiny closet and drag Michelle out as she screams. When she sees Seamus lying on the bed soaked in his own blood and the white sheets scarlet, she runs to him and screams his name. She grabs his body and screams, calling me a monster and every name in the book.

I WANT to feel something for her, but I feel nothing. I put my gun to the back of Michelle's head.

"Get up," I say to her calmly. "You're going for a swim, princess."

THERE'S no sound except for Michelle's whimpering.

I open the door and drag Michelle to the lowest possible deck and tell her to jump. She stands trembling at the edge as the Boston air whips around her.

I don't feel anything as I watch her standing at the railing, refusing to look at me.

"You aren't fucking serious, Murray," she says, gripping the railing tightly. Her fingers are ice sheets. The water will be even colder. I don't care if she survives or not.

"You know who I am, Michelle. I'm Padraig Murray's son. You know what that name means in our community. You chose to betray me. Humiliate me…"

I can't continue because she lets out an irritating sob. She didn't look so sorry when I found her. I push the image out of my head.

"Jump," I command her. "If you don't jump, I'll throw you over. You have a better chance of surviving if you do it yourself."

"You're a bastard," she whimpers through loud sobs. I wait for her to climb over the railing and she curses me one more time as she jumps. I wait until I hear a splash and I walk away as she screams. One step away from the railing is all it takes for the noise of the boat to drown her out.

I don't know if she'll make it back to shore. She can swim but… it's Boston. It's always cold here. I return below deck to the hallway where I found her to clean up, and solve the mystery of the noise at the end of the hall. Tavarius pushes the door open, his eyes wide and his body dripping with sweat.

"Yo, were you making all that noise?" I ask him, peering behind him, but discovering nothing.

If there was a woman back there with him, he doesn't drag her out. Tavarius looks me up and down and then looks at the blood on my hands.

"Did you find Kamari?" he asks. *Kamari.*

I SHOULD HAVE BEEN with her tonight. *If only that weren't fucking impossible.*

Chapter Four
Kamari

Now

I make it three days at my brother's house before his girlfriend subtly makes him kick me out.

After a lot of crying and arguing (plus pretty humiliating begging), my brother gives me $750, which is enough to cover the rent of a room for a short amount of time in South Boston. I have that much time to come up with money for the next month – including extra for a security deposit most likely.

I don't want to go back to South Boston, especially because of who I risk running into. My brother doesn't get it. He'll never understand what happened five years ago.

I drag my suitcases up three flights of stairs to the floor of my new apartment. My new roommates aren't home yet, but they don't seem like the type to sit around and talk based on my conversations with them over text message. My bank account is dangerously empty and I still don't have a job.

It takes me several hours to unpack my things, even if I don't have much. I like arranging my bedroom just the way I like it. Even if I don't stay in one place for long, I like the place to be mine. This apartment isn't bad for South Boston. This city has changed a lot since I was a little girl.

I don't walk past Darragh's boxing gym to see if it's still open, but I can't help but wonder. It's been five years. I know he still sees Tavarius from time to time, but they're not as close as they were five years ago. I think it has something to do with Darragh's birthday party. Everything terrible happened that night.

That was the last night I saw him. It was the last night I allowed myself to ever fall in love with him.

I hate him now and I'll always hate him. If I ever see that racist bastard Darragh Murray again, I'll give him a piece of my mind and throw a fist at his face if I can get away with it. I'll make up for every damn thing that happened that night on that stupid boat.

When my roommate gets home, I push the door open to meet her. I'll be living with two girls this time. Kaly Fields towers over me. She's close to six feet tall and she's wearing heels which makes her even taller. She's dressed like a fitness model in a matching lilac athletic suit that hugs her body and pushes her boobs together so they look fake.

As she stands there smacking her gum, I also notice she has a long set of hot pink acrylic nails.

"Kamari, right? Is that you?"

"Yup. Kaly?"

"Oh. My. God. You are so freaking gorgeous. You look like a hot fucking gypsy hippie girl. Your pictures do *not* do you justice," Kaly says. "Welcome home, new roomie!"

She has long eyelashes, pink lip gloss that smells like bubblegum and thick, heavy makeup. I don't bother with all that stuff, but the done up look matches Kaly's bubbly personality. It's always festive when a white girl wears a wig, and Kaly's wig is a pale, pink color and is long enough to just graze her butt.

"So. You said you were in a housing emergency. Our landlord doesn't want anyone taking over that room until he makes repairs," she says. "But we can try to make something work. As long as you have the money by the first, we can be cool."

"Thanks," I answer, feeling warm for a second and maybe like everything would be okay. Boston has a bad reputation sometimes, but people here look out for each other. All of us struggle with the cost of living here at some point or another.

Kaly nods enthusiastically and continues, "I can try to help you get on your feet otherwise. I have lots of friends in this area. Where did you say you were from? I have a baby brain, I swear."

I tell her that I originally grew up in Lawrence. After my parents got divorced, my mom brought me and my brother to South Boston. We went to the local public schools, but Tavarius was always too far ahead of me for us to ever attend school together. Kaly listens intently and then asks me about work.

"I'm unemployed right now," I say to her, trying to act all cool about it. "But I have the money to pay you and get my food, so you have nothing to worry about."

Kaly smiles. "I'm not worried about that. I can help you fix your job problem though. I don't know if it's fancy enough for a college girl like you, but you have the look for it."

"The look for it?"

"I used to work at this one place. I made $1,400 in one night. I was a fucking idiot so I blew it all taking my asshole boyfriend to Florida. But it was amazing."

"If it was so amazing, why don't you work there anymore?"

"Because it's not a job for the faint-hearted."

"The suspense is killing me."

"It'll be better if you go in blind," Kaly says. "I know the manager in charge of doing all the hiring. I'll give you the address, and you can show up there tonight. I'll call him and let him know you're coming."

"What type of job is it? I should at least know that if they're going to be interviewing me."

"It's not the sort of interview you can prepare for," Kaly says. "But if you need money, I promise you'll have every cent you need by the end of a week there. Especially with a butt like that."

"Is this some type of weird modeling gig?"

"It's better than that," Kaly says. Her phone buzzes as several text messages come through in succession.

"Fuck," she says. "That's my boyfriend. He's losing his mind over some... you know what... I'll text you the address, but I can't stay. This fucking asshole..."

Kaly mutters expletives before tapping away on her phone, grabbing her keys and disappearing just as suddenly as she arrived. What the fuck? She looks like a model, but she's all over the place.

MY PHONE BUZZES as her text comes through with the address to the mystery job. When I look up the place, the only thing that comes up is a warehouse. I guess it could be one of those shipping places where you fulfill orders, but that doesn't sound lucrative enough to make $1,400 in a night.

I plug the address into my phone and decide to walk the thirty minutes there instead of getting an Uber. I don't know what to wear, but I dress "business casual" so I can be ready for anything. I have to walk, so I slip into all white Chuck Taylors to make the journey as painless as possible. Before heading out the door, I grab my purse and throw my phone into the main pocket. I trace my steps from what I remember off Google Maps to the address since there aren't many big turns. I have my headphones over my ears and a cheap tote bag slung over my shoulder, blasting *Bed Peace* by Jhene Aiko and Childish Gambino as I walk. Her 2013 album *Sail Out* is my favorite. I know the words to *every* song and the music calms me down as I walk toward this mystery job.

Sure, I just met Kaly, but she wouldn't fuck me over, would she? This must be a pretty good gig and I just have to trust that the universe will take care of me. Maybe it's hippie bullshit, but I believe it. The closer I get to the warehouse, the more questions I have than answers. There aren't many buildings on the side street with the blue and white warehouse. All the cars parked outside are *nice*. There's a brand new red Tesla Model X, a lime green Hummer, a black lifted Ford-F150 truck and three Mercedes Benz sports cars that look like they came in a very expensive set.

I glance between the cars and the warehouse. *What the fuck is this place?* There's a small metal door with a small sign over it that wasn't on my phone's map. The sign says *Harrison Ave.*

That's a weird name for… a warehouse? Or whatever this is.

I stuff my headphones into my bag before pulling open the metal door. The smell of vanilla and cucumber body spray engulfs me in a cloud. The room is dark, illuminated only by red lights. Before I can take a step inside, a gigantic bald man who's about 6'5" and with tattoos covering every inch of his exposed skin emerges from the dark. My eyes haven't adjusted yet so it seems like he materializes out of nowhere.

"Hey, miss. What're you doing here? Are you lost?"

"No. My friend Kaly told me there were job openings here and you do walk-in interviews."

He makes a weird noise and gestures for me to walk inside before shutting the door behind me.

"Give your eyes a second to adjust to the light," he says. He coughs and wipes his forehead with a napkin. As my eyes adjust to the light, I see him giving me a once over. He chuckles.

"Your friend Kaly must have a sense of humor."

"Excuse me? Look, do you have any job openings here or not? I'm in a tough situation, so if you don't have anything for me, I'll be on my way."

"Sorry miss," he says. "Listen, don't take off. I didn't mean any harm by it. Just our history with your friend Kaly is... You know what, as long as you're ready to have an interview right away... I'll talk to the boss."

"Thank you...sir?"

"The name's Declan."

"I'm... Kamari."

"Okay," he says. "I'll tell the boss I've got someone here to see him. You look nice. Just be confident, and I'm sure everything will work out great."

His warm demeanor puts me at ease. *Thanks, Declan.* He disappears down one of the dark hallways. My eyes have finally adjusted and I can see that the walls are covered in red velvet. The vanilla smell also gets stronger the longer I'm inside. I hear men with weird accents arguing in a room that must be down one of the dark hallways. I hear other guys who sound like Southies. That accent always makes me think of him all these years later...

· · ·

Kamari

I JUST WANT to forget him already. I'll do *anything* to forget him. Because right now, I could go to him for help. He's still Tavarius' best friend, and out of some fucked up sense of guilt or obligation, he'd help me. But I'll never go back to Darragh Murray.

I'll never look him in the eye again without trying to hurt him.

Chapter Five
Darragh

Now

Declan opens my office door and she struts through like a fallen angel with all the confidence in the world until she notices the person on the other side of the desk. She turns to the door like she's going to run away, but it's too late for Kamari. Declan has already shut the door behind her. She's here, and neither of us can run away from this. When I heard the name, I suspected it might be her but I wasn't prepared to see her after all this time.

I don't know what to say. I want to say nothing, but I'm the boss and it's my job to turn this fucking strip joint around. Dad's in the hospital and Aiden's back in Boston with Valentina, so turning the business around and getting it 'compliant' for the IRS next year is my job.

I didn't know how seeing her would affect me, but this is like a punch to the fucking gut. She glares at me, but neither of us move and both of us are too stubborn to speak. I don't want to be the first, but if I don't take control of this, Kamari will, and the last time I let her have her way – I ruined everything.

.I ruined her.

She looks fucking great though. Too fucking good. My cock wants to respond to her presence, but I focus on analyzing how much she's changed instead of how good she looks. Her hips have filled out even more. She still has that pale, reddish skin, so much brighter than her brothers. Her hair is different. It's even longer and she's committed to that dark red color which shimmers against her very light coppery skin.

She still has those deer-eyes that tilt up and force you to gaze into them and think sinful, traitorous thoughts about your family.

Aiden succumbed to temptation because he's too high-strung. He never lets loose. I'm different. I've fucked women of every race and color. But I've never loved them.

That's the difference with Kamari. That's what makes everything that happened between us so fucking wrong.

"Do you know where you are, Kamari?"

"Hello, Darragh. I should have known you would be camping out in a seedy South Boston warehouse if you weren't dead in a ditch somewhere from an alcohol overdose," Kamari says calmly.

She could scalp someone with her words. I bristle, but I try not to let her get under my skin. I'm the boss here.

"My cousin told me a girl came to the front door looking for a job. Surely, that still applies?"

"McDonalds is probably hiring. I'll see myself out." She turns and starts heading for my office door.

I know this woman. She's *scared.* She's not scared of me, but she's scared of something and after all this time, after all the ways I've hurt her, I want to know *why.* It's not just morbid curiosity. If I can do one thing to make up for how I hurt her, I can do it now.

I whistle sharply. She stops in confusion, but my whistle just alerted Declan outside to barricade the door. I just got my hands on Kamari. I'm not letting her out of my sight until I get to the bottom of what could make Kamari desperate enough to wander into my strip club looking for a job. Who sent her here?

She grabs the door handle and yanks on it, but the handle doesn't budge. It's locked – automatic feature.

"Darragh, let me out of here," she yells. "DECLAN! Declan, help!"

Women. She thinks she can smile and say a few kind words to my bodyguard and win his loyalty? Men are not as simple as women like her think.

"Can you relax? I haven't moved. I don't want to hurt you. I just want to know how you ended up here looking for a job. There's no way in hell I'm hiring you."

"If you aren't hiring me, then there's no point in me being here. And by the way Darragh? Fuck you. You are a completely racist asshole who treats me and other women like dirt. Douchebags like you are going to die completely alone. I hope you rot in hell."

She pauses like she's going to say more. Then she puffs and folds her arms, waiting for my response.

"Did that feel good, princess?"

"Do *not* call me princess," she says. "Don't you ever in your entire life call me princess ever again because I am *not* your princess. Nor will I ever be."

"Fine, Kamari. Since you're interested in entering a business relationship with me, I'll call you by your first name."

"I am not interested in a business relationship," she says. "You barricaded me in here. I've already decided I'd rather settle for minimum wage than disgrace myself working for you as a janitor or whatever the hell job this is."

"Who sent you here?" I ask her, ignoring her carrying on and focusing instead on the question I desperately need answered. Her brother certainly didn't send her to this part of Boston to get a job at a place like this. Kamari could make a lot of money working here but not for the right reasons, and I'd never be able to handle her on that stage.

"My friend Kaly gave me the job referral."

That explains a lot. The Kaly incident should have never happened. She refused to work again after the dick from Baltimore wanted a little more than a blowjob in the back room. The guy didn't make it back across the border to NY State without us kicking the shit out of him, and regardless of us promising extra security, my highest earning girl quit on me.

The last thing she said to me was that men always want what they can't have. Not in those words. She said it more like, "You racist fucks always want exactly what you can't have. Maybe the next girl who walks through those doors should be a Puerto Rican and you can save this shithole for real."

Kaly was worth the headache believe it or not. And Kamari... She's worth way more than this. She might make $700 to $1000 a night working here and she could make more if she offered extras but... I could never watch her do that to herself. The girls that make it in this world were either born cold or had fucked up shit happened to them.

That's not her.

"Interesting. Kamari, do you know that this is a whites-only strip club and that the job you're interviewing for is to become an exotic dancer?"

She turns even redder. She's a burnt copper shade now and her perfect lips painted with purple lipstick part slightly. Words don't come out. So she didn't know what she was signing up for. Kaly probably knew she could never convince a normal girl to come here without keeping some things in the dark.

"I already told you I don't want the job. It's nice to see you've become even more disgusting since I left Boston."

"The clientele are whites only. The girls can be... whatever we like."

"No thank you, Darragh. Coming here was a mistake. I can get back on my feet without your stupid racist strip club job. I went to college. I can handle my shit."

"You went off to college, congrats. Looks like that didn't help you much. You think I'm wrong about so many things, Kamari, but for all your so-called intelligence, you're still in my office begging *me* for a job."

"I'm not begging you for a job you privileged sack of cow dung."

"You're just outright begging for money then?"

"I don't need anything from you except for you to let me out."

Why the hell does she want to leave so badly? Doesn't she give a crap that it's been so long since we've seen each other? My hair is longer now. I could never grow it out for boxing. I'm also more muscular since I don't have to make weight classes anymore.

I'm a completely different guy. Smoother. Smarter. Better.

There's no way she still hates me after five years. There's no way she doesn't still have feelings for me beneath those deer-eyes ruined by rage. I know Kamari. She's still a hopeless romantic at heart.

"You need something from me. That's why you're here."

"Have I told you recently that you're the most annoying man I've ever met? You're not even a man. You're a fucking boy who needs his ass kicked a few more times."

"If your brother hadn't quit boxing, that might have happened," I answer calmly. "Are you done, princess? Because you've called me a lot worse things than an annoying man-child and all I want to know is how you've been. Because if you're here, things can't be going great."

"I'm fucking fine," she says. "Even if I wasn't fine, I'd rather work at a damn strip club and shake my ass than get help from you."

"I can sit here and argue with you all night. You aren't leaving this room until you tell me why you're looking for a job in a warehouse that looks abandoned on my side of town."

"You don't *own* South Boston," she says.

"Yes, I do."

We both gaze at each other stubbornly. She's glaring, but I can't bring myself to harden my gaze towards her. I've always had a soft spot for her. My feelings for her have been consistent over the years. It's been horrible to live with, but it's something I've come to accept. I even thought I could forget about her when she moved away. Tavarius never told me she moved back.

But he wouldn't. He suspects what happened that night and we've never talked about her since. I never wanted to seem interested, but of course I was. Of course I wanted to know how she was doing. I can't be with her for so many fucking reasons, but I've known her for years. I've known her long before I had these types of feelings for her.

There's a part of me that will always care, no matter how fucking wrong it is to put a girl like her on the same level as family.

"Fine," she says through gritted teeth. "Since you're being such an asshole, I'll tell you the truth and then you'll let me go. Deal?"

"Deal," I say, crossing my arms and leaning back in my chair.

"My asshole roommate ran off with all our money, I just emptied my savings account to pay everything off, I have no money to get a new place, and can't get a job in my industry because everyone is totally panicked about the recession."

Her voice gets faster and faster towards the end. Once she's done explaining her situation and what exactly Kaly told her that led her here, she folds her arms in unrepentant revulsion towards me.

"I don't want this stupid job."

Where the hell is she gonna go after this? If she doesn't get this job, she'll be in another strip club, doing something else. I definitely don't want her up on the stage, but I'll give her a job cleaning my office or something. I don't want Kamari doing anything stupid.

"Does your brother know you're down here?"

She looks at me with outrage and also like she thinks I'm fucking stupid. She's been looking at me like that since she walked in, but her frustrated anger is kinda hot. I know it's fucked up to even think that, but I'm a guy and we're pretty much always thinking about women we're attracted to and all the ways we're attracted to them.

"What the fuck do you think, Darragh? Obviously I didn't think I would run into you here or I wouldn't have come."

"He probably wouldn't like it if he found out."

"He would have to grow the fuck up, since his bitch ass girlfriend is the reason I need to find a job so fast."

Even Kamari doesn't like her. It's good to see we still have something in common.

"What if I told you that I changed my mind?"

"Quit with the mind games. I told you why I came, now let me out," Kamari snaps with frustration.

She grabs the door handle and yanks on it again, but Declan won't budge until he hears my signal.

"I'll give you a job if you audition. It's a strip club, but it's like any other job. There's an interview."

"Fine. I'll do an interview!" She says, throwing up her hands in despair. Maybe she's considering punching me because they curl into fists once they're at her sides and then relax.

She's still the prettiest fucking girl I've ever been with. She got me harder than any other girl. She gave me the energy to go all fucking night for the first time in ages. I've never burned with so much life as I did when I was inside her. *I loved her. It felt so fucking good because I loved her.*

The second I had the thought back then, I pushed her away. She hates me and it's all my fault. It breaks me to see her like this and to think that somehow the way I fucked with her head all these years ago brought her to this point.

"Take your clothes off."

"Excuse me?"

"It's part of the interview process. You're going to be a stripper. Now strip."

Maybe she'll see just how degrading this is and she won't complain when I hand her a mop and bucket. I smirk just imagining a world where Kamari doesn't complain about something I do. Years after we last saw each other and she hasn't forgiven me in the slightest.

"Is this *legal*?"

"I'm not asking you to fuck me, Kamari. I want to see what my clients will see."

"Your *racist* clients?"

"What you call racist, I call exclusive. Now take your clothes off."

"You are such an asshole."

"Did Kaly mention how well we pay here?"

"Why else do you think I wandered down to a random warehouse? That's probably a lie you tell to trick women into your seedy prostitution business."

"It's not seedy and it's not prostitution. And anyway, even if it were, I would never let another man put his hands on you. If any of those fucks so much as touch you, they'll be dead."

Chapter Six
Kamari

Then

"She's in there sleeping," I hear Darragh whispering outside the door. "Once the boat gets back to shore, you handle this, okay? I've got you for all the money you need."

"Are you sure you got this?" another man says. My head is too foggy to regcognize the voice at first.

"Yes," Darragh says. "I'll look after her."

"Yeah, man. No problem. Keep her here tonight. I don't want her in the house."

That's my brother's voice. Both voices fade away. My stomach hurts and I want to throw up again, but I don't.

I SLEEP for a while and wake up to uncomfortable fluorescent overhead lights. My stomach doesn't hurt anymore, but I feel sharp pain behind my eyes once they contact the light. *Ugh.* What the hell happened to me tonight? I swear, I only had a little to drink before sunset, but it's dark out now. Darragh steps into the room and shuts the door behind him.

"Where's Michelle?"

He doesn't answer. He just slowly walks into the room and sits on the bed next to me clasping his hands together like he's praying. All 6'3" of Darragh sits next to me and I feel so small. I feel like a kid again – the little girl crumbling beneath the weight of her crush on her best friend's older brother.

He has a girlfriend though and they're in love, which means I need to get my stupid childish crush out of my head. Darragh loves Michelle. They're *right for each other*. They grew up in the same Irish communities of South Boston. She belongs with him.

Not like me.

I try not to think about how attractive Darragh is, but it's impossible when his skin smells like Ivory soap. The smell is so strong that it overwhelms everything. It's like he's used up a whole bar of it. He's changed and showered too. His blond hair sticks up in silly spikes and his skin looks soft and freshly moisturized.

"Is something wrong?"

His shoulders tense, flexing his arm muscles, all covered by a series of intricate tattoos. He has a Celtic knot to match his brothers' on the back of his neck. He has a dagger with a Celtic knot around the handle tattooed on his left forearm, with several more tattoos covering his exposed skin.

"Nothing's wrong," he says, looking over at me and smiling. "Your brother trusts me to look after you tonight. Everyone left. Party's over. Still hungover?"

"Where's Michelle?" I ask again. "And it's your birthday. I don't need you to take care of me. I don't mean to scare Tavarius, I'm just... whatever..."

I must still be a little tipsy because I can't hold a thought straight in my head.

"He knows you can handle it, but you're safer here. On the boat."

"Are you still drunk?" I ask him. If he smells like whiskey, I can't tell because of the soap scent emanating off his skin. The freshness makes me want to snuggle into him and use Darragh as my personal blanket. I shift so I'm no longer lying down and sit several feet away from him on the bed. I don't want to stay close to him and let him get wind of my goofy thoughts about using him as a blanket.

That could never happen. Darragh isn't available. He's never been available and that will never change. He's been with Michelle for six years and they're about to move in together – a nice place out in Brookline with all the rich people. It's the sort of thing rich white folks do when they're about to have a kid. Plus, there's the race thing. Darragh doesn't like black people, according to Tavarius. I kinda see it, but he's always been good to me, so if it's a part of who he is, he keeps it hidden from me.

"I'm too fucking sober," he says.

"Did I ruin your birthday by getting too drunk?"

Darragh laughs, but he just says one word.

"No."

He glances over at me for the first time since entering the room and for the first time since I've ever known Darragh Murray, he considers me as if analyzing me or comparing me to something in his mind's eye. I've never noticed him studying me like this before. I feel nervous, but there's a flutter of excitement too because it's like getting the tiniest crumb of what I've always wanted from him.

"College is making you different," he grunts. "I don't know if I like it."

"I don't know if I like your black eye," I say to him. Darragh runs his fingers over his chin. There's a tiny sprinkle of a white blond five-o-clock shadow spreading across his chiseled chin. He taps his fingers against his jawline, drawing my attention to the geometric symbols tattooed across his knuckles. He's so handsome and his tattoos just give him that sexy bad boy alpha look that drives me wild. I like that he looks like exactly the type of guy you ought to stay away from.

"Fair enough," Darragh says calmly. He still hasn't taken his eyes off me. "You just look so much older. It makes me feel like an old man."

"Is that why you're staring at me?"

Darragh grins. "No. I'm staring because you're very pretty and… I've noticed. I've always noticed. You're only eighteen though, Kamari. You and me, we can't ever happen. Your brother would kill me."

"I'm an adult. Tavarius doesn't get to decide what I want."

"We're not talking about us being together," Darragh says. "That could never happen, okay? I want to make it clear. It doesn't matter if

I'm available. It doesn't matter if you want me. It's never gonna happen. So sleep here tonight and I'll come for you in the morning."

"Darragh–

"If I catch another man dancing on you like that and touching you… I'll kick his ass. I still care about you, Kamari. But nothing between us can or will ever happen."

"That sounds incredibly dumb and confusing. If there's nothing going on between us, just leave me alone to dance up on whoever I like. You're not my older brother. You're not my man. According to you, you're just in here taking care of me out of obligation."

"Yes," Darragh says, suppressing his frustration. "You're just an obligation."

Then he gives me that funny look again.

"A very fucking annoying obligation," he says, leaning over and closing the distance between us on the bed with a mountain lion's speed. He grabs my cheek with one hand and pulls me against his chest as he kisses me. Darragh Murray kisses me and I instantly feel drunk again.

I try to pull away, but he grunts, "No," before dragging me tighter against his chest and kissing me harder. My lips part to allow Darragh's tongue to enter my mouth. He has a long, slow tongue that teases me gently and I can't resist how good it feels, so I kiss him back. It's a teenage dream come true. He's my older brother's best friend and he's always been completely unattainable. He's never once looked at me the way he has during this conversation.

Has he always wanted to kiss me? I can't tell. I don't even dare to touch him, even if I so badly want to run my fingers through his hair as I kiss him deeply. Darragh grunts and pulls away from me. His roughly textured palm curves protectively around my shoulder and his eyes pierce into me. They're such a pale shade of blue, like an iceberg in the middle of an ocean. They're breathtakingly beautiful with wide, nervous black pupils nearly covering up the color.

"Now go to sleep," he says, confusing me completely.

"Go to sleep?"

"If you don't go to sleep…"

"What the hell is going on here?" I say to him. I'm not afraid of Darragh. I know that his family might be filled with criminals – he has a brother in prison with several of his family members caught up on tax charges. I'm not supposed to know about this, but he pays Tavarius to beat people up with him sometimes. Still, he wouldn't hurt me. I trust him.

"You look different," he says. "It's not just that. I've had a crazy fucking night. You feel like... You look like... I'm not in my right mind. That's all."

"You seem fine to me."

Now I can't stop looking at Darragh. There's definitely something wrong with him. Darragh doesn't do emotions. He also doesn't shower halfway through his parties and my brother doesn't leave me in the care of other folks unless it's an emergency.

"Hey," I whisper. "You can talk to me."

"That's the problem," he says. "I don't want to talk to you. I want to kiss you. I want to fucking ruin you. I can't let that happen."

"You wouldn't ruin me. Tavarius would understand... eventually."

"I'm a fucking problem, Kamari. You know my reputation with women better than anyone."

"I'm different," I blurt out, embarrassed that those specific words spill out of my mouth. I want to be different for Darragh. I've always wanted him to just fucking notice me, and tonight he didn't just notice me, he kissed me.

Darragh laughs. "In some ways. In other ways, you're just like a lot of women. I can't have you. Your brother trusted me tonight and I can't betray his trust. It doesn't matter how fucked up I feel."

"I could make you feel better."

"I bet you could," he murmurs. I want to be closer to him so badly that I'm willing to do anything. I feel stupid for wanting him, but I still can't stop myself. Darragh looks too good and even if he says that he's a bad person all the time, I don't want to believe him.

I just want him.

I pounce on Darragh and grab the collar of his starched white button down that hangs loosely around Darragh's well-developed arm muscles and pull him against me to kiss him again. His shirt is different from the one he wore earlier. I hate that I notice. I grab his cheeks and run my fingers through the stubble on Darragh's cheeks.

I've never been close enough to notice the rough stubble on his cheeks. It's such a light shade of blond that it's nearly white and I don't notice the hairs glistening against his skin until I'm touching him. Darragh has perfectly soft lips and they taste clean and minty.

I want to dive into the fresh, clean smell coming off Darragh. He puts his hands on my hips and I push him back further onto the bed, straddling him so I can keep him right where I want him.

I don't know what I'm doing, but I know what I *want* to do with Darragh. I've thought about it in my secret fantasies and written about it in my teenage diaries. As my thighs spread around Darragh's, reality hits me hard. My stomach lurches as I realize what I'm feeling through Darragh's pants.

His dick.

He grips my lower back and pulls me in closer so our crotches are nestled together and his cock is pressed even harder against me. I've never experienced anything like this before. Before I can get too distracted by his cock, Darragh leans forward and kisses my shoulder.

"You are so fucking hot," he says. "We shouldn't be doing this."

He pulls away for a second, gazing at me with a contemplative look on his face as he drags his thumb over my lower lip. I don't want him to think about this if it's going to make him stop.

"I don't care. I want you."

"Are you sure you know what you want? " he growls, his sharp blond eyebrows furrowing with impossibly unfair frustration.

"I want to kiss you. Make out. Hook up. Whatever."

"I'm a grown ass man, Kamari. I don't just kiss or hook up or whatever. I want sex. I *need* sex."

The fluttering in my stomach intensifies.

"Are you a virgin?" he asks and that fluttering turns into several small bombs going off. Darragh clearly has had way more experience than I have. Up until a few hours ago, he had a girlfriend who slept in his bed. Her stuff is still in this bedroom, strewn all over the floor. My stomach lurches.

I don't want to answer.

Chapter Seven
Darragh

Now

My comments make Kamari angrier.

"Don't pretend you give a shit about me and what other guys do to me," she says. "You know what? To prove you don't give a fuck, I'll do it. I'll apply for your job, I'll get up on that stage and you'll treat me like just another woman. Isn't that what I am?"

"Kamari–

She ignores my apologetic tone and sets her purse down on my desk with an aggressive thud. Kamari takes off her shirt and drops it on the ground. She glares at me in just a bra and her pants. My cock stiffens immediately. There's no reason why her body wouldn't have the same effect on me after all this time. The last time I was alone in a room with her, I lost control of myself and made two of the biggest mistakes of my life in one night.

"What, Darragh?"

I was so fucking selfish back then, so fucking hurt that I was willing to push away the one woman who was always there for me, even more than my sisters and mother. She always saw me like an idol, like someone larger than life, not Darragh the dumbass who gets his head knocked in because he's too stupid to manage businesses like Aiden or Callum. Not smart enough to keep his ass out of jail or handle more business than a fucking seedy strip club.

She never saw me that way. Her anger now can't be contained as I force her to face the truth about who I am again. Back then, I was an idiot for pushing her away. I don't want to do that again. I want to be the guy who protects her. A man she can trust.

If she's in trouble, she can't just strut into my club looking like this and demanding to jump on my stage. This life is too dangerous for her and despite my frustration with her attitude and the way it always makes me want to throw her over my thigh and spank the hell out of her, I have to protect her.

I *hurt* her when she was the last woman to love me or to look at me like I was the strongest man in the world. Michelle never looked at me the way Kamari did. How the hell did fate bring this woman to my club?

"I made a mistake with you," I tell her, hoping she senses how much I mean it.

Kamari rolls her eyes. "Congratulations, you spent years figuring out that you're a complete asshole. Are you going to let me out of here or not?"

"No. But I don't want you to work here. I want you to see that this is a dumb idea and that you can't handle it."

"You don't know what the hell I can handle," she says, her chest bouncing as she adjusts her stance, clearly trying not to swing on me.

Fuck, her tits look incredible. Her bra can barely hold her breasts back. Kamari has always been fucking irresistible to me. If I'd resisted her the first time I touched her, she wouldn't be here right now testing me. Provoking me. Pissing me off.

She can't handle this and I'll prove it to her. I have selfish reasons for wanting this, obviously, but Kamari doesn't belong in this world. What the hell happened? She went off to college. She left the tiny apartment she shared with her family and went off to Cornell. She shouldn't be in my club trying to change my mind.

It doesn't matter how much money I pay the girls to strip for a bunch of old racist Irish bastards. Kamari is worth more. If it's money she needs, I'll give it to her.

She's too stubborn to see that she can't handle this unless I show her.

"Lose the pants, princess," I command her, ignoring her previous orders not to call her that. She'll have to hear a lot of shit she doesn't like if she dances in this club. She's not just a regular Irish woman.

"Princess?" she responds with a tightening voice.

"You're in my club, princess. You do what I say, or you walk out that door and leave the shirt behind. That's how the job works at Harrison Ave. You listen to me and I keep you safe."

She frowns but gives every sign that she's going to obey me. *She has to be kidding me.* I suppress my instinctive outrage at the thought that she could be so comfortable and emotionless about taking her clothes off in front of strangers.

Kamari slides her thumbs into the waist of her pants and struggles to get them over her full hips and soft, jiggly ass. Once she gets them off, she shimmies to get them to fall to the floor. My cock nearly bursts through my pants. *Holy fuck, her thighs are thick. Gorgeous. And...*

"When did you get a tattoo?" I ask, observing the fresh black ink on Kamari's recently exposed thigh. My cock throbs. She looks cute as fuck with a little bit of ink on her pale reddish-brown skin. I want to stroke her thighs and wrap them around my fucking face.

"I got it when some asshole broke my heart," she says fiercely. She never backs down and I fucking love it.

I lean forward to take a closer look at the swirled pattern.

"Don't worry," she says. "That asshole wasn't you. I have absolutely no feelings for you and you didn't affect me enough for me to get a tattoo."

It's a scorpion tattoo. Fierce.

"Who broke your heart then?" I ask.

Kamari pushes me again with her next words. She's so fucking stubborn.

"I'm here for a job interview, not to spill all my personal business to my future boss," she says.

"It's important for me and Declan to know in case he finds out you work here and comes around to start trouble. In fact, I need a list of every man in your life from the past five years."

Kamari snorts and crosses her arms over her stomach. It's a little softer than when I last saw her, but still sexy as hell. Watching her cross her arms and push her breasts together saps me of my will power to fuck with her. This would be so much more entertaining if I could bend her over my desk and take her right now.

"I'm not telling you about my past, Darragh."

"Fine. Leave. I'll call your brother once you're gone," I say to her with a smug look on my face that I know riles her up.

"Are you going to blackmail me every time I don't do what you want?" she huffs. She bites her lower lip hard like she's holding back a series of expletives. It's really not like her to hold back, so there's definitely a part of her that really needs the money.

"Yes. I'll also spank you if necessary."

"Fuck you, Darragh."

"I'm not joking. I have to turn this strip club around, and bringing forth forbidden fruit might work. But I have to make sure my forbidden fruit stays obedient."

"You are *disgusting*."

She looks fucking incredible in her underwear. I could have her stand here and insult the shit out of me all fucking day. I wouldn't give a fuck as long as she stood there looking gorgeous as hell without a fucking thing on.

"Did Kaly mention how much you could make working here?"

"She hinted at it," Kamari says, getting more nervous as she watches me, searching for more cruelty. Is she serious? I want to push her. To see how far she'll go. But there's no way in hell I'm having Kamari get up on a stage in my club.

I don't want her to know that yet. I run my hands over my chin like I'm stuck in deep contemplation.

"For you, I'll pay even more. I don't know how the guys will react, so I'll need you to be well compensated. $400 a night, 5 p.m. to 5 a.m., plus whatever tips you make."

"You're telling me that you pay over twenty bucks an hour plus tips?" she says, completely surprised. *She is out of her mind if she thinks I'm watching her strip for a bunch of guys.*

"Yes," I say, struggling to hide my tightening voice.

Kamari can't hide how much the numbers tempt her. It's more money than a lot of college girls around here make. I'm careful about the women I hire. I need to be, considering discretion is one of my clientele's primary concerns.

"I already did what you asked. I took my clothes off," she says. "When do I show up? How do I learn the dances?"

She's too eager for this. And I'm too petty to let it go. I push her again, hoping to find some limits, some signs of the innocent eighteen-year-old whose heart I broke on my twenty-fourth birthday.

"You'll do what I ask again and turn around," I command her.

She bites her lip to stop from verbally attacking me again and she drops her hands to her sides, turning around slowly. Kamari's hair touches the small of her back and I instantly imagine her on all fours with my hands wrapped around those curls as I tilt her head back. *Fuck, Darragh. Focus.*

I don't make it a habit of sleeping with my employees and I won't start now.

"Another tattoo?"

She has another tattoo on the back of her thigh. This time, it's a tiny aloe plant. Cute.

"Is that relevant to the job, Mister Murray?"

My cock nearly explodes in my pants when she calls me Mister Murray. She definitely doesn't mean to turn me on this much, but I can't help it. That's always been the problem with Kamari. Every time I look at her, she flips a switch in my brain that suddenly makes it okay for me to fantasize about her. It's not just her skin color, but that's a part of it. Imagining my pale hand against her dark skin gets me hard. Then there's kissing her. I shift in my seat and try to focus. It's always impossible when she's in the room.

I proceed forward confidently, "Everything is relevant to the job, including a list of all the men who have touched you since–"

"Since you fucked me and left me?" she shoots back. She's facing away from me, so thankfully she can't see the pained expression on my face. Kamari doesn't know how much it fucking killed me to do what I did. Every second she's been gone, I've thrown myself into girls, boxing, and finding my niece Tegan for a while.

Everything in my life has been a distraction because of how I hurt her.

"Yes. Since that happened."

"Why do you care?"

"I don't. I want to see the likelihood that you've picked up anything that you might give to my clients."

"Fuck you, Darragh."

"Answer the question, Kamari. I'm beginning to find your avoidance suspicious."

"I've only been with two other guys, okay? They were both complete assholes and you don't need to know more than that."

"Okay."

"Actually, what you need to know," Kamari blurts out. "Is that neither of them were entitled racist white boys who screwed with me just to rebel against their family."

She turns around to face me, taking away my incredible view of her ass and the tiny tattoo on her thigh beneath it. She looks like she wants to punch me in the face. Maybe I should let her just so she can blow off some fucking steam and we can have a real conversation.

"Okay. Now I know."

My calmness infuriates her more than me acting out ever could. I know Kamari. She wants a reaction out of me.

"Take the rest of your clothes off."

"Are you serious?"

"It's a strip club, Kamari. What did you expect? Now strip."

She glares at me like she wants to skewer me. I don't mind, because at least she's looking. At least she can see the effect she has on me after all this time. I might want to torture her a bit, but I don't want to hide anything from Kamari after everything we've been through.

She's back here... I can't let her slip out of my reach again.

"This is ridiculous."

"You clearly need the money."

"Shut up, Darragh."

I smile as she reaches behind her back and unhooks her bra. Her breasts look even better than I remember. The older she gets, the more beautiful she gets, like she's still growing into how beautiful she's meant to be. Maybe I just want her because I'm not supposed to have her. I don't really give a shit why I want her. I just want to run my tongue over her bare nipples and do some truly twisted things to Kamari's body in my office.

I shift my left leg to give my cock room to move to a more comfortable position in my trousers. Kamari reaches her palms over her breasts, probably because my office is cold enough to make her dark nipples incredibly stiff.

"Move your hands," I command her. "Prove to me you can follow instructions. The girls who work here are all very obedient."

She makes an irritated scoff, but her hands fall away to her sides. My cock lurches with unbridled lust. I can barely make out my next words. "Take your underwear off, princess."

Chapter Eight
Kamari

Then

I don't want to tell Darragh the truth about my virginity because I know him. He'll run at the slightest hint of intimacy.

"No. I'm not a virgin," I say to him, lying through my teeth.

He scowls as if he was certain otherwise.

"Who did it?"

"I'm not telling you."

He rolls his eyes. "Liar."

"I'm not lying."

"You're a liar *and* a virgin," he murmurs, leaning forward and teasing my neck with his perfect lips again. God, he smells delicious. I want that clean smell all over me. I clutch his shirt and pull Darragh's body against mine. He grunts as I touch his chest. My hands can't get enough of him. He's in great shape from boxing and whenever he bulks up, he gets even more muscular and delicious.

He holds the back of my neck as I kiss him and feel up his chest, moving my hands to his shoulders and running my fingers over the ink covering his skin, slowly moving down his arms. He flinches once I get to his biceps, and pulls away from our kiss.

"What's wrong?"

My thighs tighten around him. My biggest fear right then is that he'll push me off of him and leave. My second biggest fear is that this will happen and he'll regret it and that will make everything even worse.

"You don't know what you're doing," he says grumpily. "You don't know the type of man you're getting involved with. I want you so fucking badly, princess. I really fucking want you. But you're the one woman I can't just fuck around with."

I can feel his heart racing with one of my palms pressed to Darragh's chest. His icy blue eyes connect with mine. They're such a light shade of blue that it's hard not to stare at them up close.

"I know exactly who you are. A boxer. Irish. Maybe in the mob or something."

Darragh laughs and I absolutely hate it. He thinks because he's a little older than me, he's so much smarter than me. I'm smarter than he gives me credit for or I wouldn't be going to college. At least he doesn't push me away. His large palm moves to my lower back as he shakes his head.

"I can't ever be with you, Kamari. I'm Irish. My family has always been Irish. It's not possible for me to be with a girl like you."

"Because of religion?"

I realize it's a stupid question the second it spills out of my mouth. He means race, doesn't he?

Darragh's cheeks darken considerably. He sticks his tongue into the side of his cheek and then clears his throat. "No. Not because of religion."

His finger finds one of my curls and he twirls it around his finger. "You're just... It's not you."

"Right. It's not because I'm black."

He doesn't stop twirling my hair, which makes me want to slap him and kiss him again at the same time.

"It's because I'm white," he says.

"Screw all that stuff," I say to him. He stops twirling my hair which makes me want to drag him against me. I've waited too long for Darragh to stop messing around with other girls and finally realize my crush on him. I can't have him slipping out of my fingers now.

"I can't. Those tattoos I have on my hands right now represent a commitment I've made. That doesn't just go away because you're beautiful."

"Shut up," I say to him, my voice shaking as I say it. I don't want to accept that this is who he is. I don't want to believe that something as dark as racism could be so close to the surface of Darragh Murray.

How can he be racist? He's always been there for me. He's always cared. *No.* I want to prove him wrong so badly that I grab his face and kiss him. He lets me, of course. I run my fingers through the stubble on his cheeks and kiss him until my lips are completely numb. When I stop kissing him, I don't stop clutching his shirt, as if I could stop him from getting away from me.

I feel an uncomfortable wetness between my thighs. I've never felt this intense desire. I've never felt my body getting ready for a man and I've definitely never actually wanted anyone the way I want Darragh. His face is incredibly stern as I grind my hips into him, like I'm making him question everything.

"What would your brother think?"

He doesn't even genuinely sound like he cares what my brother would think.

"I don't care. I'm eighteen and he's not my dad. I can do what I want."

"That's not supposed to include me," Darragh replies, but he doesn't stop me from reaching for the bottom of his shirt and lifting it over his chest. I push his shirt over his shoulders and take it off.

"I don't care what you think."

Now that I have Darragh's shirt off, I see all his chest tattoos up close for the first time. I've never really had many occasions to see him shirtless up close and outside of the boxing ring and I tried to remember what he looked like in vivid detail every chance I got, but nothing beats seeing him half naked and up close. He looks even better than when he's in the boxing ring dripping in sweat, and he looks pretty good then too.

"Do you know what any of these mean?"

"No. And I don't care. They look cool. Bad ass."

Darragh flinches again as my fingers trace his chest tattoos. I move my hips forward again and his hardness presses into me. He can't hide his body's reactions to me and his reactions prove what tattoos can't. If Darragh really didn't want me, he wouldn't respond like this.

"These are my commitments to my family and to myself."

"Your dick feels very committed," I respond, my heart racing as I push boundaries with the way I'm talking to Darragh. We've never been open with each other like this and we've definitely never come this close to admitting that the stolen glances between us mean something.

"My dick is confused about my morals, but my morals are clear Kamari. I will only be with an Irish woman. I will only love and marry an Irish woman. If we fuck, it's going to be a one time thing."

"You don't mean that."

"I definitely do, which is why I say you don't know what you're getting into."

"You care about me, Darragh. You would never hurt me like that."

Darragh's grip on my lower back tightens. I don't know why I get under his skin so easily. He leans forward and kisses my chest, moving my straps aside so they fall over my shoulder and expose my breasts. Darragh runs his tongue over my nipples.

"I don't," he says gruffly. "I don't give a fuck about anyone. I'm a bad person, Kamari. I've killed people."

He pulls his head away and looks up at me as if seeking my approval. I gaze into his icy eyes, completely uncertain about whether or not I believe him. I run my fingers through his wet and spiky blond hair. I don't believe him.

"I don't care," I say to him. "If you killed someone, you probably had a good reason."

"I keep trying to tell you the truth," he says. "But you won't listen. You're making it very hard for me to do the right thing."

"Then do the wrong thing, stupid," I whisper. I wonder if I'll come to regret those words. I just want him so badly that nothing he says could change my mind. I don't believe all those horrible things about Darragh. I don't want to believe them.

Darragh grabs my thighs. He's so hot shirtless that it gets me even wetter to press my palms to his bare chest.

"You think you know what you want?" Darragh growls. "Then get on your knees, princess. Let me feel your lips around my cock."

Chapter Eight

Chapter Nine
Darragh

Now

"You can't genuinely expect me to take my underwear off as a part of a job interview," Kamari says. "And I already told you not to call me princess."

"Kamari, I own this club which means if you want to step onto my stage, I own you. Which means you do as I ask."

"You're forgetting the part where I asked to walk out of here."

"I'm not forgetting anything," I answer her calmly, wishing I had enough whiskey to draw this out longer. I'm losing my patience with Kamari and my cock's response to her. "I know what you asked for. If I let you walk out of here, you'll walk into another strip club and you'll be someone else's problem."

"Isn't that what you always wanted? You wanted me to be someone else's problem and now you can have your damn wish."

There's a beat between us. It's impossible to think straight with her standing nearly naked in front of me. Her full hips jut out and her thick thighs are just begging for me to thrust my tongue between them. It's difficult to think straight with her in the room. I've missed her more than I realized.

"That's not what I want. I want you to get the job so you can support yourself."

It's a half-truth, but it's enough to get her to reach into the waist of her underwear and expose herself to me. I nearly lose control once she's naked. Kamari has a small strip of pubic hair over her mound and the folds of her thighs remind me of what I've missed all the time she's been away.

That night with her was the best sex I've ever had. It was the night I realized how far I would go for Kamari. I came so close to burning every relationship in my life, just for her – just for the delicious cinnamon treat between her legs. So many fucking regrets with her…

How could I speak to her after what I did and said to her? Shame ate away at me for years. I thought I could repair some of that shame by helping my brother Aiden. He fell for the wrong kind of woman and I thought if I could help him, I could atone for what I did to her.

Then just my fucking luck, Kamari walks into my office, and now she's obediently taking her clothes off desperately needing something from me. She still looks at me like she hates me, but this is my second chance – my chance to win her back.

"You look very good," I say to her, trying to stay calm, but feeling warmth in my cheeks that suggest I've turned bright fucking red. *Fuck. I hope she doesn't notice.* I let my eyes linger on every inch of her, pretending to do a professional analysis of Kamari's physique.

"I've gained a lot of weight since you last saw me," Kamari says. " I don't mind it, but I know white guys like basic chicks with no ass."

Again, she's trying to get under my skin. Life didn't end up how I was taught it would. I thought I could make myself love an Irish woman. I thought I could be like every other man in my family and have my affairs on the side, enjoy the occasional hooker. I genuinely thought I could choose the color of the woman I loved and when life didn't work out that way, I panicked.

I didn't realize I'd go so many years and never meet another girl I could ever imagine loving as much as I loved her. I still love her. That's why I want her here instead of in some other guy's club. That's why I want her to stay with me – in my clutches. *One of my girls.*

Not on the stage, but still, she's pushing me. Testing me. Does she want to see if I still care about her? Of course I still care about her…

Chapter Nine

"You'll do just fine."

"What a winning endorsement."

I scoff. "Winning endorsement? Isn't it enough for you to get the job?"

"I need money," she says, folding her arms. Her arms push her breasts together. I run my tongue over my lips. This isn't her world. How long would it take for one of the assholes who comes to the club to offer her more money for *even more.*

Does she even realize what she's doing here?

I push her further. "The only girls who get winning endorsements from me are the ones who get on their knees."

"I'm not interviewing to become a hooker," Kamari responds fiercely. She pushes back against everything I say, always resisting me, always pushing me until I become completely dominant and forceful with her.

She's a little fighter, which makes winning her over that much more exciting.

"Trust me, I won't let you get on your knees for anyone else. But if you want this job, I'll want something in return."

"The second I get out of here, I'll tell Tavarius about this and he'll kick your ass."

"You'll tell your brother that you got naked in my office and sucked my cock?"

"I won't suck your cock," she says angrily. "I'm not going to let you use me like a whore when the last time I stupidly let you get in my pants, you were–

I interrupt her. "I don't want to use you like a whore. I just miss your mouth and I know the only way I can get you on your knees again is by doing this. *By making you.*"

"I hate you."

"I don't care. I'm perfectly comfortable cumming in your mouth whether you hate me or not."

"I'm not giving you a blowjob, Darragh."

"I'll give you a signing bonus if you get on your knees. $15,000 cash. Right now."

I open my desk drawer and pull out fifteen grand from my personal stash. In my line of work, this type of cash comes in handy. Declan could take care of anyone stupid enough to try to steal it. Kamari can't hide her visible reaction to the money on the desk.

"How rich are you, Darragh?"

"How much will it take to get you on your knees?"

Kamari glares. "I'm not a hooker."

"You're not. You're a family friend and you need money so you're doing me a favor. I honestly haven't had any lips as good as yours since I let you go. I'd give you all the money in the world to feel your lips again."

"Your life has you so fucked up," Kamari says critically.

"Yes," I answer. "I'll admit that. I've said the worst things in the world to you, but your lips are the ones I dream about when I go to sleep at night. It's your skin I want to touch. You have always had this incredible hold on me that God or my father will surely punish me for."

"Give me twenty-grand," she says. "Twenty-grand, and I'll do it. But I'm only doing it because I don't have feelings for you and I'll never have feelings for you again. This is a job to me. Nothing but a job."

Chapter Ten
Kamari

Then

I scramble between Darragh's legs and eagerly reach for his jeans as he sits on the edge of the bed. He groans as I touch him.

"Go slow," he groans. "You make me want to cum like... instantly."

I kiss the top of his thighs through his jeans and try to slow down as I peel them off. He watches me unzip and unbutton his pants, only shifting his hips so I can slide them over his ass and down his thighs.

Darragh's underwear can barely restrain his hardness. I gaze down at it with fascination. I've never seen one up close like this before. I've fantasized about seeing Darragh's dick, but it's nothing like what I imagined. It's so much *bigger*. During my research, I learned about the length of the average male penis. Darragh's enormous. His dick must be the length of my forearm and it's definitely thicker.

I glance up at him nervously as I run my fingers over the outline of his dick through his underwear. My heart races as slowly touching his cock allows me to feel how big it is. I'm nervous about getting it inside me. Despite my attempts to lie to Darragh, my virginity remains intact.

Not wanting him to notice my inexperience, I work on getting his underwear off. Darragh's cock looks even bigger exposed. It's a dusky pink color with clear fluid oozing from the head which looks even darker than the rest of his dick. Thick blue veins bulge along the length of his dick. It's so different from what I expected it to look like. It looks almost reddish and angry.

What does he want from me down here?

"You've done this before, haven't you?" he says, sounding as gentle as he can with his evident sexual frustration. Fluid spills from the tip of his cock onto his thigh. I can't stop staring at the gigantic head.

"No... I don't know."

"You put your mouth around it and you please me. Without your teeth."

Well, that's just common sense not to go around biting people's genitals. I would think pleasing Darragh would come with more instructions. I still don't exactly know what he wants me to do, but instinct and faint memories of sneakily reading romance novels in middle school give me some ideas.

I wrap my hands slowly around the base of Darragh's shaft. He grunts as I lift his impressive dick and run my tongue over the opening, tasting the clear fluid spilling out of his engorged dick. Every part of touching Darragh thrills me. I could stay here all night on my knees if it just meant I got to touch him. I've looked up to him for so long that it's nearly impossible for me to believe I'm really here, touching him.

Darragh groans with pleasure, dragging me back to reality. Continuing to grip the base of his shaft, I widen my mouth and slowly slide my lips down the length of Darragh's dick. His groaning becomes deeper and more forceful. He surprises me by touching my head, sliding his fingers through my hair and groaning even louder as I get my mouth halfway down Darragh's shaft.

"Fuck, you're good at this," he says. "You're a natural, princess."

My heart flutters when he says that. I gag as I try to take more of him down my throat. It's too much. I want to please him, but I just can't handle it. I pull away from Darragh's dick, gasping for breath. It flops over onto his thigh, covered in my spit. Tears stream from my eyes.

"Hey," Darragh says, grabbing my chin and tilting my head up to meet him. "You're not done. Go slower. It'll be easier to get the whole thing in your mouth."

He leans forward and gives me a deep, encouraging kiss on the lips. I lean into the kiss desperate for him not to move away, but he pulls away and gazes expectantly at his dick. Every part of him is so lean and perfect.

I regain my composure, slightly adjusting my position on my knees as I lean forward and start again. I grab the base of Darragh's dick and slowly inhale as I wrap my lips around the head again. He strokes the top of my head in a way that comforts me more than I expect.

"More," he says. "You're almost there."

His firm words of encouragement and his hand on my head make me feel completely submissive to him. I breathe slowly through my nose and ignore the tingling in the back of my throat as the tip of his cock reaches back there, nearly choking me. I gag again, and this time, I feel him explode.

I might not have been an expert at this, but I know what's happening once it starts. It's too late for me to pull my mouth away from Darragh's dick, so I have to swallow his eruption. Thick pumps of his hot cum slide down my throat and my cheeks feel swollen from stretching so wide to accommodate Darragh's dick.

He keeps his hand firmly planted on the top of my head as I ease my mouth off his dick. I keep breathing slowly through my nose, terrified I'll throw up otherwise. I don't want to offend him, but it's the first time I've ever tasted a man's cum and I don't like it. Before I can pull away and feel truly grossed out about Darragh's cum in my mouth, he grabs my cheeks like before and leans over to kiss me.

I want to stop him because of all the spit around my mouth and because I just swallowed his seed, but Darragh's in control. He easily pulls me forward to kiss him and when he pushes his tongue into my mouth, I yield to him and tease his tongue with mine. He pulls away from me again with a heaving chest.

"Your brother is gonna kill me if he finds out," he says, gasping for breath. He doesn't stop staring at me, and I don't know if I'm supposed to answer and take away his guilt, or if he's just Darragh, fighting his demons as usual.

I swallow, mostly to get the taste of cum out of my mouth, but

Darragh interprets this as nerves or something. He sighs and lets go of my cheeks, shaking his head.

"What the fuck am I doing with you, princess? This can only hurt you and it can only hurt me. It's fucking wrong."

"Don't be stupid," I fight back, terror filling every part of me. I don't want Darragh to stop this now. I don't want him to push me away when he's finally admitted that he has feelings for me as more than Tavarius' dorky little sister.

"It's not stupid. I've tried to tell you, Kamari. My family would not approve and I will not betray them. Don't you get it? I'm not choosing you. I'm using you. I've had a fucked up night and it's my birthday and... I just *want* you. It's wrong."

"What's so wrong about wanting me?"

He snorts as if I'm a complete idiot for asking. Darragh stares at me with those intense icy eyes. I feel hypnotized by them, especially when they're caught in a beam of light, and they look so clear that I'm tempted to believe I can see straight through to his heart by looking into them.

"So many fucking things," Darragh says. He can't help himself though. He toys with one of my curls as he says it. "Get off your knees, princess. Let me count the fucking ways."

I stand, barely noticing how much it strained me to be in that position until I do. Darragh doesn't leave me standing for long. He draws me in and leads me to straddle him where he's sitting on the edge of the bed. It feels lewd to have my thighs spread so wide around Darragh, but I want to be this person now.

I want to be his. He keeps toying with that one curl once he has me on his lap. His other hand sits firmly against my lower back, keeping me pressed close. Then he takes my shirt off and my bra. My heart is racing when he does that. It's so fast that I swear I'm losing myself.

He rests his forehead on my chest, his hot breath warming up my breasts and making me aware of Darragh's every movement and every emotion expressed in his breath. I've never let another guy see me like this before. It's new, terrifying and exciting, especially because it's Darragh, who seems reluctant again, even if he stares at my breasts.

"You're my best friend's little sister," he says. "That's the first problem."

"We already handled that," I answer.

"That's one way of putting it," Darragh says, sighing a bit. His breath is a little cooler when he sighs, and I squirm because he's making my nipples hard and it's a weird new sensation for me. An awkward wet gush between my thighs makes me aware of how closely our crotches are pressed together.

"You're also black," Darragh continues. "That's a big fucking problem for me, as I've made several promises to never be with a woman of your color. Not seriously. I can't be with you. I can't claim you in public. I can't... I shouldn't have even cum in your mouth. Even that was too far."

He sighs again. I feel the weight of this hurting him and it's so damn confusing. What does it matter that I'm black? Why does he act like he cares so much when his body had no problem responding to my touch? He can't keep his hands off my skin or his fingers out of my curly hair. If he's so racist, why does he look at me with so much longing?

I understand Darragh better than he understands himself sometimes.

"You aren't convincing me that you're some bad person," I say to him, wrapping my arms around him and touching his back, wondering if I still have permission to touch him now that he's cum and possibly come to his senses. He doesn't push my hands away, which means that I do, which thrills me. I tease my fingers over his back, tempted to push him away, but failing. *Why can't I push him away when I know he's racist and wrong for me?*

"I've hurt people," he says softly, his breath still teasing my breasts. "I'm worse than what I'm telling you, that's the thing. I want you to understand that."

"I don't care."

"Fuck," he grunts, as if in genuine distress. "I want you so fucking bad. I want you so fucking bad."

He repeats it with near desperation and then he pushes his hands into my underwear. The sudden movement surprises me, but I don't fight Darragh's fingers between my legs.

He slides purposefully between my lower lips and I gasp with pleasure as he rubs my small raised nub. It's too intense to bear...

Kamari

Darragh grunts as he slips his fingers along the length of my wetness and I feel his cock coming back to life, warming up against my thigh as he gets incredibly hard again.

WE'RE DOING THIS. I'm losing my virginity to Darragh tonight, on his birthday, and it's going to be perfect...

Chapter Eleven
Darragh

Now

"Fuck's sake, Kamari. Are you serious?"

"What? You're the one offering it."

"If you were in such dire straits that would suck cock for money, why wouldn't you just come to me for help?"

"Are you out of your mind?" Kamari snaps. "In fact, I know you're out of your mind because you've spent every second of your life getting hit in the damn head. I would never come to you for help. I don't have any feelings for you. I can do a job and leave the past in the past, but there will never be a future with us."

"I tried to make things right. I tried to go through your brother and help and–" I sound fucking stupid.

Kamari looks unimpressed, which I should have expected. Nothing I can say or do impresses her. I came *this* close to having her on her knees, but my better judgment pulled me away from the edge of what a previous version of me would have done.

I can't fix this with sex. That just made things worse between us after the first time.

"Nothing you do can make this right," she says.

"I'll give you the money that you need."

"In exchange for head?" Her voice brims with her disgust for me. I hate to have her think of me like I'm some irredeemable asshole, even if I shouldn't care what she thinks.

"No," I say to her. "I'll give you all the money now, but you give me your word that you never show your face here and that I won't catch word of you on the stage of another man's club."

"You can't tell me where to work or what to do."

"I can if I make your problems go away. Now... put your clothes on."

I especially regret those last four words. The last thing I want is Kamari's remarkable assets covered up. I hope I can keep a mental image of her alive long after she struts out of my strip club. I'm probably never going to see her again, and she will have lightened my pockets by a considerable amount with me getting nothing in exchange.

No, I got something. I got a chance to see her body again, to see how she changed. Her hips are still full and she still has a soft, plump looking ass. It's large, too. She has the type of ass where she needs to jump to get into her jeans. Her pale copper skin always drove me crazy. She would turn the perfect shade of brown in the summers...

I still want her more than I've ever wanted anyone. If my older brother gets to break his vows and survive because of Pa's coma, what's the harm in indulging myself now?

She's not right for me, that's the harm. But I can't stop staring at her in awe, silently blaming her for bewitching me completely. Kamari eagerly dresses and I definitely regret issuing the command, even if clothing puts her at greater ease.

Once she dresses, she continues her disapproving glare.

"If you're going to give me the money, do it and let me out of here."

"What exactly got you into this mess?"

Reluctantly, she explains with more details what exactly landed her in such financial trouble. I want to hurt the assholes who ran off with her money. I can see how much the betrayal hurt her and how much it hurt to have her hard work snatched away with no respite.

"The cops aren't doing anything," she says. "I have all my expenses piling up in the most expensive city *ever* and it's a fucking mess. So you caught me. I'm desperate."

I get up from my seat and close the distance between us. Kamari stands her ground. Even if she were to ever fear me, she would never show it. Fearlessness against hopelessness is more of Kamari's style. *It's why I was so in love with her. She was always a wild thing and I thought fuck, I'm a wild thing too. If we weren't from different worlds, we could be wild together.*

I don't touch her, because she would definitely slap me if I did, but I scrutinize her like all I'll have of her is this memory of us standing right here.

"I've changed my mind," I whisper. "Since you're so desperate, I'll give you all the money you need, $21,456.98 in exchange for one thing… *a second chance.*"

"No way in hell."

"I want you to think about it carefully."

I fight the urge to call her princess. That would definitely just piss her off.

"There are no second chances, Darragh. You shattered my heart back then. You turned me cold-hearted. This is all you. So no, you don't get a second chance. Not for all the money in the world."

"What about a kiss?"

"Fuck you."

Her brows raise a little and her mouth purses up like it does when she gets all mad at me. But then Kamari surprises the shit out of me and she leans forward recklessly to kiss me on the lips. She pulls away before I can grab hold of her and immediately lose control of myself. Her cheeks are slightly darker once she pulls away.

"You still have nice lips," she says. "Which is an impressive trait for a man who is 100% asshole."

"I'm a man of my word," I say to her, opening up my desk drawer and handing her more money than she needs. "Stay out of trouble."

"What about the job?" she says.

"You have more than enough to relax until you find a better one," I say to her. "Stay out of trouble," I repeat.

She stuffs all the money into a giant canvas tote bag I loan to her with a zipper and pretends like it doesn't weigh down her shoulder, even if I can see her face straining painfully from the weight of the cash.

"Good-bye, Darragh. Seeing you again has been an oddly profitable nightmare."

"We'll keep this between us, then…"

Kamari rolls her eyes. "Yes, asshole. Your secret is safe with me. I won't tell my brother or anyone in your racist little clan a thing."

"Funny idea your friend had. Black stripper at an Irish-only bar."

"Yeah," she says. "Funny."

"Goodbye, princess."

"Goodbye, asshole."

I watch her beautiful ass swaying with each step as she hurries out of my office. I lean back in my chair, wondering what the fuck just happened. I could have had Kamari on her knees. I could have had her the way I did all those years ago.

It feels like I've really changed and it's fucking with my head she can't see that. I'm smart enough to keep my hands off her now. I'm not smart enough to stop myself from messing with her, but it's only because she hates my guts. Not even giving her more than half the money in my work desk can change how much she hates me.

She frustrates the ever living fuck out of me. She's haunted me since my birthday. I've never been able to *perform* for another woman since her. I've tried, but after a couple times I gave up. After my ex cheated and I took Kamari to bed, I saw what I was missing.

What I'm still missing. Her.

DUTY CALLS before I can make the impulsive decision to chase after her. My brother calls – and not the fun one.

"Have you solved the strip club problem yet?" Aiden growls into the phone with all the genteel of a dog in a fighting ring. If he threw a few more punches, he would have a far more relaxed demeanor.

"An employee wants me to hire black strippers. Might work. Not sure if it's worth pissing people off."

Aiden chuckles. "Who came up with that idea? Dad has been saying it for ages. Well, he wants Puerto Rican girls naturally, but he thought there would be a lower chance of the men touching them, you know."

"I suppose the race bit could work to our advantage," I muse carefully. "I don't know. Could be dangerous."

"I don't give a fuck what you do, as long as the books look good next week. I'm having the accountant come by and I need that club to look like it makes $120,000 a week. Better yet, you make that amount and we can work out an even better deal with the accountant."

Aiden's getting on my nerves. Why the fuck is he calling me in the middle of the work day over this?

"What's the point of this phone call? I know how to do my job."

Aiden makes a gruff, impatient sound which might scare our younger brother Odhran, but won't scare me.

"I need you to get Tavarius to fight. Callum wants to do the book-making for that, get money in for the bets. We have someone lined up who will throw the fight, make it easy for him. If he comes back out of retirement and you get him into shape, it's easy money for all of us."

"Tavarius won't mess around with fights."

"He doesn't have to know what's going on. In fact, better if he doesn't. If it wasn't something we could pull off I wouldn't ask for this, D. Offer him money. A lot of fucking money. We're looking at a potential $760,000 on our end from the surveys Callum ran. Didn't you have your eye on a new Bugatti?"

No. But I have my eye on Kamari and if I get Tavarius in on this, I'll have a greater chance of running into her. Seeing her again. I feel like I'll do foolish things to see Kamari again.

"Whatever you say, boss."

Aiden grunts uncomfortably. "Dad's still alive. I'm not the boss while he's alive."

He hangs up with an unceremonious click. My brother pisses me off. I don't know how the fuck he tricked a woman into putting up with him full time.

Chapter Twelve
Kamari

Now

Darragh always thinks he has the upper hand with me. He's used to getting his way and ever since I've been out of his life, apparently his unfettered arrogance has only become worse. The money weighs down the stupid bag he gave me, and carrying the tote and my purse is a mess. I don't know how I'm going to get home like this. A ride-share app? That sounds like a horrible idea. What if the driver figures out I'm carrying a fuck ton of cash and robs my ass?

I walk past Declan and focus on struggling with Darragh's tote full of money as well as fully ignoring Declan's existence since he left me at his boss's mercy.

As I struggle to open the door to exit the warehouse, Declan runs down the hallway.

"Can I help?"

"I don't need shit from you."

"Listen, miss, I'm sorry. He's the boss. I gotta listen to the boss."

Declan catches up to me easily, thanks to the weight of the stupid bag. He takes it off my shoulder and raises his eyebrows once he feels the weight of it. Declan clearly knows better than to ask any questions.

"Do you need help walking it out to your car?"

"I didn't drive. I'm broke. I don't exactly have access to a car."

Declan purses his lips. "You can't take this on the bus or the train. I'll talk to the boss."

"Declan, no!"

I don't want to have any more engagements with Darragh, but I still can't get the hallway door open when Declan disappears into Darragh's office. Great, I'm *locked in*. This place is a fucking nightmare and Darragh Murray... Well, he has another thing coming.

He thinks I'm still the naive teenage girl high on her feelings for him. I don't care about him the way I used to. He can't just flash his icy eyes at me and expect me to melt anymore. Declan emerges just when I land my first kick against the door. He raises an eyebrow.

"The door is metal, ma'am."

"Thank you, Declan."

I try to sound composed, but I feel stupid. Declan doesn't seem to care. He gives me a friendly grin like he's trying to put me at ease.

"The boss says I can give you a ride home."

"You're a complete stranger. I don't want you knowing where I live."

"It isn't any different from using a taxi, is it?" Declan says. "Except I swore on my life that I'd keep you safe. I don't know any cab drivers offering amenities like that."

He's not Darragh handsome, but Declan has a boyish charm that I can't resist. I give him an annoyed eye roll so he doesn't think he's winning me over too easily, and then I agree to the ride home. Darragh probably only agreed to this so he can use Declan to fish for information, but he's underestimating me if he thinks I won't use my time with Declan to my advantage too. Darragh gave me enough money to get me out of trouble, but he can't get rid of me this easily.

I've done the math. If I work at his club for six months and live within my means, I'll have enough for a down payment on a house. Why won't he give me a job and let me just have money of my own? I didn't ask for his stupid charity. I'm not in any place to deny it, but I need more. *I could handle being on that stage. What if he didn't know and I just showed up to work? That might work on Darragh.*

In a place as expensive as Massachusetts, the kind of money he's offering is a big deal. I didn't realize how much money I could make working in a club. It's not just tempting — I want it. I'm tired of the grind and I'm tired of being ground to a pulp by the corporate world.

"Does Darragh work the floor every night?" I ask Declan as he drags the tote bag into the back seat of a black Lincoln town car.

"Nah," he says. "He's normally in on the weekends. If you want him to show up during your shifts—

My heart thuds. Darragh didn't tell him that I didn't get the job. He also doesn't realize that the heavy tote has Darragh's hush money — the money he thinks he can give me to pay for how badly he hurt me. I bite my lower lip. I have another idea of how Darragh can pay in mind.

"I'm fine," I interrupt, before Declan can say more. "I don't need him there. Since I start tomorrow, I wanted to be sure I looked my best for the boss."

I slide into the passenger seat as Declan closes the door to the back seat before climbing in behind the wheel.

"He shouldn't be in tomorrow," Declan says. "What time does your shift start?"

My heart pounds.

"Uhh. I can't exactly remember. The late one. I planned on getting there early."

Declan nods. "Smart move. The late shift starts at 9 p.m. Get there an hour early and I'll have one of the girls show you the ropes."

"Darragh said it started at 5?" I ask, making sure Declan isn't screwing with me.

He smiles, like he expected as much from his boss. "You'll need to ease your way into the job. Trust me."

"Thank you. I appreciate it."

Declan chuckles. "You didn't appreciate me much when he had you screaming like a wild cat in there."

"You know Darragh. He can be difficult to deal with."

"Sure," Declan says, chuckling again. "I know that. Well, if you got any problems tomorrow, I'm your guy."

"Thanks. I doubt there will be problems."

"It's a crazy idea. Black stripper at an Irish club. It's never been done before. Did the boss mention anything about extra security?"

"No. He said he trusted you to handle everything."

I feel a pang in my chest as I lie again. Declan doesn't exactly deserve to be lied to. He seems simple and loyal, and like he could get into serious trouble if he screwed with Darragh's orders. Luckily, I'm the one screwing with Darragh, not him.

"Sounds about right," Declan says, puffing his chest out while handling the Lincoln like a pro through the streets of Boston. He immediately knows my neighborhood without me having to guide him closely. "You got history with the boss, huh?"

I nod. "Yeah."

"Kinda shocking. I've known the boss my whole life and aside from that boxer, Tavarius, I've never known him to… you know what. Never mind."

"Tavarius is my brother."

Declan's eyebrows raise a little again. "Really? He's *much* darker than you are."

I never know how to respond when people say that to me. Do they expect me to take it as a compliment that I have lighter skin? Do they want me to prove that Tavarius is still my brother, even if he's a few shades darker than me?

"Yeah, he is," I mumble awkwardly. Declan clears his throat, noticing my growing discomfort and changes the subject to childhood stories about Darragh. They're cousins, I think, or close family friends who call each other cousins. Declan's stories meander, but they largely involve behavior I would typically apply to Darragh — getting into fights, running his mouth when he shouldn't, and a lot of whiskey. *A lot* of whiskey.

When we get to my apartment, Declan offers to walk the tote upstairs for me.

"I think I can manage. It's a short walk and I've taken up enough of your time."

"Yeah," he says. "Sure thing, miss. See you at your shift tomorrow."

Chapter Twelve

"See you tomorrow, Declan."

I DRAG the money upstairs and empty it out on my bed. None of my roommates are home. I have to drag my pillow against my face and press it there to stifle my screams of excitement. It's so much fucking money. I can pay off my debts and still have almost enough money to move. It's a good start and I'll be able to survive until the end of the month, but then what?

Where else will I get a job that pays as well as this? Darragh is out of his damn mind if he thinks I'll strip down in his office and show him all the goods, just so he can send me away with a tote of money. There's way more money where that came from, and tomorrow I'm heading to Harrison Ave for more of it – damn what Darragh Murray says.

Chapter Thirteen
Darragh

Then

My body burns with desire for her. Wrong doesn't enter the equation, I want her so badly. I also could've just helped kill someone. My best friend threw my ex-girlfriend overboard and she could be dead or alive. I don't know and I don't give a fuck. I'm shell-shocked from what I've done and all the rules I've broken. Touching Kamari would only make tonight worse. Touching her would also mean betraying the man who would do anything for me without a second thought, without asking any questions. *My best friend.*

I can't betray him, but I can't stop myself from wanting Kamari either. I need something pure, soft and gentle tonight. I need her. She's already offering me everything. All I have to do is take it. All I have to do is be with her. Her closeness ruins my self-control. I wonder if I ever had any in the first place. If I did, I wouldn't be here with her. I would have told Tavarius to have someone else stay with his sister tonight.

Fuck.

I'm so fucked up.

· · ·

HER BREASTS BRUSH against my chest, and I struggle to focus on pleasing her with my fingers as my dick comes to life. My fingers move in a slow circle around her hardened nub and Kamari makes a surprised little yelp like she doesn't expect a man's hands on her clit to feel this good.

"Hasn't anyone ever touched your pussy before?" I growl, using my other hand to grab her lower back and pull her closer to me so my fingers can sink deeper between her lower lips. She moans, yielding too much pleasure to come up with a real response to me.

"Come on," I whisper, continuing to tease her clit. "Tell me the truth."

"No..." she gasps. Her thighs tighten around mine. She's getting close. I massage her faster and add another finger until Kamari moans.

"Cum for me, princess," I say into her ear, licking her earlobe as she bucks her hips to get my fingers on the most sensitive part of her clit. As I lick her ear and she slides forward, it's enough to make her cum very fucking hard. Kamari leans forward, her mass of curls cascading all over me as my fingers sink between her lower lips and a gush of wetness rushes out of her pussy.

Her thighs squeeze around mine and as Kamari cums, she releases the tension. Her body loosens and she almost can't hold herself up. I slip my fingers from between her lips and use both my hands to keep her balanced as she straddles me. Kamari's hands brace against my chest and I kiss her slowly until Kamari settles back down to earth. Her breathing is ragged and her nipples are still ridiculously stiff.

I can't stop myself from teasing one of them with my fingers, playing with Kamari's hard brown nubs until she moans. I can feel a gooey wet spot on my thigh from Kamari's cum.

Her hand juts out around my cock before I think she's ready. My dick jerks in her hand as she grabs it. I don't expect her to be this forward, since she's a virgin. I flinch as Kamari's hands squeeze around my dick. She holds it with just the right grip. Holy fuck, this is amazing.

"I want you," she breathes. "Please, Darragh... Stop denying what you feel for me. Stop using your family and whatever as an excuse... You want me. I can tell."

I'm tense when she says that. *I'm doing what's right.*

"It's for your own good."

"I don't care," she breathes, tightening her grasp around my dick. "I want you."

It's my fault for letting it get this far, but I tell myself that Kamari holds equal blame because she has her hand around my dick and she's begging for me with the sort of needy urgency that keeps a man's blood pumping.

She takes her panties off and I lose complete control of myself once I have her completely naked. She's too fucking pretty. I want her so badly...

"You don't know what you're doing," I grunt as she begins stroking my staff, determined to have her way with me. She already has most of her way with me since I'm rock fucking hard and past the point of no return with her.

If I had any shot at controlling myself, her tight grip eliminates it. I grab her hips and lift Kamari over my cock just enough so that she lets go. My dick doesn't need any help standing up. Holding the smallest part of her hips, I position her over my dick.

"You lower yourself slowly," I murmur. "Go slow. It normally hurts your first time. Not always."

Not if you're wet enough, which she might be. The head of my cock brushes against Kamari's entrance and I nearly explode the second I touch her entrance. Her pussy and thighs are both soaked with her juices and as my cock pushes against her, I easily slide the first inch into her.

Her wetness makes it easy to slip my cock between Kamari's legs, but she's still tiny in comparison to me, and fucking tight. I've never had a woman this tight and I feel redness rushing to my cheeks and blood rushing to the tip of my cock. Condoms. We should use condoms.

Kamari sinks another inch onto my cock and I forget all about the fucking condoms. I just want her impaled on my dick. I want to make love to her in every position until I forget my demons and get some fucking freedom from the monsters inside my head.

I keep hold of her hips, but let her guide herself down the length of my dick. Her moans bring me close to climax before she gets my entire cock inside her. Minutes of slowly easing her onto my dick are fucking painful for me, but once she's finally there, Kamari makes the most intense moan of pleasure that every second of patience becomes worth it.

She is so fucking hot it hurts. It hurts that it's so wrong to screw her and it definitely hurts that when I'm sober, when I'm far away from this, I'll have to stop myself from ever doing something this stupid again. I'll use my drunkenness as an excuse, even if I don't exactly feel drunk anymore. Who knows how long alcohol lasts in the body? Not me.

I cup her ass cheeks and drag her closer to me. Her wet pussy engulfs my dick and nearly draws the cum straight out of my balls.

"You're not a virgin anymore, princess," I growl into her ear. "You're mine now. You will always be mine after tonight."

I mean every fucking word I say, even if I shouldn't. She moves her hips up so she slides almost completely off my cock and then slams her hips down. I nearly burst inside of her.

"Easy, baby," I whisper. "Fuck yourself with my dick. Fuck yourself until you cum. Take as long as you need."

It's fucking beautiful watching her ride me with all her inexperience and enthusiasm mixed into one. I don't care that she's a virgin. Fuck, I love it. She doesn't try to impress me with fancy tricks, she just makes love to me exactly the way she wants to without any expectations about it.

Kamari's emotions guide how she rides me. Her pussy is so tight and wet that her hip's gyrations cause her to squeeze down on my cock. Every minute with her gets harder for me to hold myself back. She tilts her head back, allowing her long hair to cascade down her back. I wrap a handful around my wrist and thrust my hips up to meet her pussy, fucking Kamari slowly as she grinds into me.

"Yes..." she moans. "Oh, yes..."

Her soft verbalizations activate my more monstrous cravings. I keep a firm grasp of her hair and lift her off my cock with one hand. Before she knows what hit her, I move our positions, flipping her onto her stomach and pushing her onto my bed.

Kamari hits the pillow with her chin, grunting as I slide my cock inside her again. I don't bother spreading her legs. Her thick thighs form a pillowy entrance around her pussy, adding to my arousal as I plunge into her from behind.

I reach around in front of her body, teasing her clit as I thrust my hips into Kamari, bouncing against her fluffy ass cheeks with each stroke.

"Fuck," I grunt. "Fuck, you have a nice pussy."

Her thighs tighten and her pussy contracts around my dick as Kamari approaches another orgasm. Teasing her clit pushes her closer over the edge. Most women need extra stimulation to cum. I make it easy for her by using two fingers on her clit and slowly down my strokes so she can feel every inch of my cock sliding against her inner walls.

In a few short minutes, Kamari cums hard and an even bigger gush of her juices coats my dick from her pleasure. I prop her up on all fours, still inside her and take her faster from behind, edged forward by what remains of the alcohol in my system. Stimulating her clit, I make her cum a few more times in that position before I feel my own climax approaching.

I don't want to wait to finish inside her, but I must.

I want to cum inside her while gazing into her pretty brown eyes and forcing her to gaze into mine. I want Kamari to see my Murray eyes fixed on her as I cum between her legs. In that moment, what I want more than anything in the world is for a place and time and city to exist where Kamari can belong completely to me. Fuck the rules.

I pull out of her and flip her onto her back. I don't enter her right away. Her thighs tremble with pleasure and the wet spot between her thighs makes her gooey center look even more attractive to me. Every biological urge that I have compels me to cum inside her. I kiss her slowly instead, easing my way to that final climax instead of rushing it.

As I kiss her, Kamari's hands immediately find my back. She strokes the length of it, whimpering with pleasure as I kiss her neck and tease her nipples. She wants more and I want to make sure that when I cum inside her, she's absolutely spent.

"You're tight," I murmur. "And you're a very good fuck for your first time."

She flinches at my brutish language, but I expect that. She's younger than me, definitely more innocent, and I've just deflowered her — taking a birthday gift that she never intended to give.

"Darragh—

She breathes my name, gyrating her hips to encourage my return between her legs.

"You want my big dick inside you again?"

"Yes," she gasps. "It's so... big."

I smirk and press the head of my cock against her entrance again. Kamari's hands cup my ass and she greedily drags me closer as if she can trick my cock to enter her again. I kiss her and tug on her lower lip between my teeth. I move my hips forward so the first two inches of my cock easily slide between Kamari's soaked lower lips.

Her softness nearly makes me cum instantly.

"Fuck me, Darragh," she begs.

Chapter Fourteen
Kamari

Now

I ask Kaly for advice about my first day. I have to skirt the truth a little bit when she asks if I got the job. I didn't exactly *get* the job, but I plan on going in. Kaly fluffs my hair over a pint of Halo ice-cream.

"You will be *perfect*. Just let that red curly hair flow wild and those Irish guys will go nuts. Don't mind them, they act all tough and racist on the surface, but they love *different*. You don't know how many times they had me pretend to be Spanish, Italian, whatever..."

"While you were dancing?"

Kaly smiles. "Oh, I didn't always just dance. But I don't do that stuff anymore. Don't worry, Darragh's not a pimp. He won't make you do it if you don't want to."

I suppose it's a relief that I can expect Darragh not to pimp me out, but these aren't exactly exceedingly high standards for a man. Kaly helps me put together an outfit from the limited items in my closet. She finds my modest peasant tops unsatisfactory and pulls out a tiny crop top for me to wear over my matching underwear. I have my best set of hot pink undies that I normally save for special occasions.

Kaly eggs me on when she sees them. I guess my first day of work at Darragh's club is a special occasion, and there isn't exactly another man in my life, nor will there be one anytime soon. The hot pink lingerie can make its debut tonight. For my bottoms, I throw on my tiniest pair of blue denim shorts. It's cold as hell out, but Kaly offers to drive me to work tonight so I don't have to walk outside with my whole ass out. After my shift, she promises she'll come back, but just in case, maybe I can beg Declan for a ride.

I don't have any shoes that would work for the job, but Kaly promises there will be heels for me at work.

"It's your first day, Darragh will make sure everything's ready."

I feel a flush of heat over my face. Darragh doesn't technically know I'm showing up, but I can't let Kaly know that. I'll figure out the shoes thing later.

"Are you sure this is a good idea? Aren't these guys… racist?"

"Yeah, but you're a woman," Kaly says. "They're racist until they get hard."

"Gross."

"Don't worry, Declan won't let any of those losers touch you unless you want to make extra cash. He's great about that shit," she says, flipping her hair out of her face and reaching into her purse for a piece of gum. She offers me a piece, but I decline.

I smiled politely and nodded with regards to her statements about Declan and the strip club clientele, but I hope and pray that I don't have to do "extra". I can't do that type of thing with strange guys. It's never worked for me. The only time sex ever felt good was when it was with Darragh Murray. It's the kind of embarrassing thing that you can only admit to yourself, but Darragh was the best I ever had.

Before he turned into a monster after our first night together, he was the sweetest, most romantic person I'd ever known.

Darragh's cruelty was so hard for me to accept because of how good I felt that first night when everything was perfect. I *knew in my heart* that night Darragh loved me. I felt his love in the way he touched and kissed me. We were so hesitant at first about falling into bed together that every slow movement towards tangling naked in the sheets with Darragh became intensely memorable.

I've tried to be with other men since him and I gave up quickly. There's never been another man as good as the one who shattered my heart into a million pieces. He was my first love, and my first hate. There's a part of me that wonders if I'm doing this to get revenge on him. I want to prove to him that he doesn't own me. He can't control me. He broke my heart, but I stayed in control.

Kaly does my makeup and I feel *really* strange with it on. Makeup isn't my thing, but neither is stripping. Kaly assures me that all I need is confidence and as long as I love dancing, I'll be fine. Dancing to hip-hop in front of my mirror has to be different from dancing in a secret warehouse strip club, but Kaly won't let my confidence falter.

She drops me off as promised, and I glance around the parking lot for any gaudy cars that could possibly belong to Darragh. Appearing to be safe, I confidently strut through the front door and immediately run into Declann. I'm happy to see him since I'm nervous as hell. Declan is dressed all in black and he looks clean tonight. He grins when he sees me.

"You look great," he says. "Man, the boss might be right about this. The guys have been itching for something different, you know? They're old school, they've got their beliefs but… ass is ass…"

"Ass is ass? Really?"

Declan's ears turn red and he stammers an apology before offering to show me to the locker room so I can meet the "other girls". He leads me to the locker room filled with the heavy scent of vanilla and coconut perfume. It's cheap and chokes the air to the point where I can barely breathe.

The three blonde women in the room neither acknowledge nor greet me when Declan introduces me. I say hello and I'm met with silence. Declan clears his throat and shows me to a locker. The women gather on one side of the room, staring at me while they snicker. I still have clothes on, but I've never felt more naked.

Declan leans forward and whispers comfortingly, "Don't let them get to you. They always treat new girls like this."

"They probably don't like that I'm black," I whisper back, although I don't expect to find sympathy with Declan. He assures me they aren't racist, but I'm not so sure. My doubts are suddenly at a fever pitch. What if those guys throw tomatoes at me?

One of the blonde women takes a step forward.

"I'm Katie, but I go by Princess Cupcake" she says. "You got a stage name?"

Okay, she has a stage name. I didn't think I had to come up with a stage name.

"Darragh didn't give me one."

"You have to make one up," she says. "I dunno, you kinda look like a gypsy."

In any of my college classes, someone would have brought up how the term gypsy is racist, but I feel like this is the closest any of these girls has come to liking me or acknowledging my existence, so I can't afford to be difficult.

Princess Cupcake decides my name is Gypsy on the spot and she explains the job to me. Declan backs out of the room and promises to be positioned nearby the stage if I need him.

I almost want to beg him to stay just in case the other girls beat the brakes off me once we're alone. The other two still haven't acknowledged me, but they are whispering about me in the corner as Princess Cupcake explains the details of the job, taking over Declan's position.

She seems more like the leader of the group despite being the shortest. Princess Cupcake has startling blue eyes which she lines with thick black liner. Her fake lashes are some of the largest I've ever seen. Should I have worn fake lashes?

In Kaly's defense, the job Princess Cupcake explains sounds as easy as she originally promised me. According to my new jobsite trainer, you can ignore the guys, dance on the stage, take as much or as little of your clothing off as you want, and once your half hour is done, Declan collects all your tips for you backstage. She has a heavy, South Boston accent which seems surprising coming from a 5'2" blond woman who is stick thin compared to me.

She tells me that we alternate spots on the stage for the next ten hours, so we get plenty of down time to collect ourselves. The guys prefer girls who go full nude, but you don't have to do more than take your top off on your first night.

She says that Darragh is lenient with new girls. My cheeks darken again. I'm doing this behind his back, which he probably won't feel too lenient about once he finds out.

"If it's too hard to dance in heels the first time, you can go bare-foot. You make more money in heels but I dunno… You might make a bunch of cash anyway," Princess Cupcake says. All the other women are thin which makes me suddenly self conscious of my thickness. I wouldn't have noticed otherwise but we are about to take our clothes off in a room full of strangers.

If they have a "type" and I don't fit that mold, what the hell could those guys do to me? I'm about to panic and back out when Princess Cupcake says, "You're on first, okay? I'll go out with you. The other girls will take the stage together. I can't help you dance or nothing, but if you follow my lead, you'll be fine."

Darragh already gave me the money I needed. What the hell am I doing? My mouth feels dry, but it's too late for me to back out. I wanted to prove to him that I'm in control. That I don't have to listen to him. That he doesn't own me.

Even if this is the only night I get up on that stage, I'll get up there and *live* for a change. Screw Darragh Murray.

Chapter Fifteen
Darragh

Now

My phone buzzes with a text from Katie. She has a stage name, but she's family, so to me she'll always be Katie. Got a bit of a drug problem though, so dad has her working at the club as a favor to his sister so Katie stays off the streets by becoming my responsibility. Hm.

Katie: New colored girl? Really?

WHAT THE FUCK is she talking about? I shove my phone into my pocket. She does lines before going on stage in the locker room bathroom and thinks we don't know about it. This is probably one of her drug induced text messages that I can ignore. *Hm.*

I'm working out right now and I can't go to the club until I hit the gym. I love when it's just me and the punching bag. I don't fight anymore, but getting Tavarius into shape might just bring back my energy for the boxing ring. He's better than I ever was, winning a few local championships and was undefeated in New England before early retirement shortly after Kamari left for college.

He said yes to my brother's proposition, so we have three months to get his ass in gear. We didn't talk about his sister when I went over there, thank fuck. I got her address from Declan, so I know exactly where she is right now. Thud. Thud. I hit the punching bag twice, gasping for air as sweat drips down my brow.

I'd fucking love to go over there. Right hook. Right hook. Kick. My abs hurt. My forearms hurt. I feel fucking out of shape. Thud. Thud.

HOLD ON.

New colored girl.

MY STOMACH SINKS. I unwrap my wrists and strip my gloves off with incredible speed. I know she's doing something fucking stupid. I'm covered in sweat, but I just towel off before getting into my work clothes for the night. I hate how my suit feels stuck to my gross body, but if Kamari is halfway across town stripping her clothes off in my club... I have to be there.

Why is she so fucking stubborn? Why does she want to take her clothes off for other men to see her so fucking badly? I give her the money she needs and she feels the need to go behind my back and do something this foolish? *Fuck.*

I speed through the streets, avoiding anywhere I know cops hang out. I don't give a fuck about red lights or anything aside from avoiding hitting pedestrians. It's a fucking miracle I make it to the club without getting pulled over. I leave my gym bag in the car and don't bother locking it as I sprint to the door.

Declan must be near the stage because Gaelan Doyle answers the door instead. He's one of Evie's in-laws, a dull-witted redheaded boy with more muscle than brains.

"Who's on stage right now?"

He gives a stupid, satisfied grin which sends an instant surge of inexplicable rage through me.

"New girl with a fat ass."

My heart sinks into my stomach. That certainly can't be said of Katie or any of the Irish girls. I wish I had one of my guns in my jacket. My office has guns. I could get one of those.

"What's her name?"

"I dunno. Gypsy or something. She's *hot*. How did you convince a black chick to come down here?"

"Fuck off, Gaelan. Stay here and don't get into trouble, okay?"

"Boss?"

To be fair, he didn't deserve that fuck off. He's just the closest target for my aggression until I enter the club stage and seating area. I throw the soundproof door open and the deafening roar of cheering nearly knocks me on my fucking ass. These assholes are screaming their heads off and it smells like they're pounding back more beer down here than usual on a typical Wednesday night.

The smell of the beer drowns out the disgusting smell of my sweat from the gym. I walk through a thicker crowd than I've seen down here in months until I get a view of the stage. New girl with a fat ass. It couldn't have been anyone else. *What the fuck does she think she's doing?*

I sensed the woman who stormed into my office with those pretty doe-eyes was different from the one I'd held against my body on the yacht, but I didn't realize how different the two were. Dorky Kamari grasps the pole with a smile on her face and all the confidence in the world. She throws her barely covered thigh over the pole and twirls around.

The cheers get louder. Twenty dollar bills are flying from the crowd onto the stage. Stacks of them. I don't know who got word out about the "new girl" but someone got it out because every Irish thug in a fucking fifteen mile radius must be in here. I recognize men from families I'm accustomed to seeing twice a year at church.

And they're all looking at her. What I feel is worse than jealousy. It's even more irrational. I pushed her too far in my office. I messed with her to the point where she felt like she had to do this for revenge. She can't hear the things those men are saying to her over the music, but I can – and I don't fucking like it.

I move through the crowd closer to the stage. She's so fucking beautiful it hurts. Kamari takes her shirt off and throws it into the crowd. They go fucking crazy. The music throbs through the night club and the dim lights make it easy for me to move undetected. I'm getting her the fuck down from there, but I can't take my eyes off her as I move closer.

She moves her hips exactly how I like it. Her soft butt cheeks peek out from beneath tiny denim pants that I sincerely fucking hope she would never wear in public. I don't want these assholes staring at her body. They don't deserve Kamari. Even if they did, it wouldn't matter. She's *mine*.

I can't make the same mistake I made years ago. I'm close enough that Declan recognizes my presence. He gives me a big wave, which tells me he probably has no clue about Kamari's little deception. I should have never left her alone in a car with him. She's always been crafty and I can't imagine what tangled web she's caught him in.

She pokes her ass out towards the audience and the crowd goes fucking wild. *Act Up* by City Girls plays in the background. Kamari's dancing is... too much.

I can't take it any more. Declan doesn't realize what I'm doing until it's too late to stop me. Most of the guys are too drunk to recognize I'm the owner when I hoist myself on stage beneath the swaying blue and purple lights, wrapping my arm around Kamari's waist and throwing her over my shoulder as she screams.

I can't hear her screams over the music, but I feel her rib cage vibrating against mine as she throws her fists into my back. *No Hands* by Roscoe Dash and Waka Flocka Flame blares in the background as she attacks.

Her screaming is the least of my concerns. Angry patrons fling wads of coins at me and they feel like fucking paintball bullets they hurt so fucking bad.

I'm probably costing us a shit ton of money tonight, but I don't care. I'm pissed out of my fucking mind that she's here after I gave her all the money she needed. After she told me she wouldn't show up. She's finally pushed me too far. I drag her all the way to my back office, relying on the club's security team to keep the throng of infuriated patrons out of the way.

Chapter Fifteen

Once I shut my office door, we can't hear the music, which allows me to perfectly hear Kamari's screaming. She drowns out *Gas Pedal* by Sage The Gemini perfectly.

"What the fuck is wrong with you? Are you out of your mind?" Kamari yells hysterically.

She pulls a coin out of her hair and flings it at me. She misses, which only frustrates her more. I hang back, keeping just enough distance between us that she can't smack me. Standing next to my desk, Kamari is in between me and the door, which means her escape from me would be far too fucking easy if I don't take control here.

"The question is are *you* out of your mind? Do you know what kind of fucking place this is?"

"A place where assholes like you hang out. So what? Men are all assholes anyway. I might as well get paid to be around you all."

"I gave you all the money you needed and I told you to stay away from me, Kamari. Why the fuck do you never listen to me?"

"I don't listen to you because women weren't put on this earth to listen to men, Darragh," she says, her voice twisted with pure hatred.

She's so fucking beautiful as she trembles with outrage. My office is much colder than the stage, so every inch of her exposed pale copper skin breaks out into goosebumps. I want to wrap my arms around her, but only as a precursor to spanking the most frustrating woman on the planet.

"If men know better, then you ought to listen. One of those men could have hurt you. If you hear how they talk about the girls–

"You are such a hypocrite," she interrupts, blazing with outrage. "You *own* this place. You allow this to happen. And you don't give a fuck about me dancing on that stage or what these men say to me because you've said so much worse."

"Years ago," I say to her, entirely doubtful that this will have any impact on Kamari. She wants to hate me. Worse than that, she wants to punish me. Her absolute loathing for me should discourage me but if she's angry enough to want revenge, a part of her still cares. That part of her belongs to me and always will. This time, I won't break her heart.

"Does it matter that it was years ago? You're the same person."

"I'm not."

"You could never prove it."

Fuck, I'm done with this. I close the distance between us, grabbing Kamari's cheeks and pulling her to me. If she won't fucking listen to my words, maybe she'll listen to my lips. She makes a shocked squeal and struggles to push me away, fighting against my chest as I tease her lips open.

No, princess. I'm not letting you get away from me this time. Pulling her body against mine gets me instantly hard. I don't have any control of my body as blood surges to my cock. Kamari's soft, bare skin presses against me. Her butt jiggles with the slightest movement of her body and her hair smells fucking great. I want to bury my nose in her hair, in her neck…

I push my tongue into her mouth and she teases me back with hers, yielding to me. *Finally.* My hands drop from her cheeks to her hips and my dick jerks in my pants. I must still smell like sweat from the gym, but she doesn't seem to care. She lets me kiss her and hold her hips and it feels like heaven.

I'm the one who finally pulls away. I'm too hard to resist her. She keeps gaping at me like I'm out of my fucking mind. Maybe I am.

"What is wrong with you?"

Her voice has finally lost its ferocious tone. My shoulders relax.

"I love you."

There. I said it. Kamari's lips tighten and as my hands grip her hips firmly, she slaps me square across the face. Fuck…

What is wrong with *her*?

Chapter Sixteen
Kamari

Then

Darragh shifts uncomfortably, giving me the strangest look. I don't like when he looks at me with uncertainty like that. There's nothing for him to be unsure about. *I love him.* I don't care if he has flaws. I can look past them as long as we can be together...

I grab his shaft, watching his body shudder with desire as I pull him towards me. He's not *racist.* Maybe he has flaws or some residual bigotry, but he doesn't hate me. He can't. If we're making love like this, he's at least conflicted about his beliefs. *He'll change. He'll change for me.*

He slides his hips forward and I cry out as he plunges his entire length inside me. He's enormous and it feels like there's a large knot tightening just beneath my belly button as he enters me completely. It hurts at first, but the waves of pleasure from his slow, gentle movements make the pain entirely worth it.

I didn't know experiencing pleasure like this was possible before tonight. My body feels like a mystery that I'm just uncovering. Darragh leans on his forearm, easing his hips forward with his giant muscular body hovering over mine. I can feel his heavy breathing and his desire for me with each thrust.

A wave of euphoria begins deep in my core as I dig my nails into Darragh's back and pull him towards me. I don't care about the consequences of our night together. I'm too young to give a crap about consequences.

I cum hard around Darragh's dick and as I lose myself to my orgasm, Darragh's body tenses.

"Fuck," he grunts. "Fuck, you're so beautiful."

He presses his lips to mine as his cock throbs between my legs, releasing Darragh's seed between my legs. I feel so full and he feels so good. I drag him closer to me, using my ankles to pull Darragh deep inside me. I moan as he settles his weight on top of me. So good.

He kisses my forehead, then my lips, and then he has that strange look on his face again. I don't like that look.

"What's wrong?"

"Nothing," he whispers. "You're just... innocent."

"Not anymore."

"That's not funny," he says sternly. I wriggle beneath him. I don't want a lecture from Darragh while he has his dick still inside me. It's not the right time for him to get all serious and boring on me. We just did it... *finally.*

"I've wanted you forever," I confess. The confession makes me nervous, but his reaction only makes it worse.

His cheeks turn dark red and he eases his hips forward, pinning me to the bed with his giant dick.

"You shouldn't say that, Kamari," he murmurs, pressing his nose into my neck and making an incredibly frustrated groan as he stiffens inside me again. Darragh's cheeks turn a brighter shade as he struggles to hide his body's physical reaction to me.

"Why not?"

"Because we can never be together," He whispers, kissing me and taking my lower lip between his. "We can only have this. We can only have tonight."

I don't believe him, so I let him kiss me and make love to me again. I like it better when he's on top. I can gaze into his pretty blue eyes and watch his face change as he makes love to me. My body feels incredible being joined with his. I moan as Darragh takes me deeper. I moan into his mouth as he kisses me.

He smells so fucking clean that I want to disappear into his soft, tattooed skin.

"I want you," I whisper. "I want to be yours."

Darragh slides his finger between my legs and slowly rubs my clit until I cum hard. As my thighs tighten around his body, Darragh grunts and cums inside me again. He makes a low growl in his throat and kisses me possessively after he finishes. His warm body sinks into mine and the scent of his hair gets stronger. As he pulls out of me, my thighs are splattered with Darragh's essence. I hate that we have to separate.

"You can't ever be mine," he says sternly. But he pulls me against him and kisses me anyway. We kiss and become completely incapable of keeping our hands off each other. I don't care that we're being reckless. I care about Darragh.

I've loved him forever.

"Who says so?" I say after we pull away from each other for a brief moment.

"Me," he murmurs. "My family. My responsibility."

"What about love? Wouldn't that change your mind?"

His eyes roam all over my face. I love when he looks at me with curiosity and deep interest. To have Darragh's eyes on you makes you feel absolutely special. He doesn't just have a beautiful face, but a raw, muscular body cut from years of fighting. I don't even care about my brother finding out. I just want to be here. With him.

"What we're doing isn't love," he says, lying to me with his words as his cock comes to life *again*. "It's just sex."

"You are such a liar."

"Am I?"

"You're getting hard again," I whisper.

"And you're the expert on what that means?" His tongue teases my neck and I stifle a moan. I don't want him to feel like he's won me over. I just want him again. I don't believe he'll ever hurt me. He wants me just as badly as I want him, and love is all the two of us need.

"Don't get lost in a fantasy, Kamari," he says. "It's my birthday and you're the hottest girl on this boat. That's all this is."

"I don't understand you," I whisper back, pushing his head away from my neck gently. "If I'm too black for you to be with, how can you say I'm the hottest girl on this boat? It's a complete contradiction."

"Stop using all those big words," he says. "Open your legs again."

"Contradiction is not a big word," I protest, but Darragh stops listening. He kisses his way down my chest until he gets to my breasts and then flicks a tongue over my nipple.

"Tonight, you're mine. That's all that matters. I need more of my birthday gift, princess."

I feel the head of his cock against my entrance and Darragh slides into me again with one smooth stroke. *How can he go again?*

We make love until the sun comes up. Neither of us smell like Darragh's ultra-clean soap anymore. I roll over on his bed to find him awake, staring at me. Normally I like when he stares but now, he looks panicked. He turns away from me. *No.*

I know something's wrong.

I JUST DON'T KNOW how wrong it's going to get. I don't know how Darragh Murray is going to break me, but one look in his eyes and I know that he will.

Chapter Seventeen
Darragh

Now

"Why the fuck did you hit me?"

"You don't get to act all possessive with me, Darragh."

My grasp on Kamari's hips tightens. I don't need her to tell me what to do with her. I know *exactly* what to do with her. It doesn't help that she smells like delicious coconut and vanilla body spray. She's nearly naked in front of me, and resisting Kamari naked takes every bit of effort that I have.

"Why not?"

"Because you pushed me away. You broke my heart."

"Let me un-break it then."

"That's not how love works. You can't just decide that you're different."

"I am."

I don't care if she slaps me again. I kiss Kamari like my life depends on our lips touching. Kissing her seemed like a good first step of fixing things between us. I don't want her getting away from me and I definitely don't want her getting back on that fucking stage.

She's so soft to the touch and she yields to my lips after a few seconds.

She can't resist me any more than I can resist her. *If I had a second chance with her, there's no fucking way I would screw up.*

I pull away from her and she scowls, but she doesn't shove me away or slap me again.

"Why the hell did you drag me down from there?"

"Did you really think I'd let you shake your ass on that stage and do nothing?"

"I didn't think you would *be* here. I wanted to get my money and run."

"I don't believe that for a second. I think you wanted me to see you up there. I think you still want me."

"You are fucking delusional," Kamari says, the familiar spite returning to her voice.

"Am I?" I say to her, my hands wandering to her ass cheeks. She never pushes me away. She doesn't resist. My cock stiffens in my pants as I become a complete slave to my desire for her. I meant what I said all those years ago. She's the hottest woman I've ever seen. Touching her ass makes me want to cum in my pants.

"Yes."

"So if I put my fingers inside your skimpy fucking thong, you won't be soaking wet?"

"That would be sexual harassment, since you're my boss," she says, squirming as if she's trying to get away, but only settling her ass cheeks deeper into my palms. Her soft flesh sinks between my fingers, and keeping a clear thought in my head becomes incredibly fucking difficult.

Nope, it's fucking impossible.

"I think we're way past sexual harassment, princess. Especially since I have my hands on your ass," I say to her, my voice nearly hitching. I want to stop talking and enter her slowly again. I want to remember what it feels like to slide my dick inside Kamari and have her want me.

I fucking miss when she wanted me. I want to break down her cold hatred of me and make her love me again. I'll do anything.

"You're the only one doing the sexual harassing. I'm trying to do my job."

"You didn't get the job. You seem to be forgetting that one little fact."

"Because of racial discrimination?" Kamari asks. She has the tiniest smirk on her face. She's not exactly joking, but she's definitely trying to rile me up. I squeeze her ass cheeks until her smug little smirk turns into a frown.

"No," I growl, continuing to hold her. "Because your ass and your pussy only belong to me. I tried to make that clear when you came here the first time."

"You are full of shit," she says. "The last time I gave in to your sugary words, you left me high and dry. You don't give a shit about me. I finally understand that you're just as racist as you said you were."

"What do you want me to say, Kamari? That I made a mistake?"

"It wouldn't fucking kill you to apologize instead of playing mind games with me."

"Mind games," I grunt. "Isn't that what you're doing walking into my club dressed like a fucking hooker shaking your ass for half my fucking relatives?"

"I'm trying to use you and your band of racists for what you're worth. Money."

That's when I laugh.

"You won't win, Kamari. I know you don't have a materialistic bone in your body. You're here to piss me off, and congratulations. You did it."

She gives me a petulant stare. She won't answer me because she knows I'm right. Kamari might be a wild thing, but I'm a wild thing too. We understand each other. I've never wanted to dim her fire. I've just known I could never run free with her. The only place I could ever be free was in the boxing ring. That's where I put all my emotions, all my anger with my father or my brothers, all the night terrors from the wicked shit I've done.

Kamari was the first time I put my feelings into a woman. She was the first one who could feel all my emotions with me. She's so fucking fierce that it scares the crap out of me. A woman like that could burn you up and break your heart. She still can.

"I'm not here to piss you off."

"Then why?"

"I didn't think you would be here tonight."

"But you suspected I might show up eventually?"

"Maybe."

"Why?" I ask, releasing my grip on her ass to wrap my arms around her.. I don't want her running away from the question and I don't want her running away from me anymore. That's done. She's mine now and nothing can fucking change that.

"So you can finally admit to yourself that you have feelings for me and I can be absolutely certain that I don't have any feelings left for you."

She gets me hard and pisses me off at the same time. It's hard to think straight when Kamari opens her mouth. She frustrates me so bad that I want to throw her up against the wall and fuck the attitude out of her. The little smirk spreading across her face as she senses my frustration drives me wild.

"If you didn't have feelings for me, you wouldn't care how I felt about you."

"I'm petty, Darragh. I will go out of my way for revenge," she sneers. I don't believe her. Kamari and I are too fucking similar and maybe that's our downfall.

"You are a liar. And I'm going to put my fingers in that ridiculously inappropriate thong and find out the truth," I say back to her. She acts like she's going to try to escape but I hold her tightly so she can't. I meant every word of what I said – she's mine tonight. She's mine forever.

She protests loudly as I slide two fingers down the front of her shorts. My dick jerks in my pants again. She's completely waxed. It's strange feeling her pussy so soft like this, but she feels exactly how I expect – completely slick.

Kamari squirms as my fingers peel her lower lips apart. She coats my fingers in her gooey juices against her will. My cock is absolutely desperate for her at this point. She can't hide her arousal more than I can.

"I knew you would be wet."

"It's sweat," she says. "Which by the way, you absolutely reek of."

I ignore her words and focus on her breath. As I spread her lower lips apart, it gets difficult for her to hold her body stiff. Kamari can't hide how she feels about me as my thumb rubs a slow circle around her clit.

"You smell like sweat. Stripper sweat. I don't normally get turned on by that but something about you really gets me going."

"You are such an asshole," she gasps, but her hips move forward to give me better access to her pussy. She gushes and gets wetter with each slow movement of my fingers. I slide my index and middle finger down the length of her pussy lips, coating both fingers in her juices. She gasps with agitated desperation as I tease her entrance but refuse to enter her with my soaked fingers.

Not yet.

"I'm an asshole? You sauntered in here dressed like a skank to piss me off and make me jealous. You had to know I would have found out."

"You deserve it," she says, accidentally letting out a moan after telling me off as my fingers rub her sweet spot. I love the sound of Kamari's moans. How the fuck could I have lived so many years without her? I made so many fucking mistakes with her and with other women, but mostly with her. I can't make those mistakes anymore. Not tonight.

"Why? Because I kept you safe from a scumbag who takes his strippers to the back office?"

She rolls her eyes. "Don't you see the irony here, Darragh?"

"Nope."

She makes a frustrated grunt and tries to keep her voice steady as she tells me off, "You weren't an asshole to protect me. You were an asshole to protect yourself."

I move my fingers again and she moans, but this time I slow down stroking her. Kamari's thighs squeeze around my hand. I grunt and shift my hips closer to her. It's hard to hear her say this. She's right, but it isn't easy for a guy like me to admit I'm wrong. It's much easier to focus on her soft pussy lips wrapped around my fingers and how fucking badly I want more.

"I fucked up."

"Is that your idea of an apology?" Kamari asks, squirming uncomfortably as I press two fingers against her lower lips.

How can words ever make up for what I did and said to her? How can I ever say 'sorry' and have her believe I mean it? What I did was unforgivable. Racist. Heartbreaking.

AND SHE'S RIGHT. I did it because I was too scared of what it meant to love a girl like her. It was easier to choose hate. It was easier to choose my family and something safe than to choose Kamari.

Hurting her was the biggest mistake of my life, but nothing I do can ever take it back. I can just step up every fucking day and try to prove to her that I'm not the same man.

Chapter Eighteen
Kamari

Then

I know instantly he's not the same man I went to bed with. This may be my only sexual experience, but my instincts can tell me when the man I love is planning on running. He sits on the edge of the bed naked, his head in his hands as I stare at him. He listens to me moving, but he doesn't look at me. He *can't* look at me.

"I've made an awful mistake," he says. His voice instantly sounds cold. I freeze and become suddenly aware of my nakedness. I feel too vulnerable. He doesn't sound like the Darragh who made love to me last night. He sounds like my brother's best friend who scared me before I fell for him.

My heart jumps into my throat.

"You didn't," I say. "I had a great time."

His voice stiffens. "That's not the point, Kamari."

"My fucking head," he grunts. "Fuck, Darragh. Fucking idiot."

"Darragh–

"Do not say my name," he says harshly. "You... This is a fucking nightmare. What were you thinking, Kamari? Why the fuck did you let me? Never mind. Never fucking mind."

He sounds like he's lost it. I want to help. I throw my arms around him, but Darragh literally flings me off. The rejection is sudden and painful. He throws me across the bed until my back slams into a pillow. The tears are instantaneous.

"Don't you dare touch me," he snarls.

The loathing in his voice is like a punch to the gut. I'm crying partly from shock and partly from the pain of his actions and his words. I've never heard Darragh speak to me with so much hate before. I've never believed him capable of hatred before.

I scramble to my knees, dragging a blanket up to cover myself. My heart races and I feel intensely shamed and terrified that he'll shove me harder or do something worse to hurt me. *I don't want him to get crazy on me.* He still won't look at me and it hurts.

"I acted in a moment of weakness last night, Kamari. A very long moment of weakness."

"There's no point in feeling guilty about it."

I know what he's feeling is beyond guilt. I don't want to admit it to myself. I want to believe that my teenage dream came true and that my brother's best friend really wanted me for more than one night. I believed that I could be his – that I could belong to Darragh Murray. He would come around to changing from how he was raised. *I believed in him last night.*

"I don't feel guilty," he says. "I feel disgusted with myself."

My gut reaction is to feel ashamed. But then there's a tug inside me that tells me I'm too proud for that. With Darragh's white sheet covering my naked body, I stiffen my body and keep my head as high as I can.

"If you feel disgusted with yourself because you slept with a black woman, that's a stain on your character, not mine."

I want to reach out and touch his back. It's still beautiful, even if every other part of Darragh is so incredibly ugly to me right now.

"Your judgment of me is truly irrelevant," he says. "You manipulated your way into my bed despite my beliefs and if you think that your pussy will change my feelings in any way, you're wrong."

"I'm not going to listen to a man who doesn't even have the balls to face me. So if you aren't going to face me, get out of the way. I'll get my things and go find my brother."

My challenge to Darragh's masculinity gets his attention. I can barely conceal my outrage with him but he meets my outrage with his fierce gaze. If I thought his eyes were ice before, they're glaciers now.

"You don't call your fucking brother. I'll take you home later. I'm not afraid to face you, Kamari."

I search his face for any emotion. Not just any emotion: love. I search Darragh's face for the love he showed me last night and see none of it. My heart sinks into my stomach. He fooled me. I was a virgin. Tears well in my eyes again. He glares as he watches the tears stream down my cheek. I don't want to look weak in front of him, but I always told myself I was saving myself for the right guy.

What's worse was that I told myself that Darragh was the right guy. I won't break his gaze. I won't let him think I'm weak for a second, even as he shatters me to a million pieces.

"You're a complete dick."

"No," he says sternly. "I was weak."

"You're lying," I whimper, hating how weak I sound. I just care about him so much. He's my first love. He's the first guy I ever had a crush on. Darragh was the one I wanted to take me for the first time. He's handsome, wealthy, strong...

He doesn't break my gaze. "I feel nothing for you, Kamari. I tried to warn you that this was a mistake."

"You also took my virginity," I yell at him, losing myself instantaneously to my impulses. "You manipulated me into your bed and now you're blaming me because you regret it."

"Yes, I regret it," he says. "I dirtied myself. You don't understand what that means to me or to my family. You don't understand what the fuck I've done."

"I didn't know you were like this. If I'd known–

"I don't need you to act like you're better than me," he says. "That's the last fucking thing I need. Get your clothes on."

"They're on the floor."

Darragh keeps his eyes glued to me as he picks my clothes up off the floor and hands them to me. It pains me to notice how handsome he is. When I notice his sandy blond hair or the way his back muscles tense as he bends over, Darragh's cruel words return to attack me and twist into my stomach. *He hates me.*

"If you hate me so much, why the hell did you sleep with me? You grew up with my brother. You didn't *have to* do this."

It hurts too much to believe Darragh. I want to give him a chance to change his mind.

"I did it because girls like you are easy. You open your legs for any white man who acts like he wants you. It was my fucking birthday, I wanted sex and you were there."

HE SHATTERS my heart into a million pieces. Those words hurt worse than any others. My ears start ringing. I feel drunk again, but not in the good way. I feel like I did before Darragh carried me into this room to rest – completely out of control.

"But Darragh," I whisper, my hands shaking. I know I shouldn't say it, but it's my last chance to reach out to him. It's my last chance to change his mind.

"I'm in love with you," I say, and he lets my words hang in the air. The silence kills me, but not more than Darragh's next words.

"And I could never be in love with you," he says. "You were just a good fuck for one night – nothing more. That's all you'll ever be to white guys, princess – a good fuck for one night."

Chapter Nineteen
Darragh

Now

Her body squirms against mine. I keep one hand on her ass and another inside her panties. I want to be wet with her juices when I confess everything – my greatest shame.

"Nothing I say can make up for how I hurt you."

"I thought about your words for years," she says. "They've played in my head over and over again…"

I slide my fingers over her clit. I can't make the pain go away, but I can make her feel good right now. I can make Kamari's pussy feel fucking amazing.

"I hurt you because I was weak," I grunt. "I'm sorry…"

I don't want her to respond. I don't want her to reject me even if I deserve Kamari's rejection. I slide my two soaked fingers inside her pussy and Kamari moans loudly. It's not exactly an acceptance of my apology, but at least I know that she feels good.

"Your fingers…" she gasps as her pussy clenches around my fingers like a vice. She still has the tightest pussy. Her hairlessness makes her lower lips and thighs completely slick. It's easy for me to thrust my fingers in a steady rhythm because of how wet Kamari is.

Our conversation transitions into a series of her pleasurable grunts and moans as I push Kamari close to a climax. With two fingers inside her pussy and rubbing my thumb in slow circles around her clit, her pussy gets nice and tight around my fingers as she gets close.

"It feels so good to finger you," I whisper. "Our night has been on replay in my head too. Whenever I couldn't cum, all I had to do was think about you and your soft brown lips..."

I thrust my fingers into Kamari deeper. She lets out a loud moan and cums hard. I nearly erupt in my pants as I feel her pussy tighten around my fingers. Her juices gush around my fingers and she loses her balance a bit as she leans forward. Her thigh brushes against my dick, making it harder to keep any semblance of self control.

Slowly, I pull my fingers out of her pussy and out of her thong. My fingers are soaked and I need them dry, so I clean them off with my tongue. Her scent gets me drunk.

"The fact that you fantasized about fucking me doesn't make me feel better."

It still jars me to hear Kamari talk like she's really all grown up. A part of me wants her to be eighteen again, but mostly so I can go back to the night that I hurt her and do it differently this time.

"I didn't expect it to. But you were right about me, Kamari. I was fucking terrified."

"What changed? Because you didn't change because of me."

My fingers still smell like her pussy, making it incredibly hard to focus on complicated questions like why I changed.

"I changed because I missed you. You were the best woman I've ever had in my bed, but I didn't realize why that was."

"And why was that? You get off screwing women you see as beneath you?"

For all her harsh words, a part of her still gives a fuck about me. My heart quickens just knowing I have a chance with her tonight. We aren't playing mind games with each other. This is real.

"No. I get off on screwing women that I'm in love with."

"I'm not falling for your pretty words again. I'm not a dumbass teen anymore."

"I mean it, Kamari," I say to her, my heart racing because I expect her to reject me. "I love you, but you couldn't possibly understand what it means for me to do this to my family."

"What changed? And don't give me any bullshit answers about how I changed you."

"Everything changed. Me. My family. My morals... I never forgave myself for how I treated you. I was too ashamed to face your brother. I was too ashamed to face you... I gave you that money and sent you away because if you're on that stage, it's because of what I said to you."

I don't mean for my voice to catch but it gets rough and raspy. I can't keep my hands off her. *I want her so badly. It hurts.* I move my hands to her smaller hips away from her full-figured ass, and imagine taking her to my bed and putting a baby in her. It's wrong. It would be wrong... but it's what my body wants whenever I'm near her.

Kamari gazes up at me with those dark eyes. They're deep pools that drive me wild with how dark they are, like they're full of something. I can't help myself. It's probably the wrong thing to do, but I kiss her again. There are no more words for what I've done or what I feel, no words that come easily to my mind.

My lips tease hers apart and as I kiss Kamari, I slide my fingers into the skimpy waistband of her underwear and slide it over her soft ass cheeks. Her butt is so soft. I can't help but want my hands to linger on her ass.

"I can't believe you're confessing this because you're mad I danced on stage in a thong," she says as I slip the thong over her ass cheeks. "It doesn't make me want you."

"Then how the hell do I have you practically naked?"

"Because you're my boss and holding my tips hostage."

I smirk at her, but she keeps her face completely stiff, betraying nothing.

"That's it? You're soaking wet because you want your tips?"

"Yes, Darragh. Your fingers have absolutely no effect on me."

"I just licked your cum off my fingers," I growl at her, cupping her ass cheeks and pulling her against me. "Your pussy disagrees with you."

I kiss her again, this time running my hand over her bare stomach until I get to her breasts. My hand cups her breasts, enjoying the size of her flesh. I take her bra off. Kamari moans as my fingers roam over her hard nipples. I don't believe she doesn't give a fuck about me.

We feel the same way about each other, even if we both seem to want to confess at exactly the wrong time.

"I mean it," she says. "I could fuck you right now and walk out of this office without feeling a thing. But I'll only do it if you let me back on that stage tomorrow."

I swear Kamari knows exactly what to say to piss me off.

"I'm not letting you back on that stage, princess."

"I have monthly expenses, Darragh. A lump sum isn't enough and I'm tired of searching for low paying jobs around Boston. I'll wear a wig. No one here will know who I really am. I can tune out the racists."

My fingers continue to move in a slow circle around her nipples. Her frustrating words make me want to hurt her and punish her for suggesting something so foolish. She's mine and I won't let her belong to another Irishman at this club for another second.

"I can't let that happen," I growl, planting my lips on her neck. She's crazy if she thinks I'm letting her on that stage again. I reach for her shorts and slide them over her butt. Her bare ass feels incredible and those shorts don't do Kamari's petite, yet curvy figure any justice.

I push her up onto my desk and spread her legs, sliding my hips between them and rubbing my hands on them. She winces as her ass touches the wood.

"That's fucking cold," she gasps.

"I'll warm you up, princess," he says. "Take my cock out."

She presses her feet against my thighs, using her strongest defenses to push me away. Kamari's strong for her size, but she's not strong enough to effectively get me away from her. I'm utterly fixed on the soaking prize between her thighs.

"Not until you agree to my terms."

"I'm hard for you Kamari, and I'm trying to fucking look out for you. You want me..."

"I'm wet," she says. "It's a biological reaction. Remember, I have no feelings for you and I never will. If you want sex, you have to agree to my terms."

"You're a fucking impossible wench."

"Did you just call me a *wench?*"

"Yes…" I grunt. "And I'm *truly* apologetic, but my cock is making me very fucking disagreeable."

"Agree to my terms, Darragh," she says firmly. "Or if you want me, you'll have to do something twisted and sick to get me."

"I'm not fucking like that, Kamari."

I'm not that cruel. And I love her. I'd never hurt her like that.

"Then agree."

"This is blackmail."

"Exactly," she says. "That's exactly what I'm doing."

"Fine," I grunt. "I'll deal with you after I've had you. Show up to work tomorrow and I'll let the men have their way with you. After that, you'll be begging for my protection."

"Whatever, Darragh. I just need the money."

With that, she leans forward and kisses me. I don't believe her. She just wants an excuse to kiss me and touch me. She needs a way to justify it because she knows that she should hate me. I know exactly what she's going through because I've gone through the same thing. I know exactly what it's like to want someone that I know I should hate.

"Take my cock out then," I murmur. "Let me feel your soft hands around my dick."

I don't want to just feel her hands. I want to feel her pussy gripping my cock. I know what will happen when I enter her. I'll feel what I felt all those years ago when she was just eighteen and I was still way too fucking old for her.

Kamari unbuckles my belt and slides my trousers over my ass. I smell like sweat and I hope she doesn't mind that I'm about to get her just as dirty as I am. She reaches into my underwear and I shudder as her perfect hands wrap around my cock. It's exactly what I need right now. Her hands. My cock. It's a match made in fucking heaven.

"Fuck," I grunt. "Your hands…"

They're soft and small. She can barely meet her fingers and thumbs around the girth of my shaft. Kamari releases her grip on my dick and shifts my trousers over my thighs before sliding them all the way down. My underwear follows soon after. I groan and push my hips forward, my cock sliding against her bare thigh. My dick touching her thigh is nearly enough to make me erupt.

"It's just an exchange," she says. "I get on that stage tomorrow and you don't touch me. You don't stop me from getting my bag."

I ignore her and push the head of my dick against her entrance. She's so wet. I swallow and think of the Red Sox for a second to stop myself from cumming before I enter her. *Control yourself, Darragh.* I kiss her for a few seconds to get control of my body and then press against her entrance again.

Sliding into her feels fucking perfect. I hold her ass and draw her against me, pushing the entire length of my dick into Kamari's incredibly tight pussy. She gushes as our hips join together and she stifles a moan as the size of my dick surprises her judging by the expression on her face. *Fuck, she's tight.*

Chapter Twenty
Kamari

Darragh eases his dick into my pussy and I lean forward and sink my teeth into his shoulder to stop myself from crying out in pleasure. I don't want him to know how good it feels that our bodies are like this again. There's never been a man that's made me feel as good as Darragh did that night, which made falling out of love with him hard, but not impossible.

He moves his hips slowly, withdrawing his impossibly large dick from my pussy and then easing into me so I can feel him slowly filling me.

"Since I'm paying for this," he murmurs as he slides into me. "Can I get extras?"

"What. Extras," I manage to say in between his thrusts.

I bite down on my lower lip to stop myself from moaning again. I can stop myself from moaning, but I can't stop the pleasure from Darragh's giant dick teasing my inner walls.

"Say that you want my big white cock."

"Have you lost your mind?" I gasp as Darragh pushes into me again. I moan as he settles his cock deep inside me, nestling his hips against mine. He's so deep that I nearly cum just from taking so much of him inside me. It's impossible for me to think straight.

"No. I want to hear you say it."

"I hate you so much," I whisper. His eyes widen like my response surprises him. My heart thuds with impossible anger. I hate him so much, but not for the reasons he thinks. I hate him because of the effect he has on me. I know he's wrong for me in every sense of the word. Look at what he's done to me tonight. He thinks he has a right to me even if he doesn't want to claim me and I hate him for it. I hate myself more for wanting him to claim me.

I want to belong to Darragh even if he's bad for me. He runs his hand over my thighs and my eyes pierce with tears. I hate him. I hate him. It doesn't matter that he gets me wet. I can't submit to him.

"I don't care," he says. "Since you have no feelings for me and this is purely transactional, you shouldn't care what I have to say either."

"Why do you always have to be a scumbag?"

"Because it's who I am, princess," he murmurs, taking my lower lip between his teeth. I squirm a little but that only makes his cock feel better inside me. I can't believe I ever had feelings for Darragh. I can't believe I ever loved a man who would treat me like this.

"No..."

He chuckles. "I knew it. You're not as ice cold as you think, princess."

Before I can protest, Darragh reaches between my legs and rubs my clit. I moan and ease my hips forward. Just because I like how his fingers feel doesn't mean there are emotions anymore.

"Shut up... And you're not paying me for this. I'm just doing this to keep my job."

"Do you make it a habit of fucking the boss to keep your job?"

"Watch your mouth, Darragh... I don't want to slap you while you're inside me."

He chuckles and kisses me again. His lips taste salty from his workout, and I know the taste should gross me out, but it doesn't. I've always loved the smell of Darragh's sweaty shirts. His clothes are fresh, but he must have just come here from the gym because that's what he smells like and as he kisses me and moves his hips inside me, I inhale more of Darragh's delicious scent.

"Okay," he whispers. "Okay, princess. I just want to feel you. I just want to feel your pretty black pussy around my dick."

Of course he finds a workaround. Stubborn asshole. He moves deeper inside me and I moan again. Darragh's words seem so taboo, but I can't help my body's reaction to his body or to his voice. He's always had this impossible effect on me.

"Shush…"

"No," he grunts. "I want you to know what I love about you. Even if it's wrong. Even if it could get us killed–"

"It couldn't get us killed."

"Hush," He grunts, thrusting with painstaking slowness to keep me still and focused on him as he moves and speaks. "I love your pretty black pussy. I love your breasts and your dark nipples. I love your big lips. I love your hair."

He punctuates each sentence with a deep thrust and I can't stop myself from being close to an orgasm when he stops talking. Darragh teases around the hood of my clit as he moves and within a few seconds, that pushes me over the edge. I cum hard and cry out loudly. Luckily, I think this office is soundproof. Darragh groans and holds me against his body as I finish.

"Good girl," he says. "Good girl…"

Those words melt me completely. I shudder and climax again as Darragh holds me and thrusts into me slowly until I'm done riding the wave of my orgasm. Why is it him? Why am I drawn to the wrong person like this?

I whimper and wrap my thighs around him. No protection, of course. But this won't be like our first time.

"I'm not done," he says. "But I want you to look at me. I at least paid for that."

"Why do you want that?" I ask, giving Darragh a fierce and hopefully unappealing look. The angry expression on my face naturally makes him smile.

"Because it turns me on to look at you when I cum."

I roll my eyes. "I don't need you to flatter me, Darragh."

"I'm not flattering you. Not at all, princess. It's the truth," he says. "I've had to picture your pretty face every time I've cum since you left."

"Shut up. And that's disgusting. You make it seem like you just thought about cumming on my face."

"Yes," he grunts, moving his hips again at a steady pace. "Among other places."

"I'm on birth control."

"Good," he says. "Because I want to cum deep inside you. I want you to feel my big white cock erupting deep inside your pussy."

He doesn't stop his steady pace until he's close. I can feel another wave of a climax entering me from the friction of Darragh's steady thrusting. I moan and move against him, grinding my hips against his gigantic dick. We move together until we both cum and my third climax is even harder than the first or second. Darragh pumps his cum deep inside me as he finishes.

The gush of his seed between my legs just makes my orgasm better. Our bodies rock together and as we hold each other, I feel a surprising burst of something I convinced myself I'd lost long ago. I wrap my arms around his neck and pull him against me, not to kiss him, but to feel Darragh's big sweaty body as close to mine as possible.

"You're mine," he grunts, continuing to pump into me after he finishes. "You will *always* be mine, Kamari."

His possessiveness sends a mix of emotions surging through me. As I wrap my arm tighter around his neck, Darragh's scent fills my nostrils and sends an unintentional shudder of pleasure through me. I don't want to be his the way I used to be. I'm not the same girl.

Darragh's large forearm wraps around my waist. It's been a long time since I've felt petite, although its always been easy to feel petite around Darragh's gigantic muscular form. He holds me against him, rocking his hips as he pushes the last bit of his seed deeper inside me.

"I was a fucking idiot to let you go."

He uses his lips to guide my face with kisses so I'm looking at him again. I scramble away from him and Darragh slides out of me, dripping my wetness and his cum over my thighs as he removes himself from between my legs.

I don't want him to drag me into a conversation about feelings again. I made myself clear – this is purely transactional and I have absolutely nothing left in my heart for Darragh. Those little flutters and tremors from having his cock between my legs are nothing more than the after effects of sexual pleasure. I can't love him – he's exactly the monster he said he was.

"I'll be at work bright and early tomorrow," I say to him stiffly as he gives me the warmest, most loving look in the world. I expect to feel good when his face falls, but I don't. It's hard to feel good about other people's anguish, even when they piss you off and rile you up the way Darragh does to me.

"Are you fucking with me, princess?" He says, taking a step back.

"No. I'm not. I told you this was purely transactional. Orgasms are not the key to winning a woman's forgiveness."

"What do you want then? You want me to let you get up on my fucking stage every night and watch men in my family holler at you while you bare your cunt to them?"

"Apparently, it's a very high paying job," I say to him, smugness in my voice. "You made a deal, Darragh. I know how important your vows are to you."

I scamper away from him and find whatever clothing I have scattered around his office, which is just a bra, thong and short shorts. Not exactly the world's most full-coverage outfit.

Darragh pulls up his underwear and pants without taking his fierce blue gaze off me. I hate how he's looking at me as if he has a right to be angry. He took my naive, precious heart and he shattered it in two. He took my virginity. Darragh took every ounce of my dignity back then and he doesn't have a right to be angry with how I cope.

Darragh scowls. "How many times do I have to apologize for what I did?"

Here we go again. How long can we keep having this same argument? Darragh needs to realize that his apologies won't work. Nothing about him appeals to me anymore. I can just view him as an attractive body to meet my biological needs and nothing more.

"An apology isn't enough. I told you, Darragh, I have no feelings for you anymore. I just proved it and nothing you say can–

BOOM!

Kamari

. . .

BOOM!

DARRAGH'S DOOR shatters as if it's made of glass as the second loud eruption blasts through the room. Before I realize what's happening, I feel Darragh's body cover mine as he throws me to the ground with the full force of his weight. The smell of smoke and burning fills the air.

With his door being gone, we can hear the unfiltered screams coming through the doorway.

I can't breathe for a few seconds as Darragh presses me into the ground. His eyes meet mine and he gasps, "Bomb. We have to get out of here."

I can't hear him very well, but I can read his lips and I nod. I'm covered in sweat, still covered in Darragh's essence, and terrified for my life. My body shakes against his as he rolls off me.

We hear gunshots outside of Darragh's office, but whoever set the bomb off hasn't made any efforts to come in here yet.

"We have to move," Darragh grunts as he rolls off me. I'm on the floor near his desk and am about to stand when he grabs my forearm forcefully.

"No," He says. "There's too much smoke. We have to crawl. There's a way out without going through the door."

"How?!" I gasp, glancing nervously at the gaping doorway.

Darragh moves the rug under his desk and pushes his chair back. I can see where the floor looks funny with the rug removed. Secret door.

I follow Darragh behind his desk as he grunts and gets the secret door open. It looks black down there and I can't tell how far it goes.

"Darragh..."

"I need a gun. You get down there and you don't move a fucking muscle, you hear me?"

"Are you crazy! You're coming down there with me?"

"I'm not."

I reach for his forearm instinctively, my nails digging into ink that he didn't have the last time we saw each other. It's the first time I notice the intricate 'K' tattooed on his forearm with violets and Celtic loops. *Violets are my favorite flower.* My throat tightens.

"You aren't going to get yourself killed."

"Trust me, Kamari," he says. "I'll be back."

"Darragh, I–

"No," he says. "We'll talk when I get back. Now go..."

He leaves me little choice since Darragh unceremoniously shoves me down the secret door beneath his desk. It's about a six foot drop, but I'm not as tall as Darragh so the impact hurts my knees. He shuts the door and I hear him shuffling overhead. Everything happening in the strip club sounds so much louder now.

What the fuck is going on out there?

I reach into my pocket, remembering that my cell phone is in the locker room. *Crap.* I can't smell any smoke down here, but I can hear footsteps and gunshots. There's screaming too, but the screaming dies down after a few minutes of gunfire.

Darragh didn't shove me into a tiny box as it turns out. There's a door that blends in with the wall and has a push down handle. My hands shake as I consider all the worst case scenarios. The door could be locked. Or whoever bombed Darragh's night club could be on the other side.

I hear a pistol fire for the first time among the shots from the semi-automatic weapons. I have a brother, so I know enough about guns to get by. I at least know the difference between a pistol and a semi-automatic weapon. Darragh must have had a pistol in his desk, right? That means he's still okay. I tell myself that as I push the door handle down and mercifully find it unlocked.

The room is pitch black, but my hands slide along the cold concrete walls until I eventually find a switch.

. . .

Kamari

SAFETY. All I want in this room is safety from the violence upstairs. I'm shaking and gasping for breath, uncertain of how I'll escape, but knowing that it's my responsibility to find a way out of here.

When I flip the light switch on though I don't quite find safety.

I FIND something both confusing and horrifying in the little room beneath Darragh's office.

Part Two

Present Day

Now.

Chapter Twenty-One
Darragh

The air is thick with smoke and she's the only person I can think about. Declan's on the floor with blood coming out of his skull. I can't tell if he's alive or dead. I also don't have time to find out. There are large fires everywhere. Tables. The bar. This must've been a hit, but I can't tell if they got their targets or not because it's a bloodbath and there's too much chaos for me to tell our men from anyone else.

Sweat glues my shirt to my skin and I struggle to breathe as I scan the room for anyone who looks like they don't belong in our club. Everyone here took vows, so they have rings. I swivel my gun around and hear the distinct blast of a sawed off shotgun.

My tongue sits in my mouth as dry as sandpaper as a frustrating bead of sweat drips down my face. The corner of my eye detects movement and I swing around with my finger dangerously close to pulling the trigger. I lower the gun as relief floods through me.

"Aiden? What the fuck are you doing here?"

"Where the fuck have you been?" Aiden growls. At least I know the owner of the sawed off shotgun. He lowers his firearm from its position at his hip. He's covered in soot and he looks like he was close enough to the blast judging by the blood dripping from his forearm.

"Busy running the club."

"It's on fucking fire, Darragh," Aiden snarls, letting out a cough that I find dramatic. My eyes are watering from the smoke.

"What happened? Who the fuck did this and where are they?"

"I don't know, but the fire department is on its way and we have bodies out here. Lots of bodies. The cops are gonna be all over this fucking place and they'll have questions."

"How long until they get here?"

Before Aiden answers, I hear a gunshot. It's a pistol and it must be a similar model to mine since it sounds the same. I raise my gun and swing around before I realize that the bullet hit Aiden. He grunts and stumbles backwards, his shotgun clattering to the ground.

"Where are you, you cowardly fuck!" I yell, swiveling around through the thick smoke, searching for the source of the gunshot. I try not to think about the fact that Aiden's been shot. There's nothing I can do at this point, and the fire department is already on its way, so they'll be bringing the EMTs.

I hear another gunshot and I just *know* the bullet hit me before I even feel it. The dull heat feels like it's in my shoulder or my arm. I can't really tell. I just know my right arm hurts like hell before my gun falls to the ground, and I follow it. I hear sirens in the distance as the shock hits me and I lie there, frozen. There's heat in my arm from the blood gushing out of the gunshot wound.

I hear Aiden groan, but it's an unearthly, deathly groan that sounds like he's dying. I call my brother's name, or at least I think I do, but he doesn't move. I'm still conscious, but stiff from shock and incapable of moving. I hear footsteps and taste blood and bile in the back of my throat as they approach.

This is our attacker, I'm certain of it. And if they came here to kill someone, it's probably a fucking Murray because we're always the ones in trouble. Hell, I'm probably the one they want to kill. I see black pants and my eyes search through the smoke for the barely visible figure of a man.

I see his face and tell myself that I'll be able to hold it in my memory. He's tall and doesn't look Irish. He doesn't have our tattoos or our rings. He doesn't even have our hair color. He stands over me and gazes down with absolute loathing.

"Which one of you is Aiden?" he asks, leveling a pistol at my face.

I stare straight down the barrel, certain this is the last thing I'll ever see.

I've thought of facing my death a thousand times. Every time I've killed a man myself, I thought about what it would be like to finally stare down the barrel of a gun and face the same fate of most men in the mob life. Irish, Italian or any other group of us in the mob faces the same demons.

"It's me. Or maybe it's him. Doesn't fucking matter. Finish the job."

"I asked you a question, Murray."

I see details of the man's face. He looks familiar, like a picture I've seen once.

"If you want answers, you'll have to answer one of mine."

"I don't have time for this. Which one of you is Aiden? Which one of you killed my brother?" he says.

"I'm not answering that, so you'll have to kill both of us if that's what you want."

My heart pounds and I won't act like I'm not scared. I've killed before, but I'm still human, and taking life away was never my thing.

"I don't want that," he says. "I need the other brother alive. The one who helped."

I try to make sense of what he's saying. My eyes are in so much pain from the smoke that I feel like they're bleeding. The dull pain where this fucker shot me only intensifies and the dampness pooling in my shirt tells me that even if he doesn't shoot me again, I don't have long in this state of consciousness.

And there's Kamari, trapped beneath my office, hopefully keeping her ass perfectly still so that she doesn't get into more trouble than she's in already. The sirens sound louder and I swear I see flashing red and blue lights.

"Go fuck yourself," I snarl and cough up a spray of red blood. That's bad. Blood in my throat, that's fucking bad. But if I'm going to die, I'll die fighting like a man.

I struggle to my feet and the man keeps his gun leveled at me, certain that I won't be so stupid as to lunge at him unarmed. It hurts to stand. Every part of me hurts and thick rivers of blood or sweat soak through my shirt and run down my back in uncomfortable rivers.

"You must be Aiden, then. I heard he was the stubborn one."

"You heard right," I snarl at him. "My brother is very stubborn. But not as stubborn as me."

I lunge for the gun and it goes off. I don't know if a bullet hits me. I can't tell. The pistol falls and I feel a fist hit the side of my face. I've taken hits before, but this one sends me stumbling backward. It's too smoky in the club for me to catch my breath from the hit, but I pitch forward and use my weaker arm to hit our would-be assassin in the face.

He ducks and grabs his gun again. Blinding pain shoots through all my limbs and I hear a loud click before I feel metal against the side of my face, sending me flying sideways onto the ground.

I'M half awake as I hear thick South Boston voices. I hear Aiden's voice snarling, "I'm fine, but he's not. And that motherfucker got out of here with the girl before I could stop him."

"What girl?"

I don't recognize the voice asking *what girl,* but it sounds like family.

"I don't know," Aiden says. "One of the bottle girls."

Good. So not her, then. She's safe. I give my brother a knowing look, but my vision blurs.

If anyone knew about me and Kamari, that could get us both killed. Red and blue lights flash again. I feel a warm hand against my forehead and groan.

"He's breathing, but he doesn't have long. We need to get him to Mass General."

Aiden mutters something unintelligible.

I SLIP INTO UNCONSCIOUSNESS AGAIN.

Chapter Twenty-Two
Kamari

It's a murder room. Six feet beneath Darragh's office is a room that has clearly been used to kill people. It smells clean, which shocked me initially, but also gave me the courage to walk into the room. I glance at the walls and my stomach turns. I can't believe I touched those walls to find a light switch.

The walls are stained with thick splatters of blood, most of which dried brown. Not all the blood dried brown yet, which makes me think this room has been recently used. That would also explain the smell of bleach.

There's a metal chair in the center of the room and what looks like a small burlap bag next to it with pieces of brown twine coated in dried blood. The metal chair has a sunken seat as if it has taken a lot of weight during its lifespan. The splatter of blood on the wall behind the chair sickens me even more.

I hear a loud scream and panic, hustling into the terrifying blood-soaked room and quietly shutting the door behind me because a bloody murder room is less terrifying than what's happening upstairs. I flick the light switch off, just in case any of the light seeps through the door and betrays my hiding space.

I nearly stop breathing when the gunshots stop. If only I had a weapon. There aren't more footsteps upstairs, which makes me wonder if I'm safe down here.

When I hear a fresh set of footsteps, I freeze. Those don't sound like Darragh's.

I hear a voice in the office. "Please... don't shoot me."

"Why not?" *That's not Darragh's voice.*

"Please..."

I don't hear a gunshot, but I hear the woman scream, one set of footsteps, and the voices disappear. I'm alone again in the dark room and frozen in place. When will it be safe for me to come out? I swear I hear sirens, but I can't tell. They sound far away if there are sirens at all.

I hear a loud thud upstairs and then nothing at all for several minutes. The sirens sound like they're directly above me, which doesn't seem possible. I keep still and quiet. My clothes are soaked with sweat from all the adrenaline coursing through me. The sirens are loud enough that I'm sure there are emergency workers upstairs.

There are no more gunshots, which means that everyone holding a gun is either dead, arrested, or headed to the hospital. I still can't make myself move towards the door.

I wait in the room beneath Darragh's office until everyone leaves. This takes several hours and believe me, it's not comfortable. I don't want to turn the light on and witness the splattered blood on the walls. When the club gets completely quiet, I push the door open and glance up at the trap door to Darragh's office. I'm about a foot too short to reach the door and shove it open. *Plus, it might be locked.*

Returning through the door, I pick up the metal chair with the sunken seat and set it beneath the trap door. It doesn't seem stable enough for me to stand on, but as long as it doesn't break down instantly, the chair ought to be plenty.

The chair wobbles as I set it up. I stand on it and push up. My rib cage feels strained and my muscles tight. It's another impact of the adrenaline. Eventually, I push the door open and use all my strength to drag my body out of the hole and onto the floor of Darragh's office. My forearms hurt as they press into the debris. Glass doesn't pierce my skin, but little shards of metal and broken glass stick to the outside. I'm too scared to brush myself off and cut my hands.

Chapter Twenty-Two

I wish I was wearing some real clothing right now. . It smells charred in here. The effects of the fire are clear even in the dark. I'm cold, for one thing, which means there must be doors and windows blown open. I don't know if any of the lights work and I'm too afraid to do something that might attract attention. I'm a stripper who just climbed out of a basement barely wearing any clothes. There's no attention I could attract that would be good for me.

Once I'm on my feet, I feel for the wall and let out a little cough.

"HELLO, KAMARI," booms a deep but unfamiliar male voice. It's the last thing I expect to come out of the darkness.

I shriek. *Loudly.* The voice isn't Darragh's and since it's dark, I have no other clues, but the voice. I whip around, my fists curled in case whoever sat up in this office waiting for me to emerge tries to fight me. They do — naturally.

I scream as I feel large biceps wrap around me. If only screaming were all I did. Having had more than enough of fear and adrenaline to last me the next decade, all hell breaks loose when the man grabs me. I kick him and I feel my heel come into contact with something soft. Despite getting a kick in the groin, he only holds onto me tighter as he doubles over, cursing and calling me a few unpleasant names.

"Let go of me! Let go of me!"

I don't see how making noise in an abandoned, burned down strip club will help me, but my instincts don't give a crap about logic. If I kick this guy in the balls once, I can do it again. I scratch madly and when his grip on me gives, I thrust another kick into his balls and escape.

Air fills my lungs along with the motivation to get away from him. It's dark, but my eyes adjust just enough in the darkness for me to see the blasted through metal office door. The firefighters must have left it open. I sprint for the door, ignoring the sharp pain in my feet as I run.

The man is faster than me and much larger too. Jesus, he's a giant. He slams me into the wall and knocks the wind out of me. It's like getting tackled by a fucking quarterback. I fly against the wall with a loud grunt. He apologizes as he throws me over his shoulder, which confuses me, much like Darragh did so many years ago on his yacht.

I scream at the man to put me down repeatedly, but he doesn't listen. He walks me out of the club into the cold parking lot where my shrieking feels even more fruitless. It's isolated out here — it's off all the train lines and far away from anywhere with gentrification or college students. The Irish mob have their own universe and their own rules tucked in the underbelly of the same city that houses Harvard University and Boston College.

My lungs are empty and my throat completely sore as the man sets me down in the parking lot, pinning me against the doors of an ancient looking red Mazda coupe convertible. I push against the man's chest as I land on the ground. I want to run away but I also want to use the distance between us to get a good look at him.

He's wearing jeans and a leather jacket with a large hoodie beneath it. I can't make out any details of the man's face with his hood up.

"Don't run!" He yells. "Fuck, you're fucking difficult. Fuck!"

It's strange. He really does sound like Darragh.

"I'm not going to hurt you!" He says emphatically. "Fuck!"

The man throws his hood back and I press my back more dramatically into the two-door coupe. He has a thick crop of dishwater blond hair and fierce blue eyes. I can't mistake those eyes. I'd recognize them anywhere. Whoever this man is, he's a Murray.

That doesn't exactly relax me. I know they're racist.

"Who are you?" I yell at him. "Where's Darragh?"

My heart thuds. Darragh wasn't in the strip club. I heard gunshots. He's probably dead, isn't he? An image of Darragh lying on the floor of the strip club bleeding out flashes into my head and it's worse than a punch to the gut.

"Where's Darragh!?" I yell with an even more hysterical tone. My panicked tone surprises me. I'm not supposed to care about Darragh this much. I'm not supposed to care about him at all.

The last thing I said to him was that I didn't have any feelings for him, and he still saved my life anyway.. I feel the weight of what this could mean pressing into me, forcing my back against the two-door coupe. There's no room for escape. *Crap.*

"I can only answer one question at a time," the man says. "Fuck."

"Are you Rian?" I press him. I'm still panicking and I don't feel entirely in control of my reactions.

I haven't met all of Darragh's brothers, but the ones I've met all have a family resemblance. I would recognize Aiden because he was always at Tavarius' boxing matches with Darragh. Plus, Aiden is older. This "man" looks more like a boy, the closer look I get at his face. He's large, don't get me wrong. He's taller than Darragh, at about 6'6" tall and once I get a good look at him, I can see why him tackling me felt like getting hit by a wide receiver.

He's thick for his height and possibly for his age.

"No," he says. "Are you going to relax for a fucking second?"

Whoever he is, he swears a lot. I nod and catch my breath, even if I'm the furthest thing from relaxed. He runs his fingers through his hair and swears several more times.

"I'm Odhran, okay?"

Orrin. Another traditional Irish name. And this time, I'm familiar with the name. He's Darragh's younger brother — the *youngest*.

"Shouldn't you be in high school?" I shoot back at him. "You didn't have to drag me out of there like a wild beast."

"I did," he says. "Now get in the car."

"Um… I'm not getting in the car with you. How do I know who you are?!"

Apparently, this was the wrong answer. Before I can duck away from him and escape, the strong and far too agile teenager lunges and wraps his arms around me, pressing his hand over my mouth so any possible screams are muffled. He's so large that he gets the tiny Mazda Miata door open and shoves me in with the ease of packing a sleeping bag for a weekend camping trip.

Once I'm in the car, I panic and scramble for the door handle, but it's locked. By the time Odhran slides into the driver's seat and I try to claw him, he shoves me back into the seat with one firm palm. He takes up the majority of the interior space in the car, making me suddenly claustrophobic.

Only a teenager would own a car this fucking tiny and insane. Now that I succumb to being trapped in the car, I realize the gigantic teenager in the driver's seat plans on driving me through Boston traffic with this death trap.

"Odhran," I say calmly. "I don't know what you're doing or what you think you're doing, but I live right in Boston and you can drive me home right now and I would be very appreciative."

He smirks and there's something cold in his eyes that's too cold. Darragh isn't like this. My bad feeling intensifies, but it's too late, because Odhran starts his tiny death mobile. I grip the sides of the seat as he skids out of the parking lot.

"I'm not taking you home," he says. "I've got orders. You're mafia property now, sweetheart."

His Boston accent is thick, but his tone is still unfriendly and cold.

"Whose orders?" I press. "And what happened to Darragh? I have connections you know. My *own* connections."

Odhran snickers, interrupting me before I can continue lying my ass off and playing up how much of a bad ass I am in hopes of scaring him off. It doesn't work.

"I don't know what happened to my brother," he says. "I just know my orders, okay?"

"You're in high school," I shoot back, my toes curling into the dirty carpet at the bottom of the teenager's Mazda as he guns it several miles over the speed limit. "Aren't your orders college applications and homework?"

"Not in my family," he says. "Now please, be quiet. It's hard enough having to kidnap someone for the first time. I can't fuck this up."

It's a remarkably teenaged thought. He's worried about fucking this up and not committing a felony? Still, I don't want to let a teenager get the better of me, even if he's creeping up on 80 miles per hour in a 55 mile per hour speed zone.

"Take me to Darragh," I demand imperiously, using a tone that might have at least worked to attract Darragh's attention. Odhran slams his iron foot on the gas and shoots the car up to 95 miles per hour. He's fucking with me.

"I won't be doing that," he says. "Now if you want both of us to make it in one piece, you'll be quiet."

I shut up, but for entirely different reasons than Odhran's commands. He's going so fast that my stomach threatens to evacuate its already limited contents. I'm gripping the sides of my seat so hard that I can barely breathe as my muscles stay rigid and frozen.

Odhran slows the car down to 85 miles per hour, still scaring the ever living crap out of me as he weaves through traffic like a maniac. I want to ask if he's planning on getting pulled over, but there's no taking control here and definitely no reasoning with a Murray kid who probably grew up getting his own way. Didn't Darragh love fast cars and petty crimes when he was this age?

I know Boston, but we leave the city and I lose track of where we are until I see the signs for Framingham, a small town a few miles west of the city. It's lowkey and ratchet as fuck, but it's not my brother's style. He prefers cities. The only nearby city I can think of heading west on Route 90 is Worcester, MA. I don't bother sharing my guess with Odhran, but when he takes the first exit towards Worcester, I know I'm right.

If I ever knew anything about Darragh or his family's connection to Worcester, I clearly didn't think it was important enough to remember. Odhran slows down once we get off the last exit into the city and he turns down a few streets before we come to a shitty looking gray house that looks like it contains several rundown apartment units.

He stops the car, and looks at me with a hand stuffed into his jacket pocket. I'm barely wearing anything, so I don't know how Odhran and his leather jacket can be cold enough for him to need to warm up his hands.

"I can trust you not to run?" Odhran asks me, his hair dusting just beneath his eyebrows. He seems both nervous and utterly in control, like he's been preparing for it, but has beginner's nerves. *He doesn't seem above using violence, so I should be careful with him. He might be more dangerous because of his age, not less dangerous.*

"No," I tell him. "I know we're in Worcester. It might be cold, but I'm sure I can get my ass to a church. I don't care what I'm wearing. I'll run"

He purses his lips with disappointment.

"I *really* didn't want to use the drugs," he says.

"Huh?"

Odhran withdraws his hand from his coat pocket wielding an uncapped syringe. Panic surges through me and I start screaming and grabbing at the door handle like a mad woman before I feel a pinch in my thighs and start to lose complete control of my consciousness.

Before I go under completely, I hear Odhran say, "By the way, I lied. I think Darragh's dead."

Before I go under completely, I hear Odhran say, "By the way, I lied. I think Darragh's dead."

Chapter Twenty-Three
Darragh

The first sensations to awaken me are a mixture of pain and discomfort. I can feel dry irritation in my nasal passages and throat. It takes me several seconds to realize that I'm awake and not dead in a fucking ditch somewhere about to face purgatory. No, this place is real. The beeping heart monitor and the unmistakable hospital smell overwhelm me.

I can't keep the smell out, but I can't cough either. Every part of me feels so fucking dry. And weak. My mind loops in and out of consciousness.

Fuck, this isn't where I want to be. I whisper her name.

Kamari.

SHE DOESN'T EMERGE. I picture her curled up in the room beneath my office. She must've turned on the lights, which means she's seen the blood. The next time I see that woman, I'm almost certain that she'll want nothing to do with me. She's just not like me — Kamari's not a killer.

Her purity is the reason I always pushed her away, and now I heard my brother say they took a girl and I don't know which of the girls on the floor they're talking about. How could it have been her? I can count the number of people who know about the secret door beneath my office — all of them family.

I cough and groan. The cough sends shooting pain through every fucking part of my body. Holy shit. I know I've been shot, but the pain is so intense that it doesn't seem possible that I'm just injured and not completely fucking dead. I call her name again, wanting her to answer, wanting to smell her, wanting to promise her that I'll keep her safe.

"If you're coughing, you must be awake."

I groan and my eyes flutter open. The room is mostly dark, but once I open my eyes, I notice a small warm orange night light next to a green faux-leather chair in the corner of my hospital room. Mass General. I'd recognize the details of these hospital rooms anywhere. If I wasn't visiting family here, I was nursing my own wounds and injuries from boxing.

"I know you're in pain," Aiden says. "But this can't wait. The dicks who bombed the club have check points all over the city. We have guards at the hospital, but we have a big fucking problem on our hands."

Aiden's right, I'm in pain and he's the head of the family while dad's unconscious, not me.

"I've been shot," I choke out, not necessarily meaning it as a complaint. It's just that every part of me hurts and I'm not in the best position to help.

"Yes," Aiden says sarcastically. "I noticed. I had some blood loss and a bullet graze myself. It's nothing that some fluids and a strong Guinness couldn't cure."

Aiden holds modern medicine in strong disregard compared to the power of Guinness.

"Tell me what happened to me," I groan, my voice sounding much raspier and weaker than I mean for it to sound. "I need to know the truth."

"There's still a bullet in your arm. You suffered mild chest trauma. You're on enough pain killers to kill a horse. The other bullet hit your neck and took off a piece of flesh. You're lucky the bastard was a poor shot."

"Who do I have to thank for my future scars?"

"Our half-brother had a brother — a brother who's out for revenge. He wanted me dead and... we may have convinced him that it happened."

"How?"

"Declan."

How? If anyone were dead, I would have expected it to be him. There was blood coming from his head.

My stomach sinks. I saw Declan lying on the floor before I lost consciousness, but I told myself that he was just injured, not dead.

Aiden continues, "It was Declan's idea to stage my death. We got him out of there quickly. He was just unconscious, no bullets. He made it out with a head injury, but Seamus wasn't so lucky."

I didn't know Seamus was there – Conner Doyle's brother. My stomach knots again. Just as you feel any fucking relief in this life, something else comes to smack you in the fucking face.

"Seamus is dead?"

"Yes," he says. "But... we have reason to believe our plan worked and they think I'm the dead one. They think they have this city. But that won't be the case, D. I promise."

"I can't be stuck in here. I need to find..."

"Kamari?" Aiden asks. *He knows.* I know Aiden is the one most likely to understand aside from Callum, but there's natural discomfort with any of my family members knowing my secrets, especially about women we aren't supposed to touch.

"Where is she?" I grunt. I try to move, but my body doesn't respond. Aiden glares at me, but doesn't stop me from moving.

"Somewhere safe. The bastards kidnapped one of your strippers. I'm sending Declan after her once he's better."

"Do you think Declan has the brain power to handle a task like that?"

I'm one to talk and Aiden doesn't hide that he finds the question funny coming from me.

"I need to see her," I groan. "Please, get me the fuck out of here."

"Not possible, Darragh. You're stuck here."

"At least tell me where she is."

"Worcester," Aiden says. "And since I'm the target of this assassination, I have to go underground."

"Lucky you."

My brother gives me a sad look. That's new. Aiden doesn't do sadness. He gets pissed off. He growls and grunts. Nothing makes him sad.

"Not lucky. I have to protect Valentina. She's due soon. I'm taking her to grandma's place in Wenham. It's empty while she's in Florida. I'll need a lot from you while I'm gone."

"I can barely move, Aiden," I say, adding despite myself. "But I will obey all of your commands."

I wonder if my brother understands what he's suggesting. He wants me to lead the family while he's gone. That's the only thing that could make him this somber. It's something huge that I would never expect from him. I've never been a natural leader in our family.

But this shift in Aiden makes me wonder if I've really changed. If I really grew up. *For her.* Aiden shifts his weight to his other leg and managed to look even more serious and menacing.

"I know," my brother growls. "I don't want to leave you, Darragh. The bastard who shot you could try again."

It's like he's fighting with himself.

"I'm not a little boy," I remind him. "I can handle a fucking guido."

I also hate for Aiden to doubt my strength. I'm old enough now and different enough that he can trust me. But Aiden still has doubts and he's not shy about putting them on display for me.

"You can't even pull a trigger right now," Aiden says bluntly. "If you can't control our family in my absence, you'll be a sitting duck. If I asked you to take that power... I could kill you."

"You don't know that."

"I do," Aiden says. "Which makes asking this ten times more difficult."

I can see the weight of it on his face. My brother has always taken his role as the eldest incredibly seriously. But I'm not a child anymore. I can handle our family.

"I told you, I can handle it," I insist. "These are minor injuries."

"I need assurances," Aiden says. "Please."

"Assurances? Since when? I'm not a weakling."

Aiden growls, "Can you stop arguing with me? There are other people I have to protect. I can't chase after you if you make a fool out of yourself. I have a family to protect."

"Valentina can handle herself and so can I."

Aiden scowls and then responds sternly, "I love her too much to put her in more danger."

"Then don't. Let me handle this."

"Assurances," Aiden murmurs. "I want assurances."

"You will have them."

He takes my good hand and shakes it.

"What are we going to do about this?" I ask him.

Aiden shakes his head. "It was a fucking blood bath. Someone has to pay."

Kamari. I hope to fuck she wasn't a part of this. Aiden still can't confirm anything for me, which worries the crap out of me.

"The Italians?" I ask, keeping the thread of our conversation steady despite worrying about my girl. "They started this shit."

"Technically, our father started this," Aiden says. "But he's still sick. Still in the same fucking hospital as you are... But we can't do anything but protect what's ours. As always."

"I'll be fine," I assure him. "I'm not the shithead brother you left behind when you went to Long Island. I was on my way to turning the club around. I swear."

Aiden smirks. "Well, you seem to have found an alternate solution. We'll have to close the place for at least six months."

"More time to focus on the gym," I respond with a grin. There's no way in hell I'm gonna be in a gym anytime soon. I can feel how badly I'm hurt, even if it sucks to admit.

"I'm trusting you, Darragh. We'll flush them out of wherever the fuck they're hiding. They can't be far and we have a lot of Irishmen in Boston."

"Is it bad to think that dad would already have known where they were?" I tell my brother. "Ever worry we aren't as good at this ruthless shit?"

Aiden responds with a grunt.

"We'll have to get on without him eventually," Aiden says. "Until then, we stay together and we stay strong. I'll be away, but I won't abandon you, Darragh. I thought I was going to lose you tonight."

"You can't get rid of me that easily."

"Hm," Aiden says. "I suppose not."

"I love you too, brother."

"Now…" Aiden says with a smirk. "I never said *that*."

AIDEN LEAVES and my life becomes a painful blur of nurses and medication for a full ten days. At least I know Kamari is completely safe. On the tenth day of my stay in the hospital, which feels worse than incarceration, Callum comes to pick me up and take me home. I can't use my arm well enough to drive.

This time, he's smart enough to bring me a fucking glazed donut and coffee before forcing me to listen to him mouth off about the news from outside. Declan's chasing the Aurelio sickos, while Odhran has Kamari tucked away in the safe house. We also have extra security at our mom's place, and Declan booked a ticket and hotel to send Orla, our sister, to Atlantic City for a week so she stays out of trouble.

I just want to get out of here. The nurse finally shows up to discharge me and Callum shows up to pick me up, giving me all the information I need as he walks me to our ride. I've hardly moved except to use the bathroom in the past ten days. I can sorta shower myself. It isn't perfect, but I can clean myself well enough to keep the nurses away from my balls.

"Be careful with the Hummer," I warn Callum as we walk outside. "We're lucky she survived the bombing."

"Yes," Callum says. "We're so lucky that your SUV was saved on the night we lost three of our first cousins."

"I'm on enough pain medication to sedate a fucking rhino, Callum. I can't keep everything straight."

"Well, you missed the funerals. They were quiet."

"I'm sorry they died. If I could have stopped—

"You were lucky you were in the back room. Odhran says you had a black stripper back there with you."

"She's *not* a stripper."

Chapter Twenty-Three

"Are you sure?" Callum asks with a grin. "Odhran said she has a big black ass."

"If I hear him say something like that again, I'll smack the shit out of him," I grumble.

Callum parks my car in the lot behind my house in Beacon Hill. I love this place even if it's far from the club and far away from our sorts of people — the tatted up, rabble-rousing Irish. The folks here are rich and uptight, but after tough nights in the boxing ring or doing dirty jobs for my father, it's the perfect place to retire.

I haven't been home in so long that the place hardly feels like my own.

"Evie's gonna bring the dog back soon," Callum says, referring to Brady.

My sister has been petsitting my Irish Wolfhound, Brady since I got shot. He doesn't like noises or the strip club or the boxing ring. He's more of a puppy at heart than a gigantic shaggy sighthound.

"I miss the sweetheart. It's been hell. We'll bring him when we go to Worcester..."

"Did Aiden send you orders I didn't hear about?" Callum asks, quite frankly testing my patience.

My eyes narrow. "My girl's in Worcester, Callum. I'm out of the hospital. I'm going to her."

"She's fine."

"She's in the custody of a high school student and there are Italians all over the state trying to fucking kill us. I can't leave her there."

"If Aiden wanted you leaving the city, he would have ordered it," Callum says. "He told me to sit your ass in front of the fuckin' Patriots game or whatever the fuck is on, hand you a bottle of Wild Turkey, and keep you there until you can use your arm again."

"I don't need to use my arm when I have a shit head little brother who can drive," I tell him, sitting at my kitchen counter because that's where I keep the Wild Turkey. Callum opens my fridge and pulls out a Coors. I keep his favorite for him because he spends more time in my place than I do.

"We can't fuck with Aiden. I had to beg to get him back here in the first place. If we want him to come back at all, we have to be on our best behavior. He's gonna kill you if you leave Boston."

"It's forty minutes away, Callum. Aiden's not here. We just need to pick her up from the house."

Callum tips some of the beer down his throat and then stares at me with irritated olive-colored eyes. His light brown hair makes a curly halo around his excessively large Irish head. *What do I have to say to convince him?*

"It's dangerous," he says, drinking more.

"It's a ninety-minute round trip. We can handle this. *Please.*"

"What's in it for me?"

"Whatever you want."

"A favor. When I need it, I want a favor."

"That's a fucking weird request," I grumble, using my good hand and my teeth to get the bottle of Wild Turkey open. Callum doesn't bother offering to help me and I don't mind. The sooner I get myself working again, the better. They say it'll be weeks before the tissue heals, but I can't sit on my ass the entire time.

"Do you want me to break Aiden's rules or not? Give me your word."

"Fine, you idiot. You have my word. Now let me finish this bottle and then we can go get my girl."

Chapter Twenty-Four
Kamari

I know I've lost weight since I've been here – ten days, maybe longer. I've lost track of time. My prison guard — that asshole teenager Odhran — subsist on a disgusting diet of energy drinks and pizza. He eats so poorly that it's almost like he didn't have parents. All the windows and doors are barricaded with thick metal burglar bars and he has cameras all over the house, except my bedroom, which has a metal door on it.

The kid locks me in at night like this is a real jail. What unbeknownst to me at the time would be my last morning in Worcester, Odhran approaches the door to my bedroom around breakfast time. We have a routine since I learned the hard way that no matter how hard I try, I can't kick a 6'6" giant's ass. He's too strong and playing football gives him the strategy he needs to knock me off my feet every time.

I hear his big shuffling footsteps and then his teen voice grunting, "I brought coffee and donuts."

"Donuts? Odhran… you promised me something healthy today."

"I'm unlocking the door. Are we good this morning?"

"Yeah," I sigh. "We're good."

I wonder why this boy isn't in school, honestly. When he's not completely overpowering me, he seems relatively soft-spoken and maybe a little boring. He spends most of the day playing video games, but maybe that's because it's his job to watch me. He works out too, doing pushups and pull-ups in the middle of the night.

I wake up to him grunting sometimes and counting off his sets. He might be a terrifying hunk of teenage muscle but I admire his dedication.

"Did you hear from Darragh today? I want to talk to him."

"No," Odhran says. "They can't call. Can't text."

He opens the door and presents the white, orange and pink bag from Dunkin'. It's not the healthy breakfast I ordered, but my long fasts between slices of pizza and energy drinks make me desperate for anything I can shove in my mouth. The coffee appears to be some creamy latte, so I don't hold back drinking as much of it as possible in my first sip before stepping out of my room.

For a prison, it's nicely tailored with plants everywhere and classic New England furnishings. Odhran tells me that Darragh loves plants, which surprises me, but I see the meticulously cared for succulents and ferns all over the place. It's like a rainforest.

"The coffee is good."

Odhran doesn't respond. He's not talkative and I don't mind since I don't have much to talk to a seventeen-year-old about anyway.

He walks away back toward the living room and his video game. I follow behind him, looking in my Dunkin bag to grab my donut. He had the kindness to include two strips of bacon. Is that what he thinks being healthy is? I don't eat bacon often, so a couple strips can't hurt. I snack on one as I sink into the same arm chair I've sat in since I got here.

Odhran flops onto the couch like I'm not in the room and launches another video game. I don't catch the title but there are guns, helicopters and soldiers. He disappears into his gaming universe for what feels like an eternity but is really just enough time for me to finish my coffee, donut and the bacon.

I can't tell if the kid is finishing his video game or not, but I curl up and try to take a nap. I'm seriously bored in this house and Odhran doesn't care.

· · ·

I SHOOT STRAIGHT OUT of my napping position in the armchair when I hear a hand jostling the front door handle. It's a distinct sound and the door rattles loudly enough to wake me up. Odhran, my bodyguard, is wide awake and glued to the screen in front of him like there's nothing happening.

I toss one of the throw pillows at his head. Odhran doesn't move and the pillow misses his head. Was I this annoying when I was a teenager? I'm not much older than Odhran, but he acts like he's from a different planet.

"Odhran," I hiss. "There's someone trying to get in."

"Yeah," he says in a regular speaking tone, continuing to move his armed character through gameplay.

"Do something!"

"There's only one person who knows about this place," he says. "Your boyfriend."

"I don't *have* a boyfriend," I snap at Odhran as the door opens and Darragh Murray steps into the house, having heard everything I just said.

"That's a relief, I suppose," Darragh says. "I would hate to kill some motherfucker in this condition."

His voice jerks my attention away from kicking Odhran's stubborn ass and I leap out of my seat. I'm not sure if I'm more excited about Darragh or an open door that I can safely run through now that he's here. The way he looks at me stops me the second I stand up. He's alive. Odhran never made it clear what was happening with Darragh and I wouldn't have believed he was alive without seeing him for myself.

I freeze for a second and take in every inch of Darragh Murray. He has an arm wrapped in bandages and cuts all over his face. He still looks strong, but he's definitely hurt and not at his best. I guess that's why he brought his brother, Callum.

My body moves before I know what I'm doing and I race over to Darragh, wrapping my arms around him and squeezing him tightly until he grunts. I release my grasp on him as I hug him.

"Sorry," I say. "I didn't mean to hurt you. I just…"

"I'm fine, princess," Darragh says with a grunt. "Princess," Callum mutters. "That's new and disgusting."

I don't care about Callum's opinion. I'm just happy to be here. With Darragh. And hopefully headed home. Odhran took my phone once we got here and refused to give it back or let me communicate with the outside world.

When I pull away from Darragh, his brows furrow.

"We're getting out of here," he says. "Odhran, your job is done. She's mine."

"Thank goodness," I say with a sigh. "I've been waiting to go home. My roommates must be worried."

Callum chuckles and I don't appreciate the intonation of his little chuckle. I give Darragh a stern look.

"Why is he laughing? You're here to take me home, right? I've been missing for ten days. People are going to wonder what happened to me."

"You aren't going home," Darragh says, his voice tightening and that stubborn wall I'm so used to manifests in front of him.

"What's the point of rescuing me if you aren't taking me home?" I fold my arms and plant my feet. If one or all three of them want to carry me off, I'm powerless. I've been in this position before too. The Murray boys feel no sympathy. Odhran doesn't bother shutting off his video game in the background and he loudly murders several other characters in the game with a series of fake rifle fire that makes me flinch.

"The point is keeping you safe."

"What about keeping yourself safe?" I shoot back at him. He looks like he's seen hell and he doesn't even care.

"That's none of your concern."

"That is *so* condescending," I snap at him.

Darragh scowls. "I missed you. Doesn't that count for anything?"

"It doesn't count if you don't respect my wishes."

Darragh huffs, "I'll respect your wishes once you're safe."

"I'm not your property," I snap at Darragh. "I climbed on that stage for all of five minutes and our little deal–

"This isn't about our deal," Darragh says more forcefully than I expect. It normally takes him much longer to lose his patience with me. "And you are *more* than my property."

Callum snickers. "Good one."

Chapter Twenty-Four

"Have you lost your mind, Darragh?"

"Yes," he says. "Because I risked death to come get you and all you can do is stand there and argue with me."

"You stripped me of my freedom," I say to Darragh, still refusing to budge. "I have to go back to my apartment and I have to find another job."

"I knew I'd have to do this," Darragh says, emitting a sharp whistle which draws both his brothers to attention.

Fuck. I know what's coming before Darragh issues the command.

CALLUM AND ODHRAN sit in the front seat. I sit in the back, tied up with the string of Odhran's sweatpants, next to Darragh. As much as I want to hate him now, I'm happy to see him alive. I can't let him see that, but I quietly examine his face with sneaky glances and then his arms.

I didn't want that night to be our last together. Unfortunately, Darragh notices me stealing a glance at him. *Damn.* He smirks, which makes me roll my eyes. I don't want him to think that I give a crap about him when he's kidnapping me and forcing me to do something against my will again.

Darragh leans across and has the audacity to kiss my shoulder. I don't know what's worse, his audacity to kiss me, or the way his lips feel against my shoulder. Reassuring. Comfortable.

"Don't you dare," I hiss.

"You're going to be in my custody until we get to the bottom of the club bombing. Why shouldn't we have fun?"

"I don't find your constant disrespect of my personal space to be fun."

"Is that why you came so hard in my office?"

Odhran and Callum both snicker. I want to shove Darragh's head through the window, but I settle on a fierce glare. He runs his tongue over his lower lips as if he hasn't just completely humiliated me. Does he think we're somehow going to have sex back here with his brothers in the front? My nostrils flare with my outrage. Darragh plants a kiss on my nose that nearly makes me sneeze from surprise.

"You're cute when you're mad," he says. "Once you accept that I'm saving your life again, this will blow over."

I don't dignify him with a response. Darragh doesn't kiss or touch me the rest of the car ride to... Beacon Hill? I knew Darragh had a place here, but I've never been to his home. I've never wanted to see how Darragh lives. Knowing his beliefs and the sorts of people he associates with, I don't know if I want to stumble upon a collection of racist flags or something.

His brothers drop us off and ask Darragh if he needs help getting upstairs. It's a gorgeous, multi-story brick home on a nice street that looks too normal and boring to be where Darragh Murray lives. The exterior is well-maintained with ivy hanging from one of the second floor windows all the way to the small yard in the front of the house.

It seems too pristine for Darragh, almost. And it's green. Lush. He clearly had landscapers outside too. I love plants, but I never thought Darragh would be a plant guy too. His arm is still hurt and it's hard to see him in this condition. That should make it easier for me not to look at him, but I still can't keep my eyes off Darragh. He hasn't been able to shave in a few days and I suppress the urge to offer to trim his beard.

Hmph. If I'm lucky, the unruly blond hair will suffocate him and I can escape. Darragh refuses his brother's help and they drive off, leaving us in Beacon Hill. I would normally feel unsafe being out this late alone but Darragh has a soothing, unbothered presence. He genuinely doesn't care that he's a complete asshole.

"I could run away," I threaten under my breath.

"Do you want to be stuck with Odhran again?" Darragh growls.

I ROLL MY EYES. I don't know what I want. But it isn't *this*.

"Whatever," I grumble. "I won't run."

Chapter Twenty-Five
Darragh

Kamari falls asleep on the couch as I make her the ramen noodles she requested. She knows my dog, Brady, and they've always gotten along well. He curls up near her feet like he's her protector. I don't mind sharing the job with him, as long as she's safe.

I don't want to wake her up because she looks so peaceful. How did I fuck up this badly? She couldn't stop talking about the plants in my apartment. If it weren't for the plants, she wouldn't have bothered talking to me at all. She can thank Orla for the plants. My sister ignited my interest in collecting all manner of greenery in my house.

I have several ferns, pothos plants, succulents and a few orchids that I maintain despite an extremely erratic approach to plant care. Kamari seems surprised, and she rolls her eyes when I tell her that I have a charming side too.

I'm not just a monster. But I suppose I'm also that – and she can't look past it. How can I expect her to?

I don't want to leave her in the living room alone, so I lie on the other couch and curl up watching her until I fall asleep. My arm hurts like fuck but I can't leave her. I don't want to. *I can't.* Whatever the fuck this woman has done to me, she has me wrapped entirely around her finger.

Darragh

I'm not letting her out of my sight.

MY RATTLING front door wakes me up. I know it's Kamari trying to escape, but I'm so fucking tired, I could keep my eyes shut and let her try for the next fifteen minutes. She'll never get out, and if she did she wouldn't get far.

"Ugh!" Kamari calls out. "I hate you so damn much!"

I know she's directing this comment to me, but I don't respond. Since she's clearly given up on escape, I can catch a few extra minutes of sleep.

"I know you're awake, asshole," Kamari says.

"You have a funny reaction to me saving your life."

Kamari's voice gets high-pitched and sarcastic, "Thank you Lord Darragh."

"Fuck, woman. Can you stop complaining? I have far better uses for your mouth."

"Are you seriously suggesting that instead of standing up for my rights, I give you a blowjob?"

"Before or after you get me a cup of coffee. Your choice."

"You are a fucking pig."

"Christ, Kamari. I'm joking. Can you get your ass over here?"

"No."

"Fine," I grunt. "I'll explain everything then. They didn't catch whoever bombed the club, and they have a hit out on me and they'll kill anyone I love if they can't get to me. These people know you're special to me."

I sit up and Kamari walks from the front door to the couch opposite mine. She's still glaring at me fiercely, but she sits and stares at me.

"I am *not* special to you, Darragh," she says plainly. Her shoulders tense up and she purses her lips with frustration.

"I would do anything to keep you safe," I reply. "Even piss you off. I fucked up the first night we had together. I got scared. I touched the one person I always promised myself I would never even look at, and that's why I pushed you away."

"You didn't just push me away," she says. "You shattered my self-esteem. You broke me and made me feel like I wasn't worthy of love. Those feelings don't just disappear because you said you're sorry."

"I hate myself for what I did to you."

She tries to stop her voice from trembling as she answers, "You should."

"I'm just glad you're safe. If anything happened to you, if anyone ever touched you, I would burn this fucking city down until I got the guys who did it."

She rolls her eyes and scoffs. "Men. You'll say all that, but I'm still not good enough for you to call your girlfriend."

"I've never liked the word."

"Good thing I'll never be your girlfriend then," she says. Her lower lip twitches and her shoulders tighten again, although they never were completely relaxed around me.

"No," I say to her. "You won't."

"Finally, we agree on something," she says, the corners of her lips sinking slightly.

"You're more than that. You're just mine. My girl. My woman. Off fucking limits to anyone else."

"You are ridiculous."

"I was a fucking pussy. It was easier to get hit in the head than to admit how fucking bad I had it for you."

"Shut up."

"I can't," I whisper. "Looking at you… thinking I would never see you again… I just want you."

"Well, you can't have sex this morning," Kamari says. "You're far too injured. I'll make you breakfast, but only out of complete pity."

"Not love?"

Kamari rolls her eyes. "Not love."

She's so fucking bad at hiding her feelings for me. I watch her ass swaying as she heads to the kitchen and cooks me breakfast. I don't know which of my siblings stocked my fridge, but boy am I fucking grateful for the smell of bacon. I drift off for a bit and wake up to the smell of coffee and Kamari telling me to get my butt up to the dining table for some food.

She has a portion of food for herself and a little coffee. She takes her coffee black, but she remembers to put cream and two sugars in mine. I grunt a thank you and Kamari grins. That's a welcome change.

"Food is still the only thing that shuts you up," she says. "I like it."

"You're welcome to cook for me any time you want. If you want, I'll pay you to come around in sexy little thongs. I'll pay better than the strip club."

"I should dip my bacon in your coffee," she says threateningly, but her lips give way to a small smile.

I can't stop myself from spilling my heart out to Kamari today. She's safe. My body hurts like hell. I can't stand the thought of losing my second chance with her.

"I was worried sick about you," I say to her once I'm done with the delicious coffee and Kamari's filling breakfast spread. "I spent every second in that hospital begging to be let out."

She moves some hair behind her ear. Her curls are messy and untamed this morning. I want to run my fingers through her hair and separate the curls. I want to wrap those curls around my wrist and watch her body squirm against mine.

She runs her tongue over her lower lip slowly and unconsciously. My cock stiffens automatically.

"I worried about you too," she says in her soft, constantly alluring voice. "Not like you deserve it."

I nod because she's probably right. I should probably lighten the mood. "At least we got to fuck before the bomb went off."

"Is that all you think about? You nearly died and you're worried about getting your dick wet?" Kamari asks.

She raises one of her very disapproving brows and my dick shifts in my sweatpants again. I don't need the use of my arm to fuck Kamari. I can watch her bounce on my dick as I sit in my living room or on the edge of my bed.

"Any time I'm around you, I think about getting my dick wet. That's my problem."

I wink at her, which makes her pale copper cheeks turn a darker shade.

Kamari rolls her eyes. "Good thing you can't pounce on me."

"I can't. But I can ask for payment for keeping you safe."

"Payment?" she huffs. "Cooking your lazy ass breakfast wasn't enough payment."

"Lazy ass? I got shot!"

Kamari rolls her eyes. "I know. I know. I'm just messing with you. But I am *not* giving you payment."

"Most women would drop down to their knees and give me a blowjob."

"Maybe women who want to be part of your gang. *We* only had sex so that you would give me a job at your business, which you got blown up. If I could, I would take it back."

This woman is absolutely frustrating. I get up and she rises too, sensing a challenge. I try to get around the table to get to her, but Kamari darts away. I dart to the left and she hangs right. I hang right, and she tries to escape to the left.

"Are you seriously trying to run away from me right now?" I say to her, ignoring the throbbing in my arm for the ultimate goal of getting Kamari close to me and putting an end to her upsetting protests. We belong together.

"What does it look like?"

She makes a last attempt at escape, but I'm faster than she is and Kamari smacks into my chest before she realizes what's happening. She emits a little shriek as she slams into me, her palms inadvertently digging into my shirt as she nearly falls over. With my good arm, I catch her, placing my hand on her lower back.

Kamari steadies herself and she doesn't pull away.

"Good job with your great escape," I tease her, leaning forward and planting a kiss on her forehead. She scowls, but doesn't move her body away from mine. *Good.* I crave her softness. She's sweeter than cream and sugar. Softer than butter. Now that I've had breakfast, I want her for dessert.

"The only reason I haven't smacked you is because of your *weakened* state," she says, dramatically emphasizing her little dig at my masculinity. Her huffy state makes me want to kiss, and eventually fuck the attitude out of her.

"Do I look weak?" I whisper, towering over her by several inches and planting another possessive kiss on the top of Kamari's stubborn head.

Her hair smells delicious and I don't mind her outrage with me. She's too close for me to feel anything other than desire for her. I regret the way I treated her. She doesn't know how much it scares me now to feel her distance and to know that my actions could be the reason I lose her for good.

I don't know how long I'll have her stuck with me in Beacon Hill, but before she leaves, I need Kamari Roberts to know how much I love her.

"You look… like a gangster. Especially with that beard."

"You can straddle me and shave it off," I say to her, running my thumb over her lip. "Then bounce on my cock when you're done."

"I'm not going to spend my morning bouncing on your dick."

I kiss Kamari before she can protest again. She makes a frustrated grunting sound, but I can't stop myself from pushing my tongue into her mouth and kissing her even harder. I can only hold her with one hand, but I put my palm on her ass and pull her towards me. *Mine.*

"Are you going to make me pay every time I want to fuck you?"

"No," she says. "Because you're not going to fuck me."

"Okay," I whisper. "You have sex with me, I'll let you go."

She rolls her eyes. "Do you really expect me to believe that?"

"Have I lied to you before?"

She rolls her eyes. "That's not the point. I'm not having sex with you. Not even considering it."

"So if I put my hand in your panties, you won't be completely wet?"

"I'll be dry," she says, her tongue darting out over her lower lip nervously.

With my good hand, I surprise Kamari by reaching my fingers into her giant sweatpants. She's not wearing underwear. My fingers slide easily between the soaked lips of her bare wet pussy.

"You're wet *and* you're not wearing underwear. Incredible."

"I'm not wet," she protests, barely stifling a moan as I move my fingers against her clit. Her demeanor instantly changes once I touch her pussy.

I take my fingers away from her pussy and push them into her mouth just as she opens her mouth to protest.

"Suck," I command and despite herself, Kamari listens to me. I pull my fingers away and she keeps giving me her signature dirty look.

"I'm not," she protests, much more weakly this time.

"Where are your panties?"

"I couldn't wear the same thong for however long you've been gone. Odhran only allowed me to either wear his boxers or go commando."

I feel the tips of my ears getting hot.

"Did he see you naked?"

"What kind of question is that?"

"Answer the fucking question."

"No!" she says. "And don't be gross. He's a teenager, so you shouldn't act all jealous."

I slip my fingers back inside Kamari's sweatpants, pressing my thumb against her perfectly soft clit. "You're mine and you're off-limits. I'm not *acting jealous*. I'm protecting what's mine."

"Again, I'm not yours," she says, biting her lower lip to stop herself from moaning as I work her clit in slow circles. I love her soft pussy. She gets so wet for me that my cock gets instantly hard.

"Your pussy disagrees," I say, pulling my hand away just when she's close to orgasm. Kamari's flushed cheeks get me so aroused that I wish I still had the full use of my arm so I could drag her off to my bedroom and worry about her protests later.

"You are an asshole," she gasps. I make it worse by licking my fingers clean of her juices.

"That's what I thought," I say after licking my fingers. "You're wet. I can taste you all over my hand."

I sniff my fingers and Kamari wrinkles her nose.

"You smell delicious," I whisper. "I *really* need to fuck you today."

"Darragh…"

"Just come," I whisper. "Give me a kiss."

She gives me a reluctant kiss on the lips and then she pulls away. I hate that she puts any distance between us at all. I close the distance and walk with her slowly until I have her almost pinned against a wall.

"You got your kiss," she says. "Now back off."

"Not until I get my morning head."

"This is your plan to get sex? Trap me and force me to suck your cock?"

"It's not forcing," I say, leaning forward and kissing her neck until she squirms. "It's convincing."

I only have one hand to touch her, but I plan on making full use of it. I slide my fingers into her sweatpants again. She gasps, but she doesn't move away.

"It's not working."

"Don't you want to cum?"

I move my fingers away from her clit, resting them on her inner thighs just to tease her. I can tell from her squirming and the flush on her face that she wants to cum so fucking badly. She's ready to slide her hands into her pants herself and touch her pussy.

"That's not the point."

"I'll make you cum if you suck my cock. I'll make you cum all morning and then I'll cook you lunch."

"With one arm?" she asks skeptically.

"I can order pizza with one arm."

"That's not cooking."

"It's better than cooking. It's pizza," I say, moving my fingers closer to her clit. She is so close to saying yes and my cock is so close to bursting out of my sweatpants. I need Kamari so damn badly.

"Pizza is not better than cooking," Kamari protests. I love it when she's wrong. Her protest doesn't last long. She gasps and moves her hips forward so my fingers touch just the right spot to make her cum. I love the way she orgasms. I push my fingers inside her to feel her tightening around them. The walls of her pussy pulse around me.

Her willingness to protest weakens as she cums. I take her lower lip between my teeth and suck on it possessively. I want her to feel me all over her. I need her to crave me as much as I crave her. She whimpers as my teeth sink into her lower lip.

"You owe me one," I whisper. "If you don't give it to me willingly, I'll have to take extreme measures."

"Like what?" she whispers, mostly ignoring my words and grinding her clit against my fingers mindlessly. Orgasms weaken her resolve against me and I love watching her body move against my hands with such needy desperation for more pleasure. I kiss her neck as she moves against my fingers before I answer.

I push Kamari's hair away from her ear and whisper, "I'll tell your brother that you begged me for a job as a stripper and then begged me to fuck you on my office desk. Our little secret will blow up and your brother will lose all trust and respect for you."

"You are a fucking asshole," she says, pulling away from me. I slip my fingers out of her underwear. Finally, I have her attention. I hate her thinking that she can act all aloof with me, like my words and actions don't affect her. She wants me just as much as I want her. The spark between us has always been mutual and we have waited long enough for each other.

She's close enough that I can kiss her again. Kissing her breaks down her resistance a little longer.

"I should have never let you go," I murmur, taking my good hand and touching her cheek.

"I broke you, but I broke myself too. I was even more of a demon back then and I'd done horrible things... I couldn't bear to taint you, Kamari..."

She closes her eyes and my lips wander to her forehead. My fingers move to her breasts. I have to feel them. She whimpers as I pinch her nipples.

"Fuck you."

"I'd love to..."

She gasps as my hard pinches turn into loving teasing. I reach beneath her clothes and rub my wet fingers in slow circles around her nipples. I want her wearing less.

"Darragh... We can't..."

"Why not...?"

"Because... If we do, I'll develop feelings for you. I know how this ends. I know you can't be with me. I can't let you break my heart again."

"I will *never* break your heart again."

"Darragh, you're in the mob. You've promised your family that you wouldn't be with someone black. You told me yourself that you couldn't picture it."

My chest tightens. It hurts to be here. In this position. She doesn't understand how hard it is to humble yourself when you're a champion, when you always win, when you've always had exactly what you wanted your entire life.

Until Kamari walked out of my life, I'd never lost anything. Losing her was hell.

"I was wrong," I murmur. Her eyes sparkle with life, like she can't believe the words spilling out of my mouth. I mean them.

"I was wrong about you. I was wrong about everything. I've been a fucking dick and I'm sorry. If I break your heart again, you get my life Kamari."

"Don't say that."

"I'm serious. If I break your heart… You get to kill me."

"That'll go over well in court," she mumbles. "Don't be dramatic."

"What do you want, then? Because I would give you the fucking world."

SHE DOESN'T ANSWER. She just gives me this puzzled look, like she still doesn't believe me.

THIS IS IT, isn't it? She's going to run. *I can't stop screwing up with her.*

Chapter Twenty-Six
Kamari

Darragh's so close to me that his scent overwhelms me. The Ivory soap brings me back to our first night together. He's different. He's really different and I don't react how I expected to react. Every logical part of me says to push him away again. He was my first everything and he broke me on purpose. He just hauled me around Boston like I was his property. He's bad news but he wriggles his way past my logical brain.

What the hell is it with me and Darragh? Why can't I let this white boy go?

I push my hands against his chest and instead of pushing him away, I kiss him. I kiss him because even if he pisses me off, I'm glad he's alive. I'm glad he's different. I want him to want me... This is what I needed from him.

When I pull away from the big kiss, Darragh's hands clutch my waist possessively.

"Just where do you think you're going with a surprise like that?"

"To think about what you just said."

"No," he says. "We're fucking. Now."

He's too agile for a man who only has complete use of one of his arms. He flips me around and presses my face and chest against the wall. Darragh drags down my sweatpants and before I can protest, I feel the soft, warm head of his dick rubbing over my ass cheeks.

Darragh slowly spreads me apart and presses the head of his cock against my entrance. I think he'll be slow and patient but once he lines the head of his dick up with my pussy, he slides in with one smooth stroke that forces me to cry out in pain. I thrust my hips back, foolishly moving backwards to get away and impaling myself deeper on his dick. We cry out together and I throw my body against his.

It's too late for me to protest. He takes me against the wall just as he wants, kissing my neck and whispering in my ear as he thrusts ardently behind me.

"You're fucking sexy," he grunts. "I love your skin. I love your hair…"

We moan together again as Darragh hits my sweet spot and then slips his fingers around the front of my mound to stroke my clit as he slides into me. He thrusts his cock with arousingly steady movements and moves his fingers around my clit.

"I love you," Darragh grunts as he thrusts into me, his fingers right on my sweet spot. I moan and he says it again. "I love you."

He keeps fucking me and saying that he loves me until I cum. He makes me cum three more times before he finishes inside me. Darragh's cum coats my inner walls as he pumps deep inside me and sucks on my neck until he spills every drop. He wraps his good arm around me and growls. "I'm not letting you out of my sight. You could have died Kamari, and I'll never let that happen. *Never.*"

WE DON'T GET out of bed until after sunset. I'm completely sore between my legs from taking Darragh's cock so many times. At least he's being a good sport about how I fell asleep. I'm curled up on his chest and wrapped around him, using his chest as a pillow. He assures me it wouldn't hurt his arm and he puts his good arm around me, clutching me against his muscles. He's warm and soothing to sleep against. I don't want to stop.

Did he mean what he said when he was inside me? I want to believe him. I always want to think the best of Darragh. I'm glad he's alive.

<h1 style="text-align:center">Chapter Twenty-Six</h1>

. . .

Since we're stuck at his place in Beacon Hill, hiding out from the people trying to kill Darragh, we have nothing better to do than to talk and have sex.

We don't talk about our past, or boxing, or the people trying to kill Darragh, but we talk about just about everything else. He tells me about what it was like growing up in Aiden's shadow, how he always got into fights to get his father's attention, which led to him entering a boxing ring for the first time when he was nine-years-old. He beat the shit out of the first kid he fought and was a champion ever since.

He makes me talk about college, which I never do. I confess how hard it was to be one of the few black students at Cornell and how I never fit in with the white kids or the black kids because everyone was from New York and I was the odd one out from Boston.

He holds me against him like I'm special. Like I mean something to him.

"How long are we going to be holed up in here?" I ask Darragh.

"Do you really want to escape me?"

"No."

"Good. Because you're mine, Kamari… My girl…"

Beacon Hill becomes my home for the next thirty days. I transition disturbingly seamlessly to captivity. Darragh keeps me busy most of the day. His mafia family delivers groceries in the dead of night and he has hushed phone calls with his brothers after he thinks I'm asleep. I can't fall asleep until he crawls into bed with me. Until I know he's safe.

Over the past month, his arm has improved significantly. He can move it now, but he still can't hold heavy weights or use a gun – which seems to be Darragh's primary concern.

We fall into a routine with each other that feels too comfortable. It's too easy to forget that he's a mobster. Even when he takes his shirt off and I can see the swirl of black ink up close for myself, I forget these are symbols of how dangerous he is. How many people he's killed. What he believes.

165

. . .

DARRAGH PULLS me close after a month, after telling me that he loves me, and he whispers something I never thought I'd hear him say. Words that hurt.

"I want a baby."

He notices how his words bring a change to my face.

"You're just saying that because we've been cooped up in here too long," I say as I stroke Darragh's chest. He has his arm around me and we're in our favorite non-sexual position in bed. I have one leg slung over Darragh and my head on his chest. He likes kissing the top of my head occasionally and reaching his good arm to squeeze my ass as he holds me.

I will never fully understand his complete obsession with my butt.

"No," Darragh grunts. "I'm saying it because I want to be with you and I'm getting old. I want a baby."

"You're in the middle of a mafia war. Is this the best time to expand your family?"

Wetness pools between my thighs instantly at the mention of making babies despite my resistance to him. It's not my body that's the problem. It's the past.

"Yes," Darragh says, turning his gaze to me. "And I'm surprised you're this resistant to it. You always wanted kids."

"How do you even know that?" I grumble. I hate when Darragh acts like he has all this knowledge of me. I want to maintain some mystery, but Darragh noses his way into all my mystery and thinks he has me all figured out.

"Because I know you, Kamari. You want to have a traditional family. Yet another reason why I didn't want you up on my stage."

Darragh won't stop jealously bringing up my extremely brief career as a stripper. With this mention, I swat his chest and roll my eyes.

"You are such a prude."

"No. I was raised Catholic. And Irish. There's a difference."

My chest tightens. I don't mind when he brings up his heritage, but it's an unpleasant reminder about how he thinks of me and my family. My heritage.

"If we have a baby, they would be the most confused baby of all time."

"I know mixed kids exist," Darragh says, twirling his finger mindlessly around my hair. The little things Darragh does are normally enough to get me going. He mindlessly plays with my hair and that tiny act makes me want to jump his bones almost more than kissing me or touching me.

"Yes, Darragh," I sigh, rubbing his firm chest muscles with my palm. "I have also heard of mixed children. That's not the point. You have beliefs about race that might affect your kids."

"You don't seem to have a problem," Darragh grumbles imperiously. He always gets so defensive when we talk about this stuff. *But we must.* I clutch his chest, so he knows this isn't me pulling away from him. I wriggle my hips so my crotch rests against him and I hold him like he's *my* property.

"Kids are different. They need a dad who loves them even if they're the palest shade of tan or the darkest shade of brown."

Darragh's eyes snap fiercely to mine. That shade of blue never fails to make my pussy throb. They're cold and captivating at one glance, but eternally beautiful in another. I love his brilliant, strange blue eyes.

"I love you," he says with confidence. "And you're brown. I'll love our children. *My* children. Especially since I'll have to spend your entire pregnancy keeping you and them out of trouble."

"Since when did I agree to this whole baby thing?"

Darragh cups one of my ass cheeks and pulls me tighter against his body. "Since now."

"I haven't agreed to anything," I protest, using my toes to push against Darragh's thighs and irritate him away from this line of thinking with my cold feet.

Unfortunately, my cold feet just wake him up even more. Even with one bad arm, he effortlessly flips me onto my back and uses his weight to pin me to the bed.

"Darragh. Solitary confinement with a woman from your past isn't a good enough reason to start a family."

"I love you," he says. "When you love a woman, you give her babies. You keep giving her babies and you don't stop until…"

He trails off as if lost in a fantasy about keeping me continuously pregnant. Considering Darragh's sex drive, the fantasy likely revolves around the process of getting me pregnant. His hand wanders beneath the giant hoodie I'm wearing to my stomach.

"Until?" I press him, wriggling to get away from his hand but failing because of Darragh's massive weight against mine. Even in his injured state, he's so much stronger than me.

"We just keep going, I think," Darragh murmurs, kissing me and losing himself in his baby-making fantasy.

"No, Darragh," I protest between kisses. I don't stop myself from kissing back. I just protest him weakly. "We can have one or two kids."

"Yes, a few batches of two would make it easier to get to seventeen…"

"You have to start way earlier if you want seventeen kids," I say, unsure about the details of it, but pretty sure I didn't want to have seventeen of Darragh's kids running around.

"We'll see…" Darragh whispers, unceremoniously sliding his hands into my panties. He demands that I give him constant access to my pussy while we share a bed and I give in to him because he knows exactly how to use his fingers and I crave him.

It scares me how much I want Darragh, but considering his beliefs and his family, I don't know if I can give him a kid.

He rubs my clit slowly with an index finger as if gentle teasing can change my mind. I squeeze my thighs together, but this just makes his fingers feel even better and I let out a soft moan, giving Darragh the wrong idea.

"See, princess?" he murmurs. "Your body wants a baby. You're getting so wet for me because you're getting ready for a pretty Murray baby…"

"No…" I whimper, my body betraying me with an arched back and hips thrusting eagerly for more of Darragh's fingers.

He grunts and thrusts them both inside me and I yield to him with an even louder moan. I touch his chest, letting my fingers appreciate his chiseled abdomen as Darragh pumps two fingers between my legs in a flawless rhythm.

"No babies…" I gasp between moans.

"I'll be a good father," he whispers in my ear as he fucks me with his fingers. "I'll fight for them. I'll love them. Color doesn't matter, princess. Just us. Just our family…"

He plants his lips on mine and pushes his fingers against my sweet spot, making me cum at just the right time. I shudder and lift my body against his, my nipples grazing his shirt.

I whimper and sink back into bed, coming down to earth as Darragh gazes at my face. He loves how I look when I orgasm. He's told me several times and he's obvious about how much he loves watching my face darken. I bite my lips when I cum, apparently, so he loves sinking his teeth into my lower lip and imagining me finishing around his dick.

He pulls his fingers from my pussy again and runs them over my lips.

"Do you taste that, princess?" he says. "That's your pussy begging for my cum. Begging for a baby…"

He might have knocked most of the sense out of me, but Darragh's begging tugs at me again. *He's forcing me to do this.*

"I can't…"

"What do you mean?" he asks, panic rising in his voice.

"Because I already got pregnant. And it ended badly. And I'm never putting myself through that hell again."

There you go, Darragh. My big secret.

Chapter Twenty-Seven
Darragh

I don't have to ask to know it was mine... but I do anyway, because I want to hear the truth from her – the way I broke her heart was entirely unforgivable. The real reason for the wall between us.

She sees the fear written all over my face and sweet, too gentle Kamari holds my hand. I don't deserve it. I'm a monster. I abandoned her when she needed me most.

"Kamari... was it..."

"This wasn't your fault. I know it wasn't your fault but..."

My grasp on her tightens. She was pregnant with my child. The words hit me slowly. The pain feels like an infection worming its way beneath my skin. *Pregnant.*

"How did you get pregnant?"

"We had sex," she says bluntly, as if I could possibly have forgotten *that.*

"We were careful," I mutter, although I can't remember if we were. I suppose I was anything but careful that night. I wanted her so badly and I lost so much that I needed someone close. I needed it to be her. I needed an excuse to yield to my urges and Michelle provided the perfect one. *Revenge.*

I didn't just break Kamari's heart, I left her pregnant and...

"Not careful enough," she says sadly. "I kept wanting to tell you but... I didn't even tell Tavarius. I didn't want him to know until the baby came."

"What happened?"

I stroke her hair out of her face and kiss her. "Tell me," I continue. "I won't leave you, Kamari. Nothing you say could make me leave you."

Her chest shudders and she shakes her head. "I don't talk about it."

"Tell me," I plead again, kissing her neck and wiping her tears away. I failed her. I failed to protect her in so many ways.

"I lost the baby. He had a genetic abnormality at five months old and the pregnancy... *self-terminated.*"

"No."

"Yes, Darragh."

I should have been there. She suffered this loss alone, but this was my child too. My burden to bear along with her. I kiss her slowly, trying to ease some of her pain, even if I know it's impossible. I love her enough to want to try.

"Were you alone?" I murmur between kisses. I still want her.

"Yes," she says.

"Fuck, Kamari... You could've told me."

I hold her against me and kiss her. I had a child. It's the most important thing – family – and I lost all of it because I pushed her away. Because of rules and beliefs that not even my eldest brother was strong enough to follow. Times change and hearts are too unruly to tame with rules and laws.

"It was bad enough that I hid the pregnancy from you. How could I tell you that I lost the baby too? You treated me like I was lower than dirt. You were the last person I wanted to come to."

"I'm here now," I whisper. "And I'm not going anywhere. I want a baby. I *still* want a baby. And the only woman I've ever wanted that with is you."

"What do you mean?"

"I think a part of me wanted you to get pregnant. I wanted you to come back. I was always so careful. That never happened with Michelle or... anyone else."

"If we were meant to have a baby, wouldn't that have worked out?"

"You don't always get lucky," I murmur. "But this time, you won't be alone. I promise, Kamari."

She lets me kiss her neck and I ease her thighs open, kissing her more and allowing my hardness to rest against her thighs. I want to fix her sadness. Kisses. Soft touches. Cuddles.

"It was a long time ago," she says. "I get sad but… a baby wouldn't have fixed us."

"What about now?"

Kamari smiles gently. Her smile is so pretty it hurts to look at. I love the way her cheeks turn into tiny apples and her eyes light up. *She glows.*

"We don't need fixing, do we? We just need to be real."

"And how do we do that?"

"We can't pretend the race thing doesn't exist," she says. "And we have to tell my brother."

That's *almost* enough to kill my erection, but Kamari's soft thigh keeps me eager for her. I press my weight into her and shake thoughts of my closest friend out of my head.

"We don't have to tell him until the baby comes, right?"

"Unlike last time, I'll be in the same city he lives in. He'll notice if I show up pregnant out of the blue."

"Can't we hide you like we've been doing?"

"I hope we aren't hiding in your house for a full calendar year," she says, drawing her thighs closer to me with great concern. "Darragh?"

It's nearly impossible to focus on the words coming out of her mouth when she gets me so fucking hard. But she's mine and I love her, so I try to listen to her.

"Hm, I'll hide you as long as I must to keep you safe."

"Remember the part where I'm not your property?" she whispers, her whisper turning into a moan as I slide a finger past her lower lips and push it inside her. Kamari's hips buck to meet my hands inadvertently. I love the way she loses control.

"Yes," I say to her, swirling my finger inside her tightness. "But you're going to be the mother of my child."

"When did I agree to that?" she says, gasping as I add a second finger inside her.

"Your pussy agrees," I whisper, tugging on her lower lip between my teeth as I tease her wetness. Kamari gasps and bucks her hips to meet me, enjoying the slow teasing between her legs. "Plus... you weren't on birth control under my brother's protection. It's the perfect time."

"Only if you promise," she says. "Only if you promise..."

This is the easiest promise I've ever made.

"I promise."

She lets go with me, easing my pants off and then grabbing hold of my shaft with her needy fingers. I almost explode the second she touches me. Her hands are soft and her gentle touch melts me entirely. Her body draws me in with every sensation. With her, I don't feel numb or achey. I barely feel any pain from where I've been shot.

She rubs the head of my cock against her slick entrance and again, I fight against my urge to erupt immediately. I thrust my hips forward, careful not to put too much weight on my injured arm. Kamari whimpers with pleasure as I push the first inch of my cock inside her. She grips the base of my dick so tightly that the blood rushing between my legs threatens to make me cum again.

I press my lips to her neck and bury myself in Kamari's scent as I drive the rest of my length inside her. I can't stay patient and reserved anymore. I want her. I want a baby. I want us to be together... *forever*.

Her moans as I fill her with my cock, and hearing her pushes me closer to the edge. I stop myself because I have to feel her cum first. I need her climax as much as I need my own. Thrusting into her urgently, I tease Kamari's clit until she soaks my shaft. To push her over the edge, I slow down, fighting my urge to pump into her furiously so I can tease her to the perfect orgasm.

Her thighs tremble and clamp down around me as she gets close.

"I want to put a baby in you," I whisper. "I want to watch you have my baby..."

I tease her with our most primitive instincts, the biological urges that push us together against all reason, all rules, all taboos about her race. She cums hard as I dig my teeth into her neck, biting her possessively as I slowly make love to her, verbalizing my intentions.

Once she cums, I pull her closer and thrust into Kamari faster.

Chapter Twenty-Seven

"I'm gonna cum inside you," I growl into her ear. "Make you mine forever…"

She wraps her body tighter around mine, making it easy for me to finish inside her. She's so close that she captures all my senses and pushes me over the edge. I push my hips into her one last time, sinking my weight into Kamari's as I cum inside her. I cum so hard it's like all the energy saps out of my body at once. I give her everything that I have. My seed. My love. *My baby…*

I know this time will be different.

"COME CLOSER," I murmur as I finish. Our thighs are sticky and we're covered in sweat. I'm not ready to pull away from her yet. Kamari obediently pushes her hips to meet me and teases my chest with her nipples as she holds onto me.

"I'm never letting you go."

Chapter Twenty-Eight
Kamari

I wake up in the middle of the night to hear Darragh arguing on the phone. He talks on the phone with his brother almost every night. It's been three weeks since he's officially been trying to get me pregnant, which means we've been here for almost two months, far too long to be cooped up in Beacon Hill. I'm going crazy and Tavarius is starting to get suspicious.

"I can't have Rian staying here," Darragh snarls. "Have you lost it? I don't care if it's his first week out of prison. I have Kamari here and I don't want him anywhere near her."

I don't hear what Aiden says, but he clearly doesn't listen to Darragh, because I hear him pace more furiously. Eavesdropping is "wrong" according to boring people who don't like getting all the tea, but I disagree. Slipping out of bed, I press my ear to the door to hear their conversation better.

"Rian's a fucking criminal piece of shit and he's a racist..."

...

"Yes, his daughter's Puerto Rican. But he hates blacks, Aiden. There's a fucking difference."

...

Blacks. Like me. This is exactly what I was worried about. The problem between us. It sounds like Darragh's defending me, but he shouldn't have to. Is this what our entire life will be like? Fights with family? Conflict over my skin color?

Did I make a mistake by letting him cum inside me so many times? After what happened the first time, I want to believe it wasn't wrong to take a chance on Darragh Murray, but life isn't a fairytale. People don't shed their monstrous beliefs overnight and it takes more than having fun in the bedroom to untangle a lifetime of hatred.

Darragh's voice snaps me out of my contemplation. "If he so much as looks at her, I'll skewer him myself."

Darragh storms back to our bedroom and before I can throw myself into bed and pretend I was sleeping, he thrusts the door open and discovers me halfway into covering up my eavesdropping. *Crap.*

He scowls. His hair has grown longer than shoulder length and he needs a little black band to keep it out of his face. The long hair looks sexy and highlights his fierce Irish features. Those eyes. *Sigh.* How lucky would my kid be to get those eyes?

I bite my lip and pretend I wasn't doing anything wrong, which won't fool him at all.

"Were you listening in?"

"You woke me up with all that stomping around."

"So you pressed your ear to the door and listened in on my conversation?" Darragh asks, raising an eyebrow and seeming more amused than upset.

"That sounds like what happened."

He sighs and thrusts his hands into his pockets, hiding his nervous and fidgeting fingers from me.

"When I fight with my brother, I normally sneak off to the gym and throw a few punches. Tonight… I just have you."

"What happened?"

"We don't have a choice, my ex-con brother is moving in tomorrow."

"What? Do you have enough room?"

I've never met Darragh's brother Rian, but I've heard his reputation from Darragh, from my brother Tavarius and from whispers amongst the Murray family. I find it amusing that he's *the* ex-con brother since most of them have spent some time in jail or prison, but I bite my tongue.

"He's sleeping in the living room," Darragh says. "I won't clean out my office for him and I don't want him near you. Rian isn't like the rest of us. He's a sociopath."

I snort and roll my eyes. "You've killed people, Darragh. By most definitions, that makes you a sociopath too."

"I kill because I have to. Rian kills, fights and hurts people because he enjoys it. Tegan deserves a better father."

I've never heard Darragh talk this way about one of his brothers. He's fiercely loyal. Even if he chose to love me, he hasn't lost any of his pride in his family. The thought of a man walking around who Darragh would call a sociopath chills me a little. Sensing my nervousness, he moves in and hugs me, gripping my butt and pulling me against him.

"Are you afraid of him?"

Darragh scoffs. "No. But you're mine to protect. I don't want you near anyone that dangerous. Ever."

"I can handle myself."

"Yes," Darragh says. "My brother ought to hurry and get the target off our backs. If he doesn't solve this soon..."

I don't like the way he sounds. *Withholding*. The only way Darragh would hold something back was if he thought it would hurt me. Ever since I confessed losing a baby I'd grown attached to in the womb, he's treated me like even more of a princess. We barely fight, even if we're trapped in a Beacon Hill brownstone with no one but each other. I don't want secrets.

I grip Darragh's hands and rub my thumb along the inside of his palm.

"No secrets."

"I can't keep you here. But if Aiden can't solve this, I'll have to do it myself. We know where they're hiding out. It's two miles away from Harrison Ave. I can shoot just fine with my other arm..."

"Can you?"

"I'll have adrenaline on my side," Darragh says with the blind confidence that only a championship boxer could have. My heart races and I understand perfectly why he tried to keep this from me. He wants to go on a suicide mission. He's trying to get me pregnant and now he wants to take his battered body into enemy territory and risk death.

My fingers hook into his forearms in a death grip.

"You are absolutely not doing that."

"If we don't get to them first, they'll find us eventually. We're Murrays and we're Irish. Our people drink and they talk. Aiden's out of his fucking mind if he thinks I'll die like a rat in a cage."

"Isn't not dying an option?"

"Not dying is the whole fucking plan, princess. But I can't leave you here alone with Rian if I need to make it happen."

"Then take me with you."

Darragh's face contorts in anger and he looks at me like I have two heads. Unlike him, my entire body isn't battered and broken. How hard can it be to fire one of those fancy modern guns in self-defense? Plus, he might need an extra set of eyes or hands or *anything*.

"I'm trying to get you pregnant, not killed."

"I'm not pregnant yet. I'm grown, Darragh. I can handle myself. I can just drive the getaway car or something and you do all the work."

And I can be close in case I need to call someone.

Darragh shakes his head. "Out of the question. When Rian comes here, I'll have you locked in the bedroom most of the day."

"Say goodbye to ever having sex again if you do something that stupid and controlling."

"It's not controlling," Darragh protests, finally pulling his forearms away from my claw grip. "It's protecting what's mine. If I have to tie you to the bed, that's what I'll do."

"If you tie me to the bed, I'll gnaw through the ropes."

Darragh smirks and tightens his grip on my ass. "Then I'll use chains."

Before I can protest, he silences me with a kiss. Mm. His lips are so pillowy soft that I could drift into a dreamland just from kissing him. Plus, he's warm from getting all hot-headed on the phone with his brother. I let him kiss me and get my fingers all tangled up in his hair, pulling it out of its knot.

"I'm not letting you turn this argument into sex," I say as I run my fingers through his hair. Darragh grunts and pushes his hips up against me. He's hard, which means that's what he had every intention of doing. I can't help but let him keep kissing me, despite having every intention of stopping him before we have sex again.

There's no sign of a missed period yet, I still have a week, but it seems impossible for us to have this much unprotected sex and not end up with a baby. Darragh's desire is relentless. He clutches me to his chest and kisses me even more fiercely.

"I'm not letting my brother move into my house without fucking you nice and loud one last time," Darragh says. "In the kitchen. In the living room. In *all* the rooms…"

Do we have enough time before Rian comes to do that? My body tingles at the suggestion despite my inner hesitation.

"Do you even have the stamina for that?" I grunt as Darragh effortlessly lifts me off the ground with one arm.

"You'll find out, princess," he says. "Your pussy will be so deliciously sore tomorrow that you won't want to leave my bed."

Chapter Twenty-Nine
Darragh

Prison changes people. Jail is one thing, especially out here in Massachusetts, but prison is an entirely different beast. Maximum security prison up in Shirley was no picnic. We have several lifers in there from our family – three of dad's cousins, two of my uncles on my mother's side, and a few more I can't remember because they've been in so long. They try to keep the mob guys separate, so it couldn't have been a picnic for Rian.

He needs to be with his daughter, not trapped with me in Beacon Hill. I drink all morning awaiting his arrival, to Kamari's dismay. She keeps hiding the whiskey, but I keep finding it and pouring more down my throat.

"If your brother is as crazy as you say he is," she protests. "Don't you think it's smart to be sober?"

I don't care what's smart. I'm tired of staying cooped up here and Aiden's latest assignment couldn't have come at a worse time. The only reason I don't outright disobey my brother's orders and root out this Italian problem tonight is that I promised Kamari I would never leave her.

I love her. I don't *want* to break my promise to her. Unfortunately, I find myself entirely committed to an extremely stubborn woman who refuses to retreat to the bedroom when Rian arrives. Callum drops him off. I can hear my younger brother's annoying truck five blocks away and my body tenses automatically. Kamari tries to rub my shoulders, but that only hurts my injury, so she stops and kisses them instead until the doorbell rings.

"I'd rather shoot us both than see him," I mutter drunkenly. Kamari clicks her tongue.

"Stop being dramatic," she says. "He just got out of prison. He'll probably just want a hot shower and some food."

I have to stop her from opening the door. I hardly want her to meet Rian at all. When I open the door, I don't see who I expect. It's Rian, but he's bigger. *Much* bigger.

"Did you spend every minute in there working out?"

My brother is my height but holds an additional forty-something pounds of muscle on his previously lean frame. His eyes are like mine and Aiden's, but bloodshot like he hasn't slept. He doesn't look like he's shaved in a while either. A pelt of copper hair with flecks of blond covers his cheeks and chin. His brown hair is otherwise cropped short and messy.

"Good to see you too, D," he grunts, but he doesn't look at me because Kamari's in the house and I'm guessing nobody warned him.

Brady bounds up to the door but once he gets to the Rian, he stops, gazes at my brother and then turns tail toward his dog bed in the living room.

"The girl for me?" Rian asks. My blood boils instantly.

"No," I say. "She's my... She's mine."

I don't trust Rian enough with the complete truth about Kamari. I usher him into the house. Aiden probably warned Callum against coming upstairs, so it's for the best that he stays in the truck.

"I'm Kamari," she says, introducing herself with an outstretched hand which Rian ignores.

"Rian," he grunts. Kamari waits before dropping her hand and sliding it down her yoga pants. Finally, she eyes Rian with the suspicion and concern she should have had from the beginning.

"I set up the guest room. Do you need anything aside from that?"

"No," Rian says, looking around my house as if he's never been inside it before. It's been a long time for him since he's had a normal life. One short sentence after another hasn't left much time for a normal life. Even the short prison or jail sentences take time to recover from and Rian hasn't had much time for recovery.

"Would you like some water or some tea?" Kamari offers. Rian glances at her and then at me, but he doesn't respond to her.

"Kamari," I say to her gently. "Wait for me in our bedroom. I'll be there soon."

She nods and disappears. I feel better when she's away from him. Rian's shoulders relax visibly once she's gone.

"It's been years since I've seen a woman," he says. "She's pretty."

"Yes."

"When you're done with her–

"She's not that sort of girl."

Rian nods. "Right. I just thought. Well... those types of girls..."

"She's not any type of girl," I say to him, trying not to let my voice betray my weakness, but failing entirely. "She's just mine."

"Dad really must be dead, then."

"No," I say to him, opening the door to the guest room, surprised that Aiden hasn't cleared up that mystery since the two of them have been in touch. "Just a coma."

Rian snorts. "Do you really think he'll wake up? He's as good as dead. That doesn't mean you and your colored girl are safe. When you lose a leader like our father, there will be other contenders for his power."

"Thanks for your advice," I respond through gritted teeth. Maybe he has a right to be cynical, but I'd prefer if he worried about his problems instead of mine. I can handle keeping Kamari safe.

Detecting the shift in my emotions, Rian sighs. "I don't wanna be here any more than you want me here. I want to see my daughter."

"Aiden's become protective of Tegan since the incident with the Italians. He just wants to make sure you're ready."

I entirely disagree with Aiden's assessment of things, but he's the boss and unlike Padraig Murray, he doesn't give a damn who I fuck. I'll take his side on everything to keep him in charge.

"She's my daughter. She doesn't need protection from me. I'm her father and I would do anything for her."

"You kept it clean in prison?" I ask him.

Rian's eyes narrow. The emotion disappears from them and the blue seems to turn black in my dimly lit hallway. "That's none of your concern. I'm out and there won't be new charges."

He looks around the guest room with blatant disappointment.

"Why do you have so many plants in there?"

"I celebrate life, Rian. Get over it. Just be happy I'm having you here at all."

Rian grunts and steps into the room. He turns to me, looking at me like I'm a stranger. We're all strangers to him. I remember what it was like the first time Rian got out of jail. Adjusting to the outside world takes weeks, sometimes months, and maximum security fucks you up in an entirely different way.

I lean against the door frame. I don't have much else to say to Rian and he probably wants to shower and sleep like Kamari suggested. He looks like he hasn't slept in weeks and he probably hasn't.

"Can I tell you something, D?" he says, putting his hand on the walls and touching them as if he can't believe the brick is real.

"What is it? Because I'd rather not fight."

Rian smiles. "No. I'm too tired and too fucking weak to fight. Both of us must be, otherwise I wouldn't be here."

"With dad in the hospital, there's not as much to fight about."

Rian shakes his head. "You're wrong. You're both wrong. Aiden is too weak to lead our family. He's too soft. You nearly died. He nearly died... But the Italians can sit in their fucking rat hole and plot on our lives because Aiden doesn't have what he needs."

"Which is what, exactly?"

"Recklessness. Ruthlessness. We need to strike and strike fast."

I lean in the doorway, considering Rian's words. Questioning Aiden is enough to get him killed. He's right that Aiden might be cautious, but *soft* isn't how I would describe our eldest brother's behavior the past few years. He can handle this shit better than Rian realizes. Rian doesn't know how life has changed him. He doesn't know what Aiden would do to protect the woman in his life. Hell, Rian probably doesn't even know about her.

Still, he's not entirely wrong.

"I agree that we shouldn't wait," I tell him. "But Aiden knows what he's doing."

Rian nods. "You trust him. But I don't trust anyone. Not even our family. Especially not our family."

He's lost a lot – not just people, but time.

"Aiden isn't our father. You might not agree now, but you will. That's a good thing."

"Yeah," he says. "I'll take some time to myself. Go be with your girl."

I LEAVE MY BROTHER ALONE, ignoring his cynical thoughts about Aiden. If it were up to Rian, we would both have guns on our hips and Italians in the trunk of our car. I belong here. With her. She sits on my bed with a piece of paper and a pencil sketching. I remember that she used to draw and paint, but I didn't know that she still sketched.

"How is he?" she asks, looking up from her drawing. Her pretty curls fall over her shoulders and she looks beautiful.

"He's fine," I respond. "Grouchy. Brooding. Typical Rian."

"He doesn't look like you at all," she says. "I can't remember if I ever met him."

I sit next to her on the bed, glancing over at her sketch. *It's me.* She glances at me and smirks. I nod.

"That looks like me."

"Bingo," Kamari responds. "He's probably just tired. He'll be fine in the morning and you'll be laughing together and watching football or whatever sport you both like."

"I doubt that. Rian and I... We're too different."

"I see," Kamari says, pausing her sketch to lean against my chest. "Well, we're all prisoners together. We should make the best of it."

"I want you to stay out of his way," I command her seriously. "He's not like me or Aiden. He's not... normal. And I don't want him getting any ideas about you."

"He implied I was a hooker to my face. He has all the wrong ideas about me already."

"I'm sorry about that."

Kamari shakes her head. "He's an ex-con and he's rough around the edges. He just needs time."

Chapter Thirty
Kamari

Darragh has refused to leave my side since Rian moved in. He's extreme about it, even waking me up to use the restroom in the morning while he stands outside the door. He listens to me shower. He watches me change. I don't eat, sleep, think or sit without Darragh's careful observation. If Rian dares to make conversation beyond "Good Morning", Darragh interrupts him.

The tension between them has been impossible to live with. Rian clearly loathes dogs, which Darragh doesn't seem to notice or care about. He's used to Brady ruling the house and doesn't see any reason why it should change. Rian's an obsessive neat freak but Darragh's hobby seems to be leaving balled up socks in his living room or hanging sweaty t-shirts to dry on the kitchen counter.

Since we've been in this safehouse together, I've grown accustomed to Darragh's untidy habits, but his brother seems ready to explode. Not like Darragh notices or cares. Whenever Rian's around, he's glued to my side and usually has his arm around me.

Rian asks questions about his daughter, Tegan, and I learn a world about what happened just before I walked into Darragh's strip club demanding a job. I can't even imagine what that poor little girl went through. The news about Tegan's struggle with recovery hurts her father — it must — but Rian's much better than Darragh at concealing his emotions. I've heard prison can make you like that. You learn to hide any weaknesses to survive.

Darragh doesn't trust his brother, but he doesn't seem evil to me. Just damaged.

WHEN THE TENSION between them finally erupts, I'm in our bedroom listening to Kehlani's album *It Was Good Until It Wasn't* and painting with some supplies Darragh ordered for me after he saw the sketch I did. Keeping myself busy makes captivity less frustrating. Taking care of Darragh and keeping him out of trouble provides some motivation, but for the cabin fever not to drive me completely nuts, my hands need to stay busy.

"Have you lost your fucking mind!" Darragh shouts, jerking my attention away from my painting. I set down the brush and tiptoe towards the door as their fight continues.

"Callum knows where they are. We have weapons. We can *walk* there for fuck's sake. It'll take us twenty minutes to kill them all."

I freeze. Rian's voice sounds so cold and emotionless as he talks about killing that it stops me cold. I know Darragh must have this side to him too, but I've never witnessed it. I don't want to. He's normally kept this part of himself away from me, but we've been cooped up here for too long and the tension with Rian has just kept building while his older brother does... God knows what.

I've lost track of my life in this house. Sometimes I can handle it. Other times, I wonder if I'm just in over my head with Darragh and I should run away.

"We can kill two, maybe three Italians without anyone giving a fuck," Darragh answers. "But we can't start a war with these people."

"They should fear us," Rian says. "Not the other way around. Who cares if we start a war? We'll win it."

They've lowered their voices, but they still vibrate with anger. Rian has a deeper, smoother voice than Darragh, but I've always loved Darragh's aggressive and masculine raspiness. He's not just aggressive now – he's outraged.

"You're suggesting I leave the woman I love unprotected in this house to hunt down Italians that we can make disappear more responsibly. We left this job incomplete last time."

"And who did that exactly?" Rian accuses, his voice filled with breath as he attempts to smother his rage. "Aiden left too many Italians alive. We can't afford to show any mercy."

"You only think that because you've never been afforded any," Darragh says. "Not everything has to be about vengeance and violence. Some problems can be solved by minimizing it. We obviously want to kill the man who bombed the club. *Obviously.* But we can't kill innocents."

"None of them are innocent," Rian says. "And they're going to die. Because if you want to stop me from leaving this house, you'll have to kill me."

I hear the somewhat familiar click of a bullet entering a chamber. *Darragh, don't be an idiot.*

I burst out of the room down the short hallway. They can obviously hear my steps as I approach, but neither of them say anything. They're just standing in the entryway of Darragh's house, glaring at each other. Rian isn't armed, but he doesn't implore Darragh not to shoot. He gazes at him with pure anger as if he has a weapon that could possibly contend with Darragh's pistol.

They both ignore my presence. My heart quickens. I want to interrupt and tell them to stop, but Darragh doesn't have his finger on the trigger. Not too late for me to intervene, then. Rian appears more than capable of defending himself.

"You shouldn't waste your bullets on me," Rian says calmly as Darragh glowers at him. "I'm going to solve Aiden's problems by eliminating every Italian asshole in that house, innocent or not, and give him someone else to pin the shit on. If I go back to prison... that's what it takes."

Darragh's face wrinkles in disgust. "You haven't even seen your daughter yet. How could you risk prison again for no reason?"

"When did our family stop making sacrifices?" Rian says. "Or was that only expected of me? Tegan has all of you. Her family is much bigger than me. And that's why we have to do this. I won't have you or even that girl imprisoned like animals when we should run this fucking city."

I know Darragh. Rian's words touch him. I can't tell if Rian Murray is sincere or a master manipulator who would say anything to his brother to get him to lower his weapon. I wish *I* had a weapon.

"Don't shoot him, Darragh," I offer, not meaning to take sides in their disagreement, but to bring about a general de-escalation. Darragh's still injured. I don't know if he can handle this. He's strong but... He'll have a hell of a time aiming with just one hand. If I know that, Rian must too, which makes him equally dangerous if he has the ability to get Darragh's weapon from him. My tongue feels like a thick, wet cotton ball in my mouth.

"I've made sacrifices," Darragh says. "Do you think I want to run a fucking strip club? I could've left this city and become an even better boxer than I was. But I chose this family. You're no better than me, regardless of the sacrifices you've supposedly had to make."

Darragh's comment doesn't provoke any outward emotional reaction from Rian. Their anger puts all of us in danger. I need them both to calm down before this spirals out of control.

"If you leave, Aiden could order your death and if he orders me to do it, I'll fucking do it," Darragh says, his rage real. His words send a chill down my spine and make me question everything I think about him. Could he really be this brutal?

"Darragh," I call his name, hoping to reach his humanity. "Stop..."

"Stay out of this, Kamari," he growls. "This is exactly why I wanted to keep you away from my sociopathic fuck of a brother."

Rian's lip twitches, but that's the only reaction he betrays before he takes his gun, and turns it on me, quickly loading a bullet into the chamber with a click. Darragh hesitates. He doesn't shoot his brother, but I freeze in place. I didn't expect this.

"I will blow your fucking brains out," Darragh says. "You pull the trigger, you hurt her in any way, and I'll fucking kill you."

"I don't want to kill her," he says. "You let me go and she gets to live."

"You're a fucking bastard," Darragh snarls.

"Just let me end this," Rian says. "Now..."

Chapter Thirty

Chapter Thirty-One
Darragh

He keeps his word and lets her go, but Rian leaving Beacon Hill doesn't make me feel any better. Kamari races over to me once he leaves and wraps her arms around me, but I can't hold her with a gun in my hand.

She shouldn't have seen me like that...

I set my gun down and then wrap my arms around her. She holds me so tightly that our bodies nearly melt together.

"You're fine," I murmur. "You're fine and I'm sorry."

"I didn't want anyone to get hurt," she says, because of course she doesn't. She's Kamari – the woman I love, the woman I want to bear my child.

"You are the only person who matters," I growl, pulling her tighter against me. "The fact that you were in danger at all pisses me the fuck off. I want to go after him but... I'm not leaving you."

She wraps her arms around me. "He won't be safe on his own."

"I don't give a fuck," I say to her, meaning every single word. "If he wants to go on this suicide mission, that's his choice. I have you... and... I won't be leaving you."

Kamari's fingers sink into the muscles on my back. She's so soft and beautiful that I want to immediately sweep her off her feet and plunge into her on the kitchen counter.

"Who are you, Darragh?"

"What do you mean?"

I hold onto her more fiercely. If Kamari thinks she's gonna push me away now, she's wrong. I won't let that happen. She's my girl. She's my everything. I don't want her to forget that for one fucking second.

"You almost killed your brother right in front of me. I… I'm gonna have your baby… But do I even know who you really are?"

"I'm the man who will die for you. I'm the man who loves you more than boxing, more than football, more than guns and fast cars. I will never abandon you. I will never lay a hand on you. That's who I am, Kamari."

She rolls her eyes, but I clutch her against me so she can't run away.

"You're not my property any more than I'm yours."

"No," I growl. "We belong to each other. And we always will. That's who we are. That's who I am. Nothing will get in the way of that any more."

"And what about your father?" she says. "I've been stuck in this house with you for months. I know he wouldn't approve and that if he finds out… neither of us will be safe."

"Neither will Aiden or Valentina," Darragh says. "We always have family, Kamari. That's the most important thing."

She nods and presses her head to my chest. Her hair smells delicious. I want to kiss her almost as much as I wanted to kill my brother.

"You could always teach me how to use a gun."

"Don't be ridiculous," I grumble, kissing her forehead and another on my favorite spot on her neck. "You don't need to use a gun when you have me. I'm your protector and I'll always keep you safe, princess."

Our lips meet in a slow, gentle kiss. I tease her mouth open to slip my tongue between her lips.

"I want you," I growl. "All I want is you."

She keeps kissing me. I can't imagine how wet she must be. I want to feel her. Calling Aiden is the responsible thing. Putting a bullet in Rian might be an even more responsible action. My life and who I am has always put a barrier between us. I don't want that anymore.

She's my girl. My princess. *My wife.* I want her to be my wife. I don't know when or how I'll ask, but the first time I saw Kamari again after all those years, I knew. *I'm never letting her get away from me again.* I want to tie the knot with this woman. Soon.

Our kisses grow more passionate and emotionally tangled. She strokes the pale stubble on my face as her tongue darts into my mouth, teasing mine perfectly. She gets me so fucking hard it hurts.

"I want you," I growl again, grabbing Kamari's perfect ass and massaging her butt cheeks. I bet her ass would be delicious right now.

"Is that really the best idea?" Kamari asks between kisses. My chest hurts. What could be a better idea than pulling Kamari against me and having my way with her? I want her so much that it aches.

"Yes," I growl. "Fuck Rian."

"He could be in danger."

I squeeze her ass harder. *I don't care. Fuck my duty. Fuck putting my idiot brother first when he doesn't even give a fuck about his own kid or his freedom.*

"You're my family too," I say. "I can't leave you."

She kisses me again. Her fingers are all over my face again, touching my stubble, feeling my cheekbones. It's like she's studying my face. I've always felt so ugly with all the black eyes and the bruises, more like a beast and a hunk of muscle than something pretty to look at. Kamari touches me like I'm beautiful, which is a strange thing for a man to feel, but her appreciative touch heightens both my arousal and desire for you.

"I've wanted you to say that forever," she says.

"I'll say it again, princess. I'll never leave you."

I LIFT Kamari off the ground effortlessly and put her right where I want her and lay her on the kitchen counter. She lets out a soft squeal, but I don't wait before spreading her legs and standing between them. I grab her hands and pin them over her head so her gentle touching doesn't push me over the edge prematurely. I'm fucking putty in her hands and I want to last long with her tonight.

Darragh

Rian should have never come here. Maybe he just belongs in jail.

I run my tongue over Kamari's neck and she lets out a soft moan as my tongue slides against her sweet spot. There's a sexy sensitive spot on Kamari's neck that smells fucking delicious and gets her absolutely weak in my arms.

Kamari's thighs squeeze against my torso, demonstrating her desire for me. She can't hold herself back and I fucking love it. This is exactly how I want her – not worried about my idiot brother, Rian.

"Darragh..." she whimpers.

"Spread your legs."

"It's wrong..."

"What's wrong?"

"Your brother..."

"I don't want to talk about my brother," I murmur. "I have you right where I want you."

"But Darragh—

Five loud gunshots interrupt Kamari's sentence and the screws fly straight out of the lock, sprinkling onto the kitchen floor of my Beacon Hill brownstone. *Fuck.* I fly away from Kamari and race for my gun.

She hops off the counter and races behind me.

"Tell me you have another gun," she says, her fingernails digging into my arm. I have enough adrenaline in me to ignore the pain from her sinking into my bad arm. We don't have time for Kamari to get armed.

"Run," I hiss as a thud sounds at the front door, probably from whoever shot out the lock trying to kick it down. "Run to the bedroom and go out the window. *Now.*"

Chapter Thirty-Two
Kamari

Darragh has lost his mind. There's no way in hell I'm leaving him here. He realizes that I won't leave, so he grabs me and we race down the hallway together. The only room at the end of the hall is Darragh's study – the only room in the house I've never entered.

I'm not allowed to go in there because of the mafia business – at least that's what I've gathered from Darragh's secret conversations on the phone with his brother. He doesn't care anymore. He pushes the door open and then locks it behind us, dragging a chair and propping it up against the door.

"Who the hell just shot your door open?"

"I witnessed what you did," Darragh says with a reddening face. "I don't know. But my arm hurts and I might've fucked it up completely. I don't know what the fuck I did…"

He's holding his right arm. *No.* Darragh's a champion fighter. He just survived his gunshot wounds and held a gun up to Rian's face.

"Fucked what up?" I hiss at him in a panicked whisper.

"The arm I need to shoot."

"What? Can I see it?"

"We don't have time," he growls. "I need you to jump out the window before he figures out where we are."

199

"He? Did you see his face?"

Darragh gives me a pissed off look and then glances over my shoulder. We're on the second floor. He can't seriously think about tossing me out of a second story window.

"There's a fire escape," he says. "You can jump out and just… run."

"You can't shoot," I tell him. "If that guy breaks in here, which he will, he'll kill you."

"I don't give a fuck. I'm tired of you arguing with me. Get your ass out the window."

"Give me the gun," I tell him. "I'll shoot him."

"Are you crazy?"

"Just show me how to work it…"

Darragh gives me another fierce look. I can tell he doesn't want me to do this, but we don't have time. Heavy footsteps get louder in the hallway. The man opens one door, probably Rian's room. My hands are sweaty and I don't know if I can point and shoot a gun, but I don't have a choice.

He loads a bullet in the chamber.

"You just push the safety. Point. Pull the trigger. Be very fucking careful…"

I nod, but my hands are shaking. The footsteps keep getting louder. I don't know if I can handle this. Darragh leans over and kisses me.

"You stand behind me," he says. "Shoot from behind me. If I get hit, your only mission is getting out of here alive."

"Darragh…" I whisper. "I… I love you."

"If you loved me enough, you would have jumped out that window and left me here. This man wants to kill me, not you. I want you safe."

"Do we really have to argue right now?" I whisper, getting behind Darragh and trying to memorize what exactly the difference between the safety and the trigger is. Guns are more complicated in real life.

He shouldn't have to be my human shield, but Darragh insists on keeping as much of his body in front of mine as possible. My right arm weaves out from beneath his right arm, which he holds around me. I can barely see and barely aim straight, but he swears it doesn't matter.

"The first thing that moves, you shoot," he whispers. "No questions. I get hit, you run."

"O-okay."

"No," he snarls. "You promise me, Kamari. You run…"

I don't want to make this promise. The thought of abandoning Darragh while he's dying makes me sick. But I know if I don't promise, he's crazy enough to throw me out the window screaming and face certain death on his own.

"There's no chance this is just Rian coming back, right?"

I want to get out of making a promise I don't agree with, but Darragh won't let me wriggle away from this verbal contract so easily.

"Promise me, princess."

My hands shake. The footsteps get louder.

"I promise," I whisper just before an elbow slams into the door of Darragh's office. I flinch, but I don't pull the trigger early. The door swings open. Once I see movement, just like Darragh told me, I shoot. It takes less than half a second to flick the safety open and it feels like I barely tug on the trigger before the explosion deafens me and I stumble back. There's no one behind me to catch me and I'm a few feet away from Darragh's desk, so I have to regain my balance.

"Did I hit him?" I yell, even if my ears are ringing and I don't know if Darragh responds or not because I can't hear a damn thing. Darragh's still standing in front of me protectively. I think I hear him yell to shoot again.

It's a semi-automatic pistol so another bullet loads in the chamber once I shoot. A black figure moves into the room with a raised gun. I don't even think. I shoot again. My arm hurts and I can't tell if I hit the person in the room, so I shoot again. This time, I definitely hit him, but he doesn't go down without fighting back.

I hear a fourth gunshot that doesn't come from Darragh's pistol. There's only one person it could hit since Darragh's body shields mine perfectly. I scream Darragh's name as the black figure falls to the floor. Red soaks through Darragh's shirt immediately and I can hear blood rushing past my ears as pure panic sets in. This can't be happening.

I can't lose Darragh Murray. He turns to yell at me, but I'm frozen in place, death-gripping the pistol and watching his shirt turn bloody as he begs me to leave.

"NO!" I yell, throwing the pistol aside and racing towards the body on the ground. I kick the intruder's gun away from him and gaze down at his face. I don't recognize him. There was still a part of me that thought the intruder might be Rian, so I'm grateful that it's not, but the man's eyes are frozen open, which makes me realize…

I let out the most ungodly shriek and try to run before I feel Darragh's giant bicep wrap around me and yank me away from the door. I'm not like Darragh. I can't face this. *I just killed someone.*

"Fuck, Kamari! I need you to calm down."

But I don't. I don't calm down and I freak out so hard, it's like I black out, not realizing what's happening until I feel Darragh's lips on my forehead, and I realize he must have used his good arm to carry me into the living room and throw me on the couch. He winces with every movement and groans.

"I need you to calm down and call Aiden," he demands. "Call Aiden and get him here… I can't…"

Darragh sits on the couch and groans, throwing his head back and gasping for breath. I don't bother pointing out that the blood soaking through his shirt is now ruining the couch. In my fear and panic, I try to find myself. Cold air blows in through the open front door and I stumble over to Darragh's half-conscious body to search his pockets for his cell phone.

We have neighbors and there were gunshots, so surely someone called. I don't know if that would be a good or a bad thing considering the situation. I fight back nausea as the image of the dead man flashes into my head. His eyes were so blue, like Darragh's. They could have been brothers, his eyes were so similar.

I find Darragh's phone in his left pocket, unlock it with his right index finger, and search for Aiden's name in his recent calls. They talk every day, so Aiden is the first number.

"What do you want, Darragh?" Aiden growls.

"It's Kamari…"

"What's wrong?" Aiden barks before I can get a word out. My voice must sound just as terrified as I feel.

"Someone broke in. Darragh got shot. I hit the guy. I think I killed someone… I… Darragh told me to call, but the cops could be on their way. I don't know."

Chapter Thirty-Two

"Where the fuck is Rian?" Aiden asks.

"I don't know."

"Don't move," he says with shocking calm. "I'll have people over there. Kamari, you're not safe in the house alone. You need to leave Darragh and trust that my people will take care of him."

"I can't do that," I protest. My heart leaps into my throat. Aiden's brother can't seriously be so cold-hearted, can he? He can't expect me to leave his brother to die after he's been shot.

"You must," Aiden says. "Take Darragh's car and drive to the address I text his phone. If you don't do this... I can't guarantee your safety and if I don't keep you safe, I'll have hell to pay."

"Hell to pay *if he survives*," I shoot back. "He's barely breathing..."

The last three words come out in a whisper. I'm not willing to acknowledge the truth that the slow movement of Darragh's chest and the placement of his third gunshot wound in the span of three months might end his life.

"That's my concern," Aiden barks. "Not yours. Take his car, take his cell phone and get out of there. *Now.*"

"Aiden... he's dying..."

I don't want to cry, I don't want to leave Darragh, but I can't argue with the mob boss's commands.

"No," Aiden says. "He isn't. He's a Murray and he's strong. Now *get in the fucking car and drive, Kamari.*"

The shock has me on autopilot. I want to fight Aiden, but his forceful voice pushes me towards reluctant obedience instead.

"Promise me you'll save his life if I listen," I say with a trembling voice, even if I already know I'm going to listen to Aiden's commands.

"I will," Aiden says. I kiss Darragh on the forehead and hang up.

DARRAGH'S PHONE buzzes with the address.

I don't want to go.

Chapter Thirty-Three
Aiden Murray

I hate leaving Valentina. Leaving our newborn son hurts even worse. Aifric Murray. I haven't told anyone in my family about him yet. It's more important for us to settle our business in Boston first. I've just had word about Darragh moving into his place, so I'll have to break the news soon.

Since the strip club bombing, I've had to keep Valentina safe away from Boston, in a small town named Shirley that nobody has fucking heard of while I have men tracking down the men coming after us over Owen.

It's not that I didn't think the bastard had family. He's Italian, clearly connected to a mob family or even rogue mobsters. I don't fucking know. All I know is that I'm still cleaning up my father's mess, even with a wife and kid.

After kissing my wife and son goodbye, I drive the backroads 20 miles over the speed limit until I get to Massachusetts General Hospital, a place we visit so much it feels like a second fucking home. I should be livid because my brothers (or at least one of them) screwed up. I've just learned over the years, and especially because of Valentina, that I handle the family bullshit better when I keep my mind calm.

Dad handled everything with violence. I don't want to be that person, even if it sometimes feels like I'm suppressing the part of me that wants to beat the shit out of Rian or strangle Darragh for never keeping his ass out of the line of fire. It's like he thinks his body parts are fucking disposable.

I don't spend four minutes in the emergency room before a pair of anxious nurses in lilac scrubs usher me out of the way and drag me to Darragh's room.

"Is he stable?"

They're South Boston girls. I can tell from their straightened shiny blond hair and blue eyes rimmed with black. They recognize me, or at least they've heard of my family reputation, so they are on their best behavior, treating me with the utmost respect as they deliver the report on my brother's condition.

My phone buzzes with a text from Darragh's girl. I glance at it briefly. She sent me her location, exactly as requested, which means for the time being at least, she's safely out of trouble. We still have a body on our hands across town, but I owe Darragh my immediate attention before I clean up the crime scene. First, deal with Darragh, next find my jackass brother Rian. The list goes on, but those are my main priorities.

When I burst into Darragh's room, he's awake, but disturbingly pale.

"Where is she?" he says. "The nurses won't tell me where she is."

He almost died, but the first question out of his mouth is about Kamari. I can't act like I don't understand entirely. When I fell for Valentina, my entire world changed. I couldn't be the guy who took pleasure in causing pain for the sake of it. She taught me that I didn't have to be a monster. Without her in my life, I might've shot my brother right in this fucking hospital bed for how much trouble he's dragging to my doorstep.

."She's safe," I say to him. "Unless we can't handle the cops combing through your Beacon Hill place who are gonna want to charge someone with murder."

The remaining color in Darragh's face drains away.

"I need her here," Darragh says. "I should have never put her in danger. I *tried* to get her to leave."

I haven't said much, a tactic which has always worked well to get my brother to confess everything he's ever done wrong to me. He's always respected me as the eldest brother, even if he's the third of the seven of us and not as irresponsible as most of our siblings.

"What you *need*," I answer, withholding as much of my anger as physically possible. "Is to tell me where the fuck Rian is and why he left. If Rian had been there, that bastard wouldn't have been able to break in so easily."

"Kamari handled him well. I remember that much."

Darragh groans as he tries to move his body slightly. He must be on enough painkillers to knock out a horse, considering what he's been through. He looks more fucked up than he did after championship fights.

"She could go to jail because we had nothing in place to stop the police from getting to the scene first. Callum's at your house. He has positive identification of the man Kamari shot."

"Who?"

"Another Aurelio. Most likely another half-brother."

Darragh considers me carefully. My jaw tightens as I await a response from him.

"Are more of them going to come after us?" Darragh asks. "I'm sick of getting shot at. Maybe Rian was right to fuck off."

"If Rian had any sense in his head, he would have stayed where I fucking asked him to and you wouldn't have had to go through this. Where the hell is he?"

"Tracking down the motherfucker who tracked us down," Darragh says. "That was the last he told me. I tried to get him to listen but..."

His voice strains and slurs a bit from the medication. He leans back against his pillow, exhausted after this short conversation. I don't need Darragh to finish his thought. I've been in his position before. This is about Kamari.

Maybe my father has a point about romantic entanglements distracting us, but I can't deny my brother the happiness that I experience with Valentina.

"I warned him this would be dangerous," Darragh says. "And I told him that Tegan needed him. If he cares about his daughter, he does a poor job of showing it."

"He just got out of jail. I should have kept a closer eye on him. He's just itching to get back into the action. And dad…"

I trail off. Dad's been in Mass General for months and I've barely come in to see him. I show up once a month when I'm in town, refresh the flowers on his side table and leave without saying anything. Our visits are brief and quiet, but at least we aren't fighting. We get along better when he's in a coma. Hmph.

"Dad would've ordered him to go blow a hole through as many heads as possible," Darragh says. "He wouldn't care about Rian going back to jail. Or Tegan."

"Exactly."

Darragh's eyes meet mine. "I trust you, Aiden. I might not always agree with you, but I trust you. Our brother doesn't trust anyone. After the shit he's been through, maybe he's just too fucked up to adjust to normal society."

"He *will* adjust. I don't run this family like our father. Until those fuckers blew up the strip club, we'd made more money in the past six months than ever before. War might be good for business but… peace is good for business too."

"Amen to that," Darragh groans. "*Fuck,* this fucking hurts."

"The nurse says you have another six months like this. What are you going to do about Kamari?"

Darragh scoffs. "*Do* about her? I'm officially too weak to control her. She does whatever the fuck she wants."

"That won't work if Rian fails to properly account for everyone he puts a bullet in. If he kills even one person not involved in this, he'll have to kill all of them."

Darragh nods in agreement. While I disagree with the totality of my father's brutality, there are some situations that require ruthlessness if you're foolish enough to stumble into them.

"I'm behind by over three hours," I grunt. "I'll try calling him again and see if Odhran has any luck tracking him down."

If Rian won't answer my calls, Odhran will have a much higher chance of contacting him. They get along with each other much better than I want to admit.

"I want to get out of here and see Kamari."

"You got shot. They won't let you out of here tonight."

"Then bring her here with an armed guard or something," Darragh says, his voice getting a little more incoherent.

"She's safe where she is," I remind him. "Better off out of sight. You'll have her again soon, Darragh. I promise."

MY BROTHER DOESN'T WANT to let me go unless I promise him to keep Kamari safe. *Hm.* I never pried too deeply into Darragh's personal life, but I never expected him to fall for anyone. He never had a serious girlfriend in high school, just flings, and then there was his on-again-off-again relationship with Michelle, who hated me and Callum. He never told me how that ended, but his twenty-fourth birthday party had something to do with it.

I JUST WANT him to be happy, so I promise, and then I call Valentina in the car as I drive towards the Boston Harbor from Mass General. That's where we normally conduct business. It's quiet at night, and easy to get rid of anything you don't want the cops to find.

It's a forty-minute drive with Boston traffic and if I don't hear her voice, I'll just get all wrapped up in the messy thoughts in my head about our Irish family and our future.

If I lost any of my brothers, if we experienced some great loss that exposed us as weak...I might have to become the man I hate — a ruthless mafia leader rather than one who rules without the use of an iron fist.

Valentina might have agreed to a return to Boston, but she didn't agree to this. She answers after one ring.

"Did Darragh make it?"

She knows how much my brother's condition worries me. I had to see him awake and breathing for myself before running after Rian.

"Yes. He's in terrible shape," I answer. "I miss you. I should be home right now, rubbing your feet, not tracking down Rian."

"I just put Tegan to bed," she says. "She wants to know when her dad is coming to pick her up."

"If I kill him tonight... never."

Valentina is too quiet.

"That was a joke," I mutter.

"It didn't sound like a joke," she says. "Rian disobeyed you and in the history of mob families, that normally doesn't end too well."

I hate how far away she is from me. If I could have her next to me, I would.

"Is Aifric sleeping?" I ask her, changing the subject from my irritating brother as I wait at a stop light.

"Yes," Valentina says. "But I think he misses you. He sleeps much better in your arms than mine."

"I'm bigger," I remind her. "I make a better bed."

"I'm his *mom*," Valentina says. "But he's already allied with you against me. It's not fair."

I chuckle. Aifric might fall asleep more easily in my arms, but his bond with Valentina isn't lacking in the slightest. He's happiest during his feeding times and he loves being near her. He only likes *me* when he needs a wall of muscle to fall asleep on. *Hm.*

"He loves you plenty," I mutter. "He loves you just as much as I love you."

Valentina's voice gets soft. "Will Rian be okay?"

"Yes. He's a bastard, but he always makes it out alive," I say to her, willing myself to believe it.

ONCE I GET close to the harbor, I tell Valentina I love her and beg her to go to bed, even if I know she'll stay awake until I get home. Because of her history of living under a cruel man in the sex slave business, Valentina often struggles to sleep. She sleeps best when I'm in bed with her, wrapping my arms around her and holding her close. I wish I could be there for her tonight.

BUT IT'S work like this that keeps our family safe. Maybe I should have been more thorough in killing the first Aurelio, checking into his past or any potential allies, but I was blinded by love enough to think that one bullet would be enough to fix my father's mistake...

Five minutes away from the harbor, Odhran calls me.

"Tell me you have news."

"Rian's at a warehouse on the Harbor," Odhran says. "He has bodies. Lots of bodies."

"Who?"

Please let this be good news.

"EVERYONE," Odhran says. "He killed everyone left in their family, in their warehouse... about twenty people?"

My stomach lurches. *Twenty?*

"How the fuck does he think we're gonna cover up twenty murders?"

Technically, twenty-one murders since Darragh still has a body up at Beacon Hill that I sent Callum to take care of.

THERE'S no rest for the boss of this fucking family. No fucking peace.

Chapter Thirty-Four
Kamari

The woman standing in the doorway raises an eyebrow in my general direction. I don't know exactly where I am, but the house seems fancy, which puts me at ease. Maybe that's wrong, but I would feel a lot more nervous approaching an apartment door than... this.

"You're Darragh's girlfriend?" she says. "Aiden never said you were black."

The white woman in the doorway wears loose-fitted boyfriend jeans with white and red paint splattered over them. Her hair is a wild, tangled mess of short curls and she smells like cigarettes. Her white-button down shirt is crisp and starched in direct contrast to her messy artist's jeans.

Before I can answer her question, she blurts out. "I'm Orla. Welcome to the safehouse. I'm your fucked up guardian angel. Literally. I had half a bottle of wine earlier. Oops. Come on in, Calamari."

"It's Kamari..."

"*Fuck.* Aiden warned me not to screw that up. Sorry. I'm his sister, by the way."

Darragh never mentioned any of his sisters. I know he has four sisters, but he's never even told me their names. I assumed they weren't very close, or maybe they had cut Darragh off for his obnoxious attitude. This one seems nice, but a little strange. She ushers me into the house and I learn very quickly that we're not alone. Nope. This house is packed with people.

Two guys in black t-shirts, who are covered in tattoos, are standing in the kitchen holding guns. A black woman is sitting at the table next to a white woman who looks exactly like Aiden, but with darker hair cut in a blunt shoulder-length hair cut. The black woman's presence surprises me, since this *is* an Irish mobster's hideout, so I'm pretty sure I'm staring at her.

She has a pretty long dress on, thick curly hair and skin several shades darker than mine. Her smile is her most noticeable feature. *Who is this woman?*

"I'm Evie," the white woman with the brown hair says. "This is Valentina. Orla's the drunk. We're all trapped here for the night while my brother makes sure we don't all get murdered in our sleep. Want a drink?"

I politely decline the drink. Darragh's been trying to get me pregnant and even if I'm not entirely sure it's working, I don't want to risk going through anything like I went through before. Evie shrugs. "I'm not drinking either," she says. "Husband wants to get me pregnant."

Valentina laughs. "Orla's the only one drinking. I'm trying to get pregnant again."

Orla makes a disgusted gagging sound as she puts her arm around me and drags me towards a stool where I can join them at a table. "I feel like I'm in a maternity ward. It's gross."

Evie snaps, "Orla, can you relax for *five seconds?*"

"Says the most uptight bitch in the room," Orla mutters under her breath. "No alcohol. Can I get you tea?"

I agree to a mug of Constant Comment tea from Orla and notice that Valentina's staring at me. That at least makes me feel better for the way I stared at her when I walked in the room, but I still don't know what to say without making the entire situation awkward.

"You are not who I expected when Evie said Darragh's girlfriend was coming."

Evie shrugs. "He didn't tell me she was black either."

"He didn't mention she was *young*," Orla says. "No offense doll, but you look about seventeen-years-old."

"I'm twenty-three."

"Still too young for him," Evie says. "He doesn't deserve a pretty girl like you. No offense."

Valentina shakes her head and rolls her eyes. "Don't listen to them. They're very cynical about their brothers. Aiden says Darragh took a bullet for you. That's love."

"Nothing more romantic than giving a woman a traumatic experience by dying in her arms with your blood all over her clothes," Orla says. "Trust a Murray boy to conjure up something so intelligent."

I can't help but smile at Orla. I can tell instantly that it's not just the liquor, she says whatever the hell is on her mind the second it comes up.

"Can you keep it down?" Evie says with frustration. "Tegan might wake up again. The girl hardly sleeps and now her idiot father might be getting himself killed days after getting out of prison. She needs as much rest as she can get."

Orla serves me my tea and Valentina offers me some snacks – homemade mini-Cinnamon rolls that smell *delicious*. They ask me questions, tell me about Tegan and all the other people in the house (including Valentina's newborn) and do their very best to keep my mind off Darragh and Aiden and the potential assassins after the entire family.

They make me *feel* like their family after sitting there for only an hour. I sense I'm not the only one who will be up all night with worry, and I have these women sitting with me who understand what I'm going through. Especially Valentina. She's a few years older than me and absolutely stunning with a face that tells you she has a story.

Evie is more of a mother hen and she reminds me a lot of Aiden at first, but more like Darragh when she makes snippy comments at Orla over her bad posture, her drinking too much or talking too loudly. That's very Darragh. Orla's the funny one, the one who clearly gets into trouble and I like that she's not afraid to point out the flaws in her brothers – even the one I love.

After two hours of drinking tea and chatting with my new sisters, Orla presses me to tell the story of how Darragh and I first got together and how we knew each other. They all react when I mention Darragh and my brother boxed together.

"Does your brother know that he snatched you?" Orla asks. "Because if he kicks Darragh's ass, I want to be there to film it."

Evie purses her lips disapprovingly at Orla. "That really isn't funny, Orla. Hon, my advice is to tell your brother *before* he finds out. If he's anything like our brothers, he's hot-headed and completely irrational. He's a *man* and he's going to feel betrayed that you lied to him."

I mean... I didn't *lie* to Tavarius, I just casually neglected to mention that I shared several special moments with his best friend. After that incident on the boat, I didn't want to get my brother involved since I assumed I wouldn't ever see Darragh again. With how chaotic the last few months have been, there hasn't been any time for me to tell him about the relationship Darragh and I have now. But Evie has a good point. I don't want my brother to get pissed off and have this turn into something more than it is – two grown folks who fell for each other. Or something.

The later it gets, the more I worry we'll never see or hear from Aiden or Darragh again. Our conversation moves over to the living room. There's a huge piano in the room and Orla informs me that Valentina is *really* good at playing.

"If the kids weren't asleep, I'd play something," she says. "But maybe we'd better rest here until they call..."

Curled up on the living room couches, the four of us toss and turn, except Valentina who spends the night with Aifric in his room so she can feed him throughout the night. The presence of bodyguards doesn't make it any easier to sleep. The women did a great job of distracting me, but whenever I close my eyes, I see flashes of the man I killed and I'm sick to my stomach. Once the immediate threat to my life ends, that won't just go away. I could go to jail for murder and then what?

My life would be over. I'm not built for jail physically or mentally. Anxious thoughts twist around in my head and I doze in and out of sleep until the smell of freshly brewed coffee wakes me up just a little after sunrise.

Orla and Valentina are still asleep, so Evie must be the one making the coffee. I slip into the kitchen and whisper good morning to her. I don't know how the hell she looks so good considering she slept on the couches with the rest of us and couldn't have slept very well at that.

"Would you like coffee? It's decaf."

I nod, desperate for something to warm me up. I still haven't heard from Darragh and I doubt Aiden dropped by during my brief time asleep. Evie pours me coffee in a bright yellow mug with sunflowers on it.

Once I sip it, Evie smiles at me.

"Well," she says. "I heard from my brother this morning. They finished the job."

"Do I want to know what that means?"

Evie shakes her head. "It's not our job to know. It's our job to look after our families. There's nothing wrong with us having different roles, you know?"

She at least has a point that I might not want to know the details of what happened.

"What about Darragh?" I ask after another sip of coffee. I'm almost too scared to know. How many times can the human body withstand the shock of getting shot?

Evie attempts to suppress her disapproving pursed lips, but she's unsuccessful. She doesn't seem to think much of her brothers, even if she's helping them out.

"He called complaining and asking questions about you," she says. "Aiden doesn't want him talking to you. He thinks Darragh will make plans to run off after you when he shouldn't be leaving the hospital until he recovers."

"Will I have to stay here until then?"

Evie shakes her head. "No. You're free to go. I just expected you might want some decaf and a little breakfast before Orla drops you off. She likes to smoke when she drives, so be ready to crack a window."

I offer to help Evie with breakfast, but she declines and instead has me sit there drinking decaf and listening to her complaints about her various brothers. She's almost as funny as Orla in a clipped, sarcastic sort of way. She calls Aiden too brutish (and stupid), complains that Darragh's impulsiveness will get him killed, suggests that Rian belongs in jail much longer, describes Callum as an idiot and Odhran as so useless it hurts. By the time she finishes breakfast – a delicious mushroom and feta quiche – I'm starving and have every detail of the Murray family drama from Evie's point of view.

As Evie cooks, Valentina wakes up and emerges with her baby, Aifric bundled up against her chest. With all Darragh's talk of babies, I have a new interest in them. Wow, Aifric is cute. Valentina brings him over to me and asks if I want to hold him while she wakes Orla up. Orla's snoring on the couch, audible from the kitchen.

"Did you wake Tegan?" Evie calls to Valentina in the living room as I hold baby Aifric. I don't hear Valentina's response because I'm mesmerized by Aifric Murray. He is *adorable*. I don't know many mixed babies. It's just me and Tavarius, and he's never wanted kids, so I've never even held a mixed kid. Aifric has this adorable baby smell like clean wipes and baby powder.

His skin is the color of a very milky latte and he has these long pale brown lashes that make his face look all cute and sandy colored. When he opens his eyes, very confused about who the hell I am, his eyes surprise the hell out of me. They're Murray blue. My heart gushes as I hold him close.

"Don't worry, little guy. Your mom will be right back…"

He doesn't cry or squirm in my arms, so I take that to mean he likes me.

Valentina drags Orla off the couch for breakfast and takes her baby back. I feel a tug at my heart strings as he leaves my arms. Is this what I'm missing out on? Orla stumbles outside with a cigarette and coffee before saying good morning. As she walks past us in the kitchen to head to the patio, she lets out a loud and very disruptive fart which makes Evie mutter, "Disgusting" under her breath. Valentina stifles a giggle and then kisses her son on the forehead. Aside from his eyes, he looks just like her, but a paler boy version.

Evie serves up slices of quiche and sliced cucumbers for breakfast and Valentina balances Aifric in one arm as she eats.

When Orla returns from her cigarette, Evie complains about the smell while getting her coffee and then she leaves to get Tegan.

Darragh's niece, Tegan, is his brother Rian's daughter and she spent several weeks held captive by the same men who want the Murray brothers dead. I've never met a little kid who has gone through so much trauma.

I can't imagine what it must have been like for a girl that young. Evie emerges after a few moments with Tegan. She's the picture of Rian, but much smaller and thinner. She has shoulder length chocolate brown hair brushed into a middle part with a tartan headband holding her hair back.

She has her father's eyes and his severe expression, which looks significantly less imposing on a girl who must be ten or eleven years old. Despite her youth, her eyes look wide and terrified. She doesn't speak when she enters the room and she doesn't smile except when she sees Valentina and Aifric.

"Hi," she says softly, sidling up to Valentina and then peering over at the bundle in her arms.

"She hardly eats," Evie comments out loud, but not to anyone in particular. "Tegan, you're gonna have something this morning, okay? Your dad's coming and he doesn't need to worry about feeding you today."

Tegan's expression changes, her blank face suddenly becoming illuminated with emotion.

"I don't want to go with my dad," she says. "So no thanks."

Evie's pursed lips return. Valentina interrupts before the situation escalates into a full-blown disagreement and she convinces Tegan to at least *try* Evie's quiche before swearing off food for the day. Valentina's approach works and Tegan picks apart pieces of the quiche from her without complaining.

"She has to go to her father," Evie mutters eventually. I don't want to get involved, but it's hard not to feel for Tegan. She clearly doesn't feel close to her father and if she had a mother in her life, I assume her mother would be here.

Darragh's phone, which I've had in my custody all night, vibrates against my thigh. I hadn't exactly forgotten that I had it, I just wasn't paying much attention. I immediately answer it without checking to see who's calling.

"Kamari?"

Darragh's voice sounds gruff and urgent. But he's alive. *He's alive.* I can hear his heavy breathing on the other line, suggesting this isn't a courtesy call and the purpose might not even be particularly positive.

"I'm here." I wouldn't have said something so muted and boring if

I didn't have an audience, but this doesn't seem like the time or the place for romantic gushing.

"Thank fuck," Darragh says, punctuating the statement with a pained groan. I assume the groan is from his injuries and my heart pounds. He could be in real danger.

"Darragh? What's going on?" I ask him, trying not to sound as panicked as I feel...

Chapter Thirty-Five
Darragh

I wish Callum would drive faster. After screaming at Aiden on the phone, I finally have permission to get the fuck out of the hospital and get Kamari the fuck out of here. Everything is different now. Rian might have successfully hunted every remaining member of the Aurelio clan, but our problems are far from over.

Evie's husband Conner has his eyes on the cops over at Beacon Hill, but because of the odd circumstances of the crime, and the involvement of neighbors, making the second Aurelio murder go away might cost. A lot.

That's not the bad news. That's not the news that makes me call Kamari in a panic, questioning everything.

"Fuck's sake, Callum, can you run the fucking red light?" I yell at him.

Callum grunts, adjusting his excessively large (and potentially excessively stupid) body in the driver's seat before gunning it through the red light, nearly missing a red Chevy Silverado.

Dad's awake.

EVERY SECOND of Padraig Murray's consciousness, Kamari's in danger. So is Valentina, but Aiden has his hands tied up with sorting out Rian's pile of bodies across town, so he's trusting Evie and Orla with the situation. My sisters love Aiden. They would gladly take a bullet for him or his wife, especially now that she has one of his sons and they're trying for another baby already – at least Aiden wants to try. He's eager for fatherhood. Hm.

I don't trust anyone but myself with Kamari's protection. She's my responsibility, even if I need an extremely high dosage of painkillers to sit up in the car. I don't know how much they're killing the pain rather than turning it into anger that I direct towards Callum, who suddenly seems like the slowest driver in the entire city.

"Fuck's sake, Callum. He could have had her killed and eaten by now."

"We left five minutes after you found out he woke up," Callum says. "Can you relax? He's an old man who just got out of a coma. He's barely had time to get a cup of water."

"It doesn't matter. It takes less than a minute to give an order. If he so much as finds out about Kamari…"

I don't need to finish the sentence. Callum knows. He was the first one of us who tried bringing home a woman of a different race. He was young and foolish enough to think that our family's talk was just talk. It's like he willed himself not to notice the tattoos spreading across Aiden's arm as he hurt more people, or the dotted tattoos covering mine as I did the same.

He wasn't like Rian, who lusted after women just because he couldn't have them. Callum made the mistake of falling in love.

She's gone. Not dead – just gone. And I doubt she'll ever come back.

"He won't find her," Callum says, his skin turning almost red enough to match his russet colored hair. "Just calm your fucking tits. Aiden's on this."

"Aiden cares about himself and his image," I reply cynically. "His interest in Kamari extends only as far as that."

"He wouldn't let anything happen to her," Callum says, edging on the defensive. "It's dad. It's always been dad."

I can't disagree with him, but now that dad's awake, the challenge to Aiden's authority exists. Once my father can stand on two feet, Aiden won't run our family anymore which means we return to the old ways of doing things. Killing. Fighting. Getting my ass handed to me every fucking week because I can't stop being such a disappointment to him.

I BARELY WAIT for Callum to park the car before jumping out of the passenger seat and hurrying to the front door. Each step hurts, but my determination to see Kamari surpasses the pain surging through every part of me. She opens the front door. Thankfully, Aiden didn't leave her alone.

Valentina, the children, and Evie left together, but Orla stayed with Kamari until my arrival.

"I want to hug you," I say to her, groaning. "But I can't move my arms much."

Kamari wraps her arms around me, careful not to squeeze me too tightly, but getting close enough to me that I can feel her. And smell her. My cock grows semi-hard in my pants just from her closeness. She kisses my cheek and I struggle not to get erect instantly.

"I am so happy to see you alive."

"I don't know why," Orla chimes in from behind her, ruining our romantic moment. "He's the most annoying brother I have aside from Callum."

"What the fuck did I do?" Calllum asks, raking his fingers through his hair and putting on a backwards Red Sox trucker hat that makes his hair stick out all spiky in the front.

"We don't have time for this," I snap at Orla. "Kamari, get in the car. Callum will be taking you to safety."

"Where exactly *is* safety, Darragh?" Kamari asks, folding her arms and looking very much like she intends to argue with me. "Your father just woke up from a coma. I don't see the big deal. There isn't anyone trying to kill us anymore."

She glances at Orla for support, but my sister knows my father too well to agree with Kamari. Orla returns Kamari's glance with a half-smile.

"Honestly, dad is gonna lose his fucking mind when he finds out *two* of his sons broke the family vow of blood purity."

Kamari bites down on her lower lip awkwardly, since she always tries to ignore or forget this side of my world. The dark side of our obsession with family is the belief that the only people who can be family are Irish. *White* and Irish.

"Wait," Orla says after a few seconds of contemplation. "There was the situation with Callum and the mixed race girl too. I forgot about *that*. Do all of you have some kind of fetish or something?"

"Orla. This is why I never talk to you. Kamari, let's go."

"Not until you *explain* where you're taking me. I'm tired of you dragging me around and fearing for my life. I don't want to run away for months and months."

Is she seriously picking a fight right now?

"You don't have a choice."

Orla reaches for a cigarette. "Are you sure? I could take her somewhere."

"Kamari, get in the car," I command her, ignoring Orla's attempts to undermine me. This is too serious for Orla's games for once.

"Where am I going?" Kamari demands again. I'm too weak to do it myself, but I suspected Kamari might protest, so I give Callum "the nod" we agreed on and he tosses Kamari effortlessly over his shoulder. Orla protests and tries to help her, but Callum is too big for Orla's efforts to make any significant impact.

Callum played football in high school and although he wasn't as good as Odhran is now. They were both linebackers, twice the size of the other kids and fierce as fuck. Nobody could get through Callum and the same holds now – not Orla's shrieks, nor Kamari's violent kicking make a difference.

He tosses Kamari kicking and screaming in the back of his truck like we discussed. Orla gives up fighting us and turns to swearing at us and name-calling once she realizes her attempts to get Kamari back are futile. I get into the front with Callum as we drive off.

Kamari tries climbing between the seats to escape the car through the front doors, but Callum takes a gigantic hand to shove her back, which works to send Kamari flying back into her seat with a loud squeal. She fights him again, but she's powerless against Callum's gigantic palm.

After that failed escape attempt, she folds her arms and glares at both of us in the rearview mirror. Poor Callum can barely handle it. He's red with embarrassment the entire time, but I don't give a fuck.

"I promised I would keep you safe, didn't I?" I grumble after I finally grow tired of Kamari's ungrateful pouting.

"You didn't promise me that I would never have a life again," she says. "I thought I would have some damn freedom."

Callum clears his throat. "I find Cape Cod very freeing."

I wish I had the strength to give my brother a slap. Kamari would have had plenty of time to find out about my second home once we arrived there. Looking back at her in the rearview mirror, she no longer looks completely pissed off, just a perfect mix of pissed off and confused. *Great.*

"The beach? You think your dad is gonna kill me so you take me to the beach? Is this *serious*, Darragh? Because the last time there was a threat to my life we were stuck in a three bedroom house. No beach views. No cocktails."

Aiden would never choose a safehouse for the views. But Aiden doesn't know about this safehouse. It's *mine*. When I won the state lightweight boxing championships at nineteen, I took the $250,000 worth of prize money and invested it in a two bedroom Cape Cod cottage in South Dennis. It's nothing compared to some of the impressive homes on the coast, but it's quiet, right on the beach, and it's mine.

Not even my father knows about it. I always imagined I would take girls from the city out here when I wanted to keep my liaisons private, but there was really nobody after my twenty-fourth birthday party. After her. This is the first time Callum has heard of this place, but Callum is the secret keeper. I think he shuts up mostly because his brain is filled with sports scores and lust, but I don't care about his motivations as long as he can keep my secrets.

"I don't want to fight with you," I grumble. "If you would just be quiet and do what you were told for once, we wouldn't have to fight."

"I know you didn't just talk to *me* like that," Kamari says.

Our argument escalates and by the time we get to the beach house, Kamari has called me every terrible name she could think of and insinuated that getting hit in the head has made me "crazier than a coon hound". When we get to the beach house, Callum asks Kamari if she wants to be escorted inside and she calls him an idiot too.

I guess this is the best I could hope for. At least she walks into the beach house herself, which spares Callum a lot of injury. He stuffs his hands into his pockets and surveys the house as we walk to the front door.

"Probably best I leave you here," Callum says.

"Yes. Probably," I say. "Don't worry. She won't run."

Kamari glares at me and rolls her eyes, but she doesn't run. Callum has to return to Boston. He shouldn't have come out here, but he tries to be a good brother to all of us, even when we're asking him to keep our secrets or handle our dirty work.

I unlock the door and Kamari drags her feet inside. I shut the door behind us, pleased that we're finally alone but concerned about Kamari's expression.

"I just want you to be safe."

She whirls around on me, fiercely angry. "When will I stop living in danger? I want to be with you, Darragh, but we never get to *be* together. It's been one safehouse or threat to our lives after another. This isn't a relationship."

"This is absolutely a fucking relationship."

Kamari's eyebrows shoot up in surprise and she folds her arms with that familiar sass again. "Excuse me?"

"I'm not fucking losing you, Kamari. I know you're tired of running. I'm tired too, but I'm more tired of getting so fucking close to having you and then losing you again. There won't be any breaking up. There won't be any running off. We're here because you and I are in danger and this is the last time I'll accept that."

"We're at a beach house 45 minutes outside of the city. We've run off! I haven't been back to my apartment in months. I keep giving Tavarius excuses about why I can't see him…"

"I just needed to get you here to think. We're not leaving Boston. I just have to make sure you're safe. And I needed to see you."

"You nearly died! Surely you only left the hospital because my life was at risk."

"I had to see you."

I close the distance Kamari keeps trying to put between us and shudder as I raise my arm to her cheek. My entire body hurts, but I would walk through fire if it meant I could touch her. She grows weak once I touch her, the will to yell and chastise me for saving her leaving her body.

"I know you're fucking worried," I tell her. "But you have to calm down. I'm here. You're gonna get your life back. Not just that... We're gonna start a life together."

"What kind of life?"

"The life you wanted with me. A baby. A family. I'm not gonna let my dad get in the way of that."

"How?" she says, her panic real and rising.

"My father isn't gonna make it. Aiden hasn't realized this and probably none of my other brothers except Callum. Rian's out of prison, we all have so much shit on our hands... We're his sons, but my father has his limits and he doesn't want change. He rules our family. There's only one way to unseat a boss."

Kamari's face contorts in horror. "Are you talking about killing your father?"

The plans aren't set in stone, but I know how Aiden thinks. If he hasn't come to this conclusion already, he will soon. Padraig Murray cannot walk out of that hospital and see what's become of his world. It's not just me, it's Valentina and his kid. Aiden would do everything to protect his family, even if it meant ending our father's life.

Knowing the fights they would get in, I'm sure Aiden has at least thought of it. But this isn't Kamari's concern. It's mine.

"I'm talking about protecting my family. I need you to trust that you *will* be protected. I just need you to stay here. For now. To trust me."

"Of course I trust you," Kamari says. "But I don't need to be kidnapped and carted around like your property. I just want you to *tell me.*"

"Telling you puts you in danger. Or it could."

"I don't have to worry about danger when I have you," she says. "So I'd rather know the truth. I don't want to feel like some... side-piece."

"Would you rather feel like my wife?"

"Is that supposed to be a proposal?" Kamari asks.

. . .

"No," I reply. "But since you seem ready to bite my head off over everything, I thought I should at least warn you that I will be proposing to you, with your dream ring, and we're going to get married."

"Do you realize the point of a proposal would be to give me a choice?" Kamari says. I kiss her forehead.

"Yes. And you choose me."

"You are ridiculous," Kamari says.

"Fine," I murmur, kissing her again on the lips. I'd rather kiss her than argue. "I'll let you choose when I get your ring."

"How gracious of you," she mumbles between kisses.

"I agree that I'm very generous," I say to her. "But I'm also in terrible pain. And I don't want to fight. So will you lie with me for a while and trust that we won't be running away and we won't be backing down. We're going to have a normal life."

"Do you promise?"

"Yes. I promise. I promise that I will look after you forever and I promise that when we lie together tonight, we will never have to spend another night apart."

"You can't promise *that*. You own a strip club."

"Fuck the strip club. We're starting a family. That's more important than any fight and any strip club."

"And Tavarius?"

"Do you have to worry about everything? At all times?"

"Yes."

"We'll tell him. And maybe he'll kick my ass. But I think you're worth an ass-kicking. Or several bullets."

"No more bullets or ass kicking. I want you to be with me, Darragh. To stay with me."

Leaving her is no longer an option.

Chapter Thirty-Six
Kamari

I wake up to the smell of cigarette smoke, which isn't normal. I follow my nose to find Darragh sitting in the window sill. His cheeks are red and he has a cigarette between his lips. I don't know where the hell he found that.

"Why are you smoking?"

I take a step back from the cigarette smoke. I'm trying to get pregnant, Darragh. He throws the cigarette out the window and shrugs.

"Because I can't sleep."

"Elaborate, Darragh."

"Aiden called. We discussed it and... we need to return to Boston. He gave the order, but my father returns to my mother's house tomorrow afternoon and we need to act like everything's normal. I need to visit him and... I suppose we need to leave. I can let you return to your apartment."

"Doesn't that sound like everything is working out... perfectly? I mean, I won't celebrate the man's death, but if he wants me killed just because of my race or anyone else for that matter... you might be doing the right thing. I don't know..."

I don't want to be too insensitive, but I don't know Darragh's father particularly well and everything I've heard about his cruelty makes me want to be as far away from him as possible.

"It's not that," he says. "I don't want you going back to your fucking apartment. I don't want you leaving me."

"Where do you expect me to go then, Darragh? I have a life to get back to."

"I want to be your life. I'll move out of Beacon Hill. We can stay in a hotel until I get us a new place. You can get a job or just stay at home, whatever the fuck you want. I just don't want to spend even one night away from you. I can't."

"Are you on a bunch of painkillers or something?"

"No," he growls. "I love you. I... love you so much that I even called your brother while you were asleep and told him."

"You did what?" *Has Darragh lost his mind?*

"He reacted poorly and said that when he gets his hands on us, he's going to kill us both."

"Darragh!"

"He's all talk. I know him. He'll be fine. I just... I'll do fucking anything to keep you."

"You don't have to freak out about keeping me, Darragh. I'm right here."

It's like he's not even listening to me. He shakes his head and reaches into his pocket for a small black box.

"You wouldn't believe how long I've had this," he says. "I know violets are your favorite flower... so I got you a ring with purple tanzanite stones and diamonds on a gold band. Something pretty and soft. Like you. Something that would look good against your skin."

"A ring? What type of ring?" I stammer awkwardly. Darragh winces as he uses his less damaged arm to pull me closer to him. His fingers interlace perfectly with mine.

"An engagement ring," Darragh says. "I'm Irish Catholic enough to marry the mother of my children. Not a complete failure at that, at least."

My heart races as Darragh opens the box for me. The ring is so beautiful that I nearly gasp out loud. I don't want to sound like I've never seen nice things before, but this engagement ring is beyond anything I could have imagined. I've only ever seen engagement rings with tiny little diamonds in them or maybe a sapphire. Nothing like this.

"It's *fancy*," I blurt out, failing to stifle my surprise.

Darragh laughs. "Thank you for noticing. You deserve fancy."

His fingers tease my palm.

"Will you be my wife, Kamari?" Darragh says. "It's a serious question. And your choice. I don't want you to be my property. I want you to be safe. I want your heart."

"You *have* my heart," I remind him. I'm here, aren't I? Callum didn't have to drag me through the door. I can smell the ocean coming in through the open window now that Darragh's cigarette has mostly faded away.

"I want more. I want commitment. I want it to go both ways. For all we know, you could be pregnant already and... whatever happens with my father and brothers, everything will change."

"You aren't just saying this because you don't want me to go to my place?"

"I'm saying this because I want to move in with you. I want to be with you. I don't care if you go back there as long as you come back to me."

"Okay," I say, nodding excitedly. "I'll be with you. I want to pack my things and I have to get a job and... we can try this."

"Not try," Darragh says sternly. "We're getting married. We're going all the way." "Yes, Mr. Murray," I say, mocking Darragh's sudden seriousness. It's not like I mind him getting all serious. Especially if it's about us.

"Then take the ring. Put it on your finger," he says. "I want to see how beautiful you look with it."

He takes my hand and helps me slip the ring on. It fits me perfectly and it's stunning – beyond anything I could have dreamed of. My chest tightens with happiness. Real happiness.

"I love you, princess," he says. "I will always love you."

CALLUM ARRIVES to take us back to Boston and he brings me a bouquet of flowers from the grocery store as an apology for manhandling me. I carry them in my lap all the way back to my apartment, where I finally explain to my roommates where I've been for the past few months. I don't tell them the truth – it would probably implicate them in several crimes – and I obviously don't mention that I killed someone.

Callum is my unofficial bodyguard as I pack my things, and I notice Kaly giving him come hither looks as he hangs around our kitchen. He doesn't seem to notice and tries to engage her in conversation about football – a subject Kaly doesn't seem to know anything about.

After I pack my things, I explain to my roommates that I'm moving in with my boyfriend and give them a check for the rent for the rest of the year, just in case they can't fill my room. Callum carries most of my things down to his green Dodge truck, but Darragh promises he'll have movers come get the rest of my things on the weekend.

Darragh picks up Brady from his sister's house and brings him to a pet friendly hotel in the city center while Callum takes me to the hotel where we're going to live until Darragh finds a new place for us. When I meet up with Brady again, he nearly knocks me over with excitement.

Callum pulls Darragh aside to talk to him as I take Brady into the hotel room and check out the spot we're gonna call home while we settle back into Boston. I don't hear the conversation happening on the other side of the door, but it's probably family related. Brady would have torn around this hotel when he was younger, but now that he's a bit older, all he wants to do is climb on the bed next to me.

I don't *prefer* him on the bed, but the dog is so damn big that I can't exactly fight him. I give in to Brady resting his paws and head on my lap while Callum and Darragh discuss *mafia business* outside.

I must have dozed off for a while because when Darragh returns to our hotel room, my eyes snap open. Crap. How long was I out? Brady still has his head laying on me.

"You two look comfortable," Darragh says. "Sorry I took so long."

"I fell asleep," I murmur. "Didn't notice."

Darragh approaches the bed and pushes my hair away from my face.

"Good," he murmurs. "It's family business. Nothing for you to worry about."

"Okay," I whisper, ready to fall asleep again. Darragh takes his shoes off and climbs into bed with me fully clothed. Our heads and shoulders press together as Darragh tries to push Brady over to give him room. Eventually, all three of us snuggle up together in the hotel bed.

"I CAN'T WAIT," Darragh murmurs. "I want to spend my life with you, princess. Every last minute..."

Chapter Thirty-Seven
Darragh

Padraig Murray's home and he's spent the past two weeks there – alive, but not yet himself. All he does is sleep, which suits me fine.

I visit him at home and avoid the question of my personal life, which takes some doing since Kamari and I just moved into our new place together. She's pregnant. We found out the day I closed on the mansion in Wellesley. Aiden gave me half of the insurance check from the strip club fire and I couldn't think of anything more important to invest in than my family.

Than her.

Aiden maintains strict control of our family home, watching everyone who comes and goes, monitoring every conversation with our father. Dad doesn't know about Valentina or his grandchildren yet. He doesn't ask about Tegan when he wakes up, but he inquires after Evie's kids, Patrick and Katie. I pretend like I don't notice and talk to him about boxing matches, books I'm running for the upcoming Patriots game, and opening a new nightclub (no strippers) in the same Italian neighborhood where Rian killed our half-sibling and his family.

Relief floods me when I leave my mother's place. Family can be difficult sometimes. I text my brother that I visited dad, giving him the information he needs, and I drive my lime green Hummer just outside the city where everything feels much safer and peaceful. The rich, boring university types in Wellesley make good neighbors.

Kamari's right that this is a better place to raise a family than right in the city center. And it's her dream home. I would have bought any house she asked for if she told me it was her dream to live there. Our $1.4 million Tudor mansion sits at the end of a private drive. Kamari can probably hear my Hummer purring from the end of the driveway.

I can't wait to see her.

I know my visit with my father has had her on pins and needles all morning. Not even my stack of wedding catalogs from Valentina could take her mind off it. The visit with my father went better than expected. He was mostly unable to speak, which accounted for the majority of my positive feelings towards the visit.

This was the first time I've ever been in my father's presence without feeling any fear. It's strange to be in this position – *not* fearing him. He lies in his bed with all his intravenous drips attached and a weak, sallow expression. His tattoos look ashy and gray, like the rest of his skin. His lips are chapped and when he speaks, he sounds audibly weaker.

I know he can hear the weakness in the same voice that once made men tremble and knowing Padraig Murray, he hates it. Meeting with him, I accept the truth of what must happen. I don't know when but... it must.

Leading the mob is a lifetime position. Dying is the only way to retire and most men in my father's position don't die of old age. Many of them consider dying of old age a sign of weakness. A man who lived by our rules would have provoked someone to kill him before he got old. *Maybe that's what he would prefer.*

Callum gave me my orders from Aiden, which I carried out successfully for the entire visit. Not like it was anything complicated – Stay quiet. Act normal. Trust Aiden. I can handle that.

Once I finish the business of lying to my father, Aiden's next orders involve integrating Rian into society. My younger brother acts like he wants to be integrated into a fucking cemetery. If he doesn't settle the fuck down, Aiden won't be able to cover up for him anymore.

I suspect Aiden's only helping him because he needs him. If he plans to kill my father and take his place as head of the mob, he can't do it himself. Rian's the only one of us who could kill his own dad unflinchingly. I couldn't. I couldn't even kill Michelle when she had betrayed me in the worst way.

Orla and Callum got Rian's place ready for him and Tegan to move in. I helped secure the purchase of an all black Victorian mansion in Brookline. Evie thinks it's a dreadful place to raise a child, but Tegan insisted on moving out of Evie's and in with her father. Really makes me wonder what type of shitshow Evie's running for Tegan to choose her fucked up dad.

Maybe Rian will leave all his murderous unhinged bullshit behind once Aiden covers his ass, we handle the shit with our dad, and he has his daughter back. He's off to a decent start by sparing no expense on Tegan's bedroom. She asks for a *Harry Potter* theme like her cousin and by the end of it, her bedroom looks right out of the movies. (Kamari made me watch them with her.)

Kamari and Valentina accompany Tegan to the animal shelter once she moves into Rian's place. She adopts a pretty cat with fluffy white fur and blue eyes named Camilla, who Rian allowed to move in, and there's been talk of hiring a nanny. Rian and Tegan can't spend more than a few hours together without fighting viciously and everyone else thinks a nanny will help.

I think Rian needs to get his shit together and be a better father, but Aiden demands that Kamari use her college connections to find someone who could be a *discreet* au pair.

"Preferably someone desperate for money," Aiden grunts crudely when he asks her to find someone. Kamari finds Aiden's brusque ways terrifying, but she thinks helping him find a nanny for Rian will endear her to him, so she wants to go full speed ahead in hiring an au pair from her alma mater.

"I wouldn't call them desperate like Aiden," she says. "But everyone I know needs help with student loans."

"Everyone?"

"Yes," Kamari says. "I got mine taken care of though."

"How?"

Kamari shrugs and launches into a list of potential candidates for the nanny gig from her college days. I can't keep track of all the names, so I tell her to get in touch with the best five candidates and we'll narrow them down through a series of interviews. We need someone willing to be discreet, sign NDAs, and someone who can handle Rian's sour fucking personality.

Despite having been in prison multiple times, it's not what caused him to have a terrible personality. Rian has always been a grouch. At his impressive height and along with his strength, this caused most people to stay out of his way throughout highschool. He barely graduated, preferring to spend his time fucking cheerleaders, smoking weed, or getting into fights. He ran a secret fight club from the time he was a freshman until a kid punctured a lung and the whole thing got shut down.

Rian didn't get expelled because our father helped the principal out of some gambling debts five years back, but he had to toe the line until his graduation. Right after graduation, he kept running into the cops and getting in trouble. Not even Tegan stopped him from repeated run-ins with the law. He craves violence more than the rest of us and he's willing to risk too much to get a taste of it.

Kamari brings her finalized list of potential nannies to me after a week of communicating with the new hires. We arrange interviews and inform Rian of our progress. He seems uninterested in the entire nanny situation, but Aiden doesn't care. I suspect Aiden also wants a willing spy. He's grown fond of Tegan and even if it's her father's right to have this reunion with his daughter, Aiden doesn't completely trust Rian. Not with a girl so fragile after the fucking hell she's been through.

The first interviewee shakes like a leaf the entire time. Even Kamari knows her nervous friend would crumble at a single glare from Rian. The next two girls are visibly indiscreet and glued to their phones. But number four stops me in my tracks. I know she's the one and tell Kamari to cancel the fifth interview.

HEAVYN WAGNER STUNS me with a broad smile and a yellow dress the second she steps in the room. She's curvy, darker than Kamari, about 5'5" in height and wearing yellow wedges that make her even taller. Her classy yellow dress hugs her curves, but suits her and looks very professional.

Wow.

She carries the conversation and stuns me with her credentials. Since college with Kamari, Heavyn went on to earn a masters degree in education. She speaks several languages, one of Rian's preferences since Tegan knows some Spanish, and she *loves* children.

She's bubbly and has the personality of a sunny preschool teacher. Eyeing her for signs of weakness that Rian might exploit, I detect none. She's assertive enough to handle herself and she doesn't balk at the NDA.

When I warn her about Rian, Heavyn brushes me off. "I've never met a guy I couldn't handle," Heavyn says. "I grew up the youngest of five. They were all boys and always beating up on me."

Once we hire Heavyn and set up the meeting with her, Rian, and Tegan, my future wife and I can dedicate ourselves completely to preparing for the baby. Aiden calls me at the last minute insisting that I go to the meeting.

When I remind him that Rian tried to kill me and put Kamari in danger, Aiden "reminds" me that he doesn't give a fuck and that if I know what's good for me, I'll smooth things over with him and the new nanny. Fucker.

Kamari doesn't mind me leaving the house because she's painting a mural in the baby room of "black heroes" for our future child. MLK Jr. looks good, but I'm not sure she's doing Rosa Parks justice. I bite my tongue. Kamari's a good artist and I'm sure she'll sort out Rosa Parks strange hair color.

I kiss her goodbye, careful not to get paint on my nose before I leave. Rian's house looks fucking haunted. I can't believe he bought a black house for his daughter after what she's been through but... he had his specifications. Questioning him wasn't my job.

Rian appears disinterested throughout the entire meeting with Heavyn. He barely says a word, leaving most of the talking to me at first and then the rest of the talking to Tegan. She bonds with Heavyn immediately, which makes me like Heavyn even more.

"She seems fine," Rian says once Tegan takes Heavyn's hand and leads her upstairs to show Heavyn her Harry Potter themed bedroom upstairs.

"That's all you have to say? Don't you have any questions? Aren't you worried about her being a meth head?"

"I trust my family," Rian says grumpily, swirling a glass of Glenfiddich whisky around with ice before downing the entire glass and pouring another without hesitation. It's nine in the morning.

"Nevertheless, she's a good match. Tegan likes her."

"Tegan likes everyone who isn't me."

"You spent most of her life in jail. Give her time to warm up."

Rian grunts and sips the whisky, making a face after just one sip and sliding the glass across the counter as if it's no longer satisfying.

"That woman…" Rian grumbles. "Are you sure she's competent?"

"She has a masters degree."

"Interesting."

"You don't sound interested."

Rian gives me a languid expression that he's definitely dramatizing for the effect. "How riveting that someone attended university. Absolutely fascinating."

"She loves kids."

"I can see that," Rian says, bristling with discomfort. "She also has an insanely fuckable body and an ass like a goddamn pumpkin."

"How drunk are you?"

Rian glares at me. "Get out of my house. You've done what you came to do."

"I asked a question, Ri. How drunk are you?"

"Drunk enough to do what Aiden just called and asked me to do," Rian says. "So kindly, dear Darragh, get the fuck out of my house."

I don't budge. There's only one thing Aiden could have called and asked Rian to do that could send him into this state.

"Did he really?"

"Yes," Rian mutters. "It's not a secret. He wants you to be there to make sure I don't fuck it up. Surprise."

"So it's happening then."

My body tenses and I reach for Rian's favorite whisky. I prefer Wild Turkey, but this expensive shit is good too. I don't bother with a glass as Rian confirms my suspicions.

Chapter Thirty-Seven

"Yes, Darragh," he says. "We have our orders. Aiden needs me to kill dad."

THE END

Rian & Heavyn's story, *Mafia Surrogate,* Book #3, will be released on June 1st 2023.

Click here to order the book.
bit.ly/bostonirishmafia3

Click here to receive text message updates when the next Jamila Jasper book releases:
bit.ly/textjamila

About Jamila Jasper

The hotter and darker the romance, the better.

That's the Jamila Jasper promise.

If you enjoy sizzling multicultural romance stories that dare to *go there* you'll enjoy any Jamila Jasper title you pick up.

Open-minded readers who appreciate **shamelessly sexy romance novels** featuring black women of all shapes and sizes paired with smokin' hot white men are welcome.

Sign up for her e-mail list here to receive one of these **FREE hot stories**, exclusive offers and an update of Jamila's publication schedule: bit.ly/jamilajasperromance

Get text message updates on new books: https://slkt.io/gxzM

Dark Mafia Romance
Preview #1

Sample these chapters from my Amalfi Coast Brotherhood Italian mafia romance series while you wait for the next mafia romance series.

If you enjoy dark & twisted mafia romance stories, you can binge the entire completed series on your eReader.

Enjoy the free chapters.

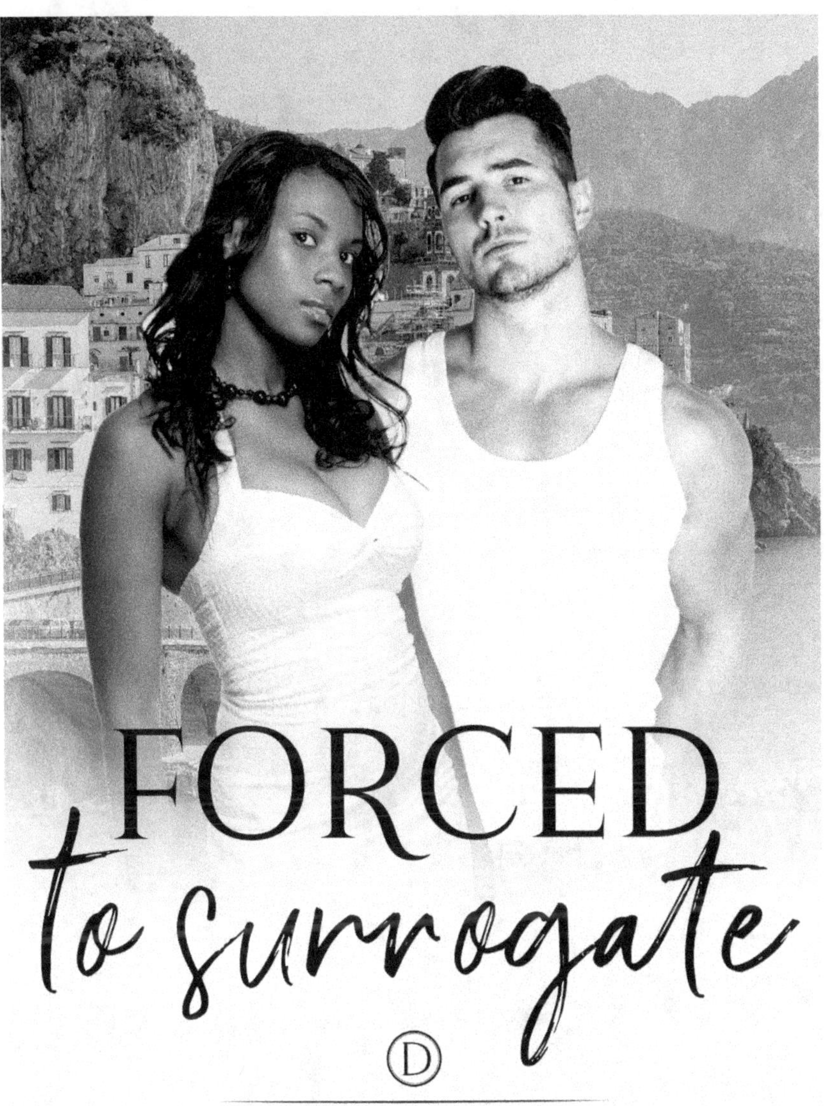

FORCED
to surrogate

the amalfi coast mafia brotherhood #1

JAMILA JASPER

Description

The last thing Jodi remembered was a shot of tequila.
Next thing she knows,
Italian sociopath Van Doukas has her chained in his basement...
And he's claiming she agreed to become the mother of his child.

There's a detailed contract and everything... with her signature.
Jodi will do whatever it takes to get away from him...
But she doesn't count on the 6'7" Italian Stallion being skilled with his
tongue and excellent in bed.

Series Titles

Forced To Surrogate
Forced To Marry
Forced To Submit

Content Awareness

dark bwwm mafia romance

This is a mafia romance story with dark themes including potentially triggering content, frank discussions and language surrounding bedroom scenes and race. All characters in this story are 18+. Sensitive readers, be cautioned about some of the material in this dark but extremely hot romance novel. The character in this story is *forced by circumstance* into her situation.

Enjoy the steamy romance story…

Chapter 1
Produce A Pure Italian Heir
Van Doukas

There aren't enough cigarettes in the world for meetings with my father. The boss. Tonight, I meet with him to discuss something 'very important'. He calls everything 'very important', but tonight, I know exactly what he wants from me.

He wants me to kill again, this time for my foolish sister, who can't seem to keep herself out of trouble. Everyone in the family heard about what happened to Ana by now. That idiot Jew was foolish enough to put his hands on her with witnesses and expect nothing to happen? That's not how the Doukas family works, which he'll soon learn.

You mess with the Doukas family, we retaliate. If the Jew had any wits about him, he would disappear from the Amalfi Coast and head for the mountains or Sicily, or somewhere we don't have ears. He could go to Albania like Matteo. Maybe then we wouldn't find him. But fuck, I don't want to carry out another hit. Why can't that lazy fuck Enzo do it? Or better yet, Eddie. I carried out my first hit when I was two years younger than him. We spoil the new generation and wonder why our family falls apart.

None of this would be my responsibility if Matteo would get over himself and come down off his fucking mountain.

I stop my motorcycle and approach my father's front door. The all white old European style mansion sits on an excessive and opulent lot on the coast, right above the cliffs with a long path to the beach, a 'fuck you' to the tax collectors and the government who want to stop us from doing business.

Most of my siblings still live here, but I prefer keeping myself far away from papa and his... associates.

I can hear the party from the entrance. Seriously? On a fucking Tuesday afternoon? I assumed he called this meeting because he was working for once. He's intertwined in a different business based on the noise filtering outside. Please, Lord, let me not walk in on my father having sex with a model... *again*.

I open the front door to our old family home without knocking and immediately regret it when a completely naked foreign woman runs giggling toward the door, too high and drunk to feel self-conscious, exposing her completely nude body to a stranger. At least I didn't find her twisted in bed with papa, although this isn't much better.

"Oh! Good afternoon, sir!" she teases me in crude Italian, spinning around to show off her assets. *Whore. Foreigner. Her tricks possess little interest to me.* My brothers Lorenzo and Matteo would sway more easily.

"Where's my father?"

She giggles and spins around again. Fucking hell, I wish the ground would swallow me up. My father's prostitutes do not interest me.

"Your papa?" she says, standing to face me with her legs slightly apart, daring me to ogle more of her body. I have no interest in whores and I want her to answer my fucking question.

Before I can answer, another one of my father's toys saunters into the foyer, naked. This one is young—she looks eighteen just about— far too young for my father. I grimace and keep my gaze firmly fixed away from the nude females. Just because the men in my family are bastards doesn't mean I have to follow suit.

If we don't conduct ourselves with respect, how can we expect the respect of the Amalfi Coast?

"Yes. My father. Sal," I grunt, failing to hide the irritation in my voice.

The woman ignores my irritated tone with her response.

"Oh, he's in the back with Boyka. I can take you there after we take you to bed upstairs."

How much is he paying these women? We're still struggling to get Jalousie off the ground and he spends all his money on Slavic hookers.

"Not interested. I have a meeting with him."

"Are you sure?"

I don't dignify them with a response. I walk past the girls, keeping my eyes away from their bodies. Where the hell is my father? I pass the long hallway with the family portraits and follow the loud music and the louder giggling from near the pool. The familiar sound of pool jets betrays papa's location.

He's in the fucking hot tub again, I know it. He spends all fucking day in the hot tub, dishing out orders and expecting work to happen without him lifting a fucking finger. It's a fucking miracle anything gets done around here.

My father chuckles loudly, and I brace myself before approaching him. He's the boss and you don't question the boss, even if he's your father and even if he cares more about partying and women than our family — than our future.

When I enter the back patio, the pungent smell of tobacco and marijuana surrounds me. Judging by the bottles of vodka on the ground, the piles of cigarette butts and the other piles of detritus, they've been at this fucking party since last night.

Fuck. I put the cigarette tucked behind my ear into my mouth and approach my father's outdoor speakers, unplugging them and stopping the little dance party happening around his hot tub. Three women, each wearing next to nothing with their tits out belly dance for him while he chuckles loudly, his fat stomach causing waves in the hot tub. When the music stops, they stop too and look up at me indignantly.

They don't have to ask who I am. The ones who don't know Van Doukas can tell that I'm related to Sal. I have my father's eyes, but thankfully, I don't have his overweight body or his bald head. The girls make booing sounds at me, but I brush them off.

"I'm here for our meeting," I say sternly to papa.

He chuckles and nods. "Yes. The meeting. I almost forgot."

Almost? He doesn't look like he's fucking prepared for a meeting.

Papa dismisses the girls, except for one — Boyka. She slides into the hot tub next to him, twirling his thick plumes of chest hair around her fingers and sliding his freshly cut cigar between his lips. Nauseating. Papa coughs after a puff and taps the cigar over the edge of the hot tub.

"You're early."

"I'm twenty minutes late."

"Oh?"

"Papa, you said it was important. Shouldn't we conduct this business alone?"

None of the girls are dumb enough to rat on Salvatore Doukas, but unlike my father, I don't see the sense in taking risks.

Boyka's hand moves down my father's chest and I don't want to imagine what sorry shriveled part of him she touches next. I just want my orders so I can get the fuck out of this bachelor pad.

"I'm getting old, Van," he says. "I'm getting old."

He didn't call me down here to bitch about his old age. I furiously puff on my cigarette, waiting for him to get to the fucking point. Papa grunts as Boyka touches something... sensitive. Cristo...

Watching my father grunt through a hand job might be the only thing worse than watching him stick it to a woman.

"Do you mind postponing your fucking hand job until later?"

Boyka's hand rises guiltily from the water and I choke down bile. She really was touching the old fuck. I shouldn't swear at him or set him off. Papa might seem old, but he can have me killed. Any of my brothers would do it if he gave the command. Tread carefully, Van.

"Maybe I should leave," Boyka says, giving me a flirty glance as she plays with her tiny pink nipples.

"Yes," I snap. "Please get the fuck out of here."

Papa scowls. "Be respectful, Van. Boyka is a very dear—"

"I said please."

Papa smirks. "Boyka, return in thirty minutes. If we're not done..."

"We'll be done," I interrupt, glowering at my father. I don't have all afternoon for his games when I have the club to attend to.

Boyka reluctantly leaves.

"Are the women in this house allergic to fucking clothes?"

"None of them are allergic to fucking anything."

I'm not doing this with the old man today.

"Why did you call me here?"

I start another cigarette. I keep swearing I won't touch another, then I spend five minutes around papa and change my mind.

He leans back in the hot tub, displacing several pints of water over the edge.

"I'm tired, Van," he groans, leaning back and rubbing his forehead.

"From working?"

My father doesn't pick up on the sarcasm. He hardly leaves his fucking hot tub anymore, and he hasn't done anything even remotely resembling working at either of the nightclubs, restaurants, apartment complexes or construction sites around town.

If it wasn't for me and Enzo, he wouldn't have the fucking time to boink Boyka or whatever the fuck he does with all these young Slavic women.

I still have to tread carefully around him. He's still my father, my boss, and I must obey him.

"Yes," he says, coughing. "From working. I need someone to take my place and lead the family soon. I want to retire, Van. You and I both know I need a break."

He spends every fucking day on vacation while his sons and nephews run his businesses. Vacation? We're the ones who need a fucking vacation.

"Perhaps you should contact Matteo about that."

My older brother spent his entire life preparing to be the boss. It's not my fault he fucked off, leaving his worthless children with us, I might add. I'm already halfway through my fucking cigarette and he hasn't closed in on the point.

Papa scoffs. "Matteo hasn't left Albania in four years. He left his children, his business, his fucking money, and he's not coming back. Give up on him."

"You're the one who trained him for the role. Send Enzo after him. Better yet, send his fucking son."

I don't want to go into the mountains to bring my jackass older brother back and I don't want to have this conversation with my father.

"Why don't you go to Albania?"

"Every time I'm in the same room as Matteo, he tries to kill me," I remind papa. I love Matteo, but he isn't exactly easy to get along with.

I'm surprised a woman tolerated him long enough to allow him to give her Eddie.

"Fair. But I need a replacement, Van. I don't want to be the boss anymore. I can't take the stress much longer."

Stress? What stress? Does my father seriously think sitting in his fucking hot tub banging whores counts as a job?

"Have you considered the role?" He asks before I can spew something disrespectful in my father's direction.

"Why would I want to be the boss of this fucking family? It's filled with degenerates, fuck-ups, people who need more violence to be kept in line. I kill enough as it is. You don't want me to be the boss and nobody in this fucking family wants me as the boss."

"People respect you, Van."

"People fear me. There's a difference."

Papa nods. "Exactly. Personally, I think you would make a good boss."

"I disagree."

But I don't completely. Yes, the job would be horrific and I'd have even more blood on my hands than I do now by the end. I could bring honor back to our family, clean the streets of our scum, stop the Jews from fucking with our shit... but I can't. Not with Matteo gone. Even in the fucking Albanian countryside, he would find out what I did and Matteo would kill me.

"No," Papa replies calmly. "You don't. But I agree with your assessment that you're not quite ready."

"I never said that. I said I didn't want the job."

Nobody smart wants my father's job. He spent twenty years walking around with a target on his back before he built up enough trust, enough loyalty, enough captains in the streets of Italy to ensure his safety. I don't want to lose my freedom.

"You didn't have to say anything. I know my son."

"Hm."

Arguing with my father is entirely senseless.

"You need an heir, Van."

"What?"

"I will give you the leadership of this family without the ritual, without the sacrifice and without the financial investment required. All I want is an heir."

"Why don't I go up to fucking Albania, then? Because I can't produce a child out of thin air."

Papa chuckles. "Don't you have women? If you want a woman... I filled this house with them. I have very young ones too. Eighteen. Nineteen. They make good mothers."

"I am not interested in fucking teenagers."

"Then find a whore like that old Greek Pagonis fuck. I don't care how you get the heir. You can prove how serious you are by giving me a child. I'll be generous. I'll give you a year."

"I don't want this role," I snap. "So the likelihood I'll produce an heir is slim."

Papa laughs, which only infuriates me further. There's nothing funny about bringing a child into the world.

"You can't lie to me, Van. You were always the most ambitious child. Maybe it's because you were smack in the middle and we didn't pay any attention to you. Who fucking knows?"

My father spent little time raising any of us, except for Enzo, and look how that fucking turned out.

"Thank you for the psychoanalysis."

Every time I visit my father, my desire for alcohol increases exponentially, along with my cravings for nicotine. He brings the worst out of everyone, especially me.

"No problem," he says, again ignoring my sarcasm.

"What happens if I don't produce an heir? Eh? You still need someone to take your place."

"I make this offer to Lorenzo if you don't produce what I want."

"What?" I would have at least expected him to mention one of our cousins, one of the very obedient captains from the northern coast, or even fucking Eddie, Matteo's 18-year-old son, would be better than my irresponsible fuck of a brother. That old fuck really knows me well because he just said the only thing that could get me to reconsider his stupid fucking offer.

"You heard me."

"Lorenzo would ruin this family. For fun."

"I know. And it would become your responsibility to save it. You would have to act as the boss to save Lorenzo from himself. You might as well earn the position."

Fuck this old man…

"I don't want a family life, papa. I don't want the fucking wife or the fucking family. I want this life. It's what I'm good at. Business. Killing. More killing. That's who you taught me to be."

I'm not a man who can picture himself kicking around a football with my children or taking them to the beach. I'm not built for seducing women for more than a night and dealing with the danger of introducing them to my life or worse, hiding it the way papa did with our mother.

He can pretend it's not his fault what happened to her, but we all know the truth. No woman deserves our life. I can't afford to react. He loves when he can draw a reaction out of me.

Papa continues, as if my reaction is irrelevant. "Part of this life means having a family. I can't expect my other children to carry on my bloodline."

"Matteo has a son. You have a fucking bloodline. Why don't you make him the fucking boss?"

"Eddie? Eddie will not survive long the way he lives."

"That's a way to talk about your grandson, eh?"

"Have another cigarette, Van."

I'm already on my fucking third. But I'm not in a position to turn down his offer, considering the shit he wants me to deal with right now. An heir? I thought he wanted me to kill someone. Producing an heir in a year… It's just fucking impossible. I stick the cigarette in my mouth and light it.

"You can't let the family fall apart. We aren't the only people who would suffer. What would happen to our people, good Italian people, when the only people around they can get money from are the fucking Jews, who hate our guts?" He says.

I can't let his guilt trip work on me.

"I want an heir."

"Hm."

"Consider what you would sacrifice by turning down my offer, Van.

It's not just about the family. It's power. You act like you're a fucking saint, but you are my son. You enjoy power. You're just too much of a stuck up cunt to let yourself enjoy it."

"Thanks papa."

"You're welcome. Now, onto the matter of the Jew."

Fuck. I hoped my father would only piss me off one way today, but if we're discussing the matter of the Jew, I won't leave here tonight without an assignment. Someone else could easily do this job, but he wants me to kill. Because I'm good at it.

"I suppose none of my other brothers have the free time to do this?"

"I don't care. I need you to do it. The cunt offended this family."

"Perhaps we waste too much time retaliating for every offense. Ana told you to drop it."

I'm taking a risk just questioning his order, but he's pissed me off so much that I stopped caring.

"Decision making isn't women's work. It's our work. The man signed his own death warrant. I want it done soon. Call me when you finish the job."

"Hm."

"If you don't like the way I run this family, Van, you know what to do. I want to retire. Make an old man happy."

Drugs and whores are the only things that make my father happy.

"An heir," I scoff. "You want me to have a fucking bastard child to continue your bloodline? A bastard won't have any loyalty to his family. Children have a mother and a father, a mother they spend all their time with. If I fuck some poor woman, you won't have an heir. You'll have a problem on your hands."

"Then get creative. If you need to get the baby and kill the mother, do what you must."

What's happening to this family? When did we lose our way and talking about murdering women for our own ends? Papa... This life changed him. It was slow, but it changed him completely. Too bad there's no getting out.

"Thank you for the advice."

"You're welcome. Now get Boyka back in here and get the fuck out. I need relief."

"Good evening, papa."

I drop my cigarette on the ground without bothering to step on it. Maybe my father's right — it's time for him to retire. But how the fuck will I get an heir? I need help.

There's one person I can call on for assistance in these matters. I don't like involving the Greeks in Italian business, but... they're our cousins. She answers after a few rings and it sounds like she's at a nightclub. She has an inordinate amount of time for parties...

"Ciao?"

I can barely hear her over the sound of the music.

"Miss Pagonis. It's Van."

She giggles. "Duh. What's happening? You finally have work for me?"

"How soon can you come back to Italy?"

Chapter 2
Single AF On The Amalfi Coast
Jodi Rose

I'm the last single woman in my family.

Three months in Italy, and I haven't had so much as a kiss, but my younger cousin Raven gets married to her college boyfriend and he looks like a dream. I drop a congratulatory comment on her photo, but my heart sinks.

You ugly, Jodi. Get used to it and stop chasing all these men out of your league. Settle with Kyle. He's the best you can do. Maybe mama was right. I'm not the marrying kind, anyway. I spent all my dating years focused on school and look at where that got me…

"Edo!"

The bartender gives me a sympathetic look. Ugh. Edo is so hot. Too bad all the hot guys are gay, especially in Italy, apparently.

"What happened?"

"Look at this."

I show him my phone and Edo cracks a smile. "Beautiful! Is she your sister?"

"No, my cousin. She's getting married and here I am… single… again."

And I'm running away from my problems with a one-way ticket to Italy. When my family finds out I'm not coming back, they're going to lose their minds. Everyone already thinks I'm crazy for leaving Kyle…

"Fuck your ex, Jodi. Seriously, fuck him," Edo says with all the passion of a best friend, even if we barely know each other.

I have major regrets about getting drunk my first night here and spilling all the drama about my ex-boyfriend to a bartender, but at least it made us fast friends. Although I'm not sure if Edo just likes the fact that Americans tip, unlike our Italian friends. He always has a way of scamming some extra euros out of me. At least he's a damn good listener.

I groan and dramatically lean against the bar as I make a proclamation that I wholeheartedly believe.

"I'm never going to get with another guy again. This is it. I'm dying alone."

I've read the statistics. Or at least I've read what women on Lipstick Alley say about the statistics. I'm a thick, well-educated black woman who is tired of the dusties and has real ass standards — according to the internet, I'm dying alone.

Edo grins and shakes his head. Since he learned I was American, he's done everything in my power to take me under his wing since I got here. I just hate getting too far out of my comfort zone, so I've ditched all his invitations to visit the local clubs in favor of spending my nights drinking cocktails alone and checking social media. I'm in Italy. I should have daily adventures and bread. I can't forget the delicious ass bread.

"You will not die alone," Edo says. "At least not without trying... my latest cocktail creation."

Edo does a dramatic dance before revealing some clear beverage that looks like some horrible mix of vodka, vermouth and orange juice.

Good. I want to get completely fucked up.

"That looks... clear."

"You'll love it, I promise."

"Will drinking really make the pain go away?" I muse, twirling the glass around so the little orange peel swirls inside it. Kyle. Why do you always miss the ones who fuck you up the most?

Hopefully, this drink will get my ain't shit ex off my mind, but let's be real. What I really need is a summer romance. Ha. Like that's going to happen in a country where half the people think I'm a prostitute because of my skin color.

"Yes. It will. Absolutely." Edo replies with a wink.

"Cheers." I swirl the drink around despite Edo's repeated claims I ruin his creations by doing that. I pour it down my throat and taste a pleasant citrus flavor before a powerful vodka burn. It takes everything in my power to get the rest of the drink down my throat. Whew! That was a damn burn.

"What the hell did you put in that?"

Edo winks, but offers no response. Tricky ass Italian.

"My shift ends in ten," he says. "I'll take you out tonight to Jalousie. No getting out of it this time to watch *Empire* in your apartment."

How the fuck does this skinny ass white boy know me so well already? I shake my head, prepared to reject his offer to take me to the club, but Edo won't let it go. He wriggles his brows suggestively.

He loves regaling me with stories about all the shenanigans that go down at the Amalfi Coast nightclubs. I'm not really a nightclub girl. Small bars like this one fit me better, but didn't I come to Italy to have fun? Meet someone? I should put in some effort.

The only men who give me any attention are the creeps on the beach who say so much nasty shit to me in Italian that I'm glad I don't understand.

Maybe I'll meet better men at the club, especially a club with a fancy ass French name like this one. Jalousie. Wait... Edo's mentioned Jalousie to me before in the past.

"Ain't that the club with the mafia shootout you told me about?"

I don't believe half the shit that comes out of Edo's mouth, but he loves regaling me with stories about the real Italian mafia, which he claims is apparently far worse than any mafia in Long Island or Staten Island. How could anyone who lives in one of the most beautiful parts of the world hurt and kill other people? I think he likes telling tall tales to impress tourists.

I get people on Staten Island killing each other, but the Amalfi Coast? Hell fucking no. The sea is perfectly blue, the air smells fresh constantly, and it's plain peaceful out here. Italians have a rich culture, amazing food, better wine and the guys here are hot.

Not every guy, but when you walk down the streets here, you definitely encounter more than a few hotties. They all dress like supermodels, too. I've never seen so many regular ass people sporting Gucci and Fendi.

"Yes," Edo says. "But you're here for 9 more months, right? Have a fling. Don't tell him your real name... and disappear. You can find a hot and incredibly rich man to spoil you during your trip."

"Wait... is this a gay club or my type of club?"

Edo chuckles. "The guys are hot. I didn't say they were gay. You haven't earned your way into going to a gay club with me yet."

"Wow, Edo. I thought we had something going here."

Edo shrugs. "My private life is my private life. That's how it is in Italy. Your private life, on the other hand, is my playground. I'll introduce you to people. I know people who frequent Jalousie."

"Hot guys?"

"Eh..."

"Hot straight guys?" I correct myself before he answers. I don't want Edo tricking me into going out for nothing.

"Not exactly... I have a girl friend in town who goes all the time — Cassia Pagonis."

He says the name like I'm supposed to know who the fuck that is.

"Who the fuck is that?"

Edo chuckles. "A very fun girl with very hot brothers."

I perk up a little until Edo tells me they're all married. Great.

"Great. They're married..."

Before Edo can reassure me (again) more customers wander into the bar and Edo scurries to the other end of the bar to take orders.

I gaze into my phone again, looking at pictures from Raven's wedding. My cousin looks gorgeous, but I can't help a twisted pang of envy. I know it's wrong but... will that ever happen for me?

My homegirls from college keep sending me articles about the sorry state of marriage for black women. Alyssa says that we need to divest completely from marriage and just have fun.

My idea of fun isn't keeping a collection of all "my dicks" in a private folder on my phone. I want the real fucking thing! Even if the world loves reminding me that 'the real thing' only happens for white women or black women with the lightest dusting of melanin... I want to believe in love.

I scroll past Raven's pictures and my feed is all babies, new puppies, new jobs, new houses, new apartments, new husbands... new everything. Before Italy, I was just doing the same old shit. I wanted to shake things up. I don't know why my life hasn't transformed entirely. I'm in the prettiest place on earth — the Amalfi Coast.

Edo's shift ends, and he calls my name from the other end of the bar, beckoning me over to the cash register.

"Any tip for me today?"

"I saw you slip that five euro note out of my wallet. I think we're good."

Edo shrugs. "Sorry, this job doesn't pay well."

"I get it. I'll pay for our drinks tonight. Happy?"

"Incredibly."

I shouldn't be offering to pay for anyone's drinks, honestly, but I tell myself that I'll worry about all the damn money I'm spending once I get back to America. I have nine months of freedom and then I can worry about these damn bills and loans and everything else.

Edo drags me off my stool, and we step outside into the cobblestone street. I'll never get over how beautifully blue everything is here. The streets smell like the ocean, pastries, wine and cigarettes, of course. People sell jewelry and fruits on the streets and the Italian accents are... gorgeous. My Italian's still crap, despite Edo's best efforts to teach me a few phrases.

At least I don't have to hear all the street harassment thrown my way, which is plentiful. Edo replies defensively to a grey-haired man who calls something lewd in my direction and grabs me tighter. "Fuck these guys," he says. "You aren't that fat."

I swear, I'll never get used to how fucking blunt they are. But I appreciate Edo doing his best to defend me. We can hear the music from Jalousie echoing down the street before we get close.

"Isn't it early for the club?"

"Why are you so fucking American?" Edo asks, linking arms with me. "Relax."

"EDOARDO!" A shrill voice with a strange accent calls from across the street. I know Italian accents by now, at least how people from the Coast sound when speaking English, and this girl sounds different.

"That's Cass," Edo says to me, a smile breaking out across his handsome face. "Chin up. She'll love you."

Edo waves to the girl across the street and she struts over to us, sticking her hand out to stop the cars making their way down the cobblestone streets. They don't even honk as she passes.

The first thing I notice about her is how striking she is. She's tall, with curly dark brown hair pinned up out of her face and flowing down her back. She's wearing crazy high heels, like all the European girls do, a short leather skirt and a tight black leather crop top.

With her dark red lipstick, she looks like a film noir femme fatale… and she stares like one.

"Edo… is this your American friend?"

She turns to me and smiles. Shit, her accent might be strong, but her English is perfect. Cass's hair falls over her shoulders, her curls carrying a soft eucalyptus scent.

"Jodi Rose," I say, happy to have some female company around here, not like there's anything wrong with Edo. "Nice to meet you."

She takes my hand, three silver Cartier bracelets sliding down her wrist. Wow. Her bracelets aren't the only expensive item of clothing she has.

"Cass Pagonis. I'm sure Edo has told you all sorts of horrible stories about me."

"I did not!"

Edo definitely did. But Cass doesn't seem like a crazy party girl. She rolls her eyes and brushes him off.

"I'm here on the Coast working for my cousin's family," Cass says. "I'm from Thessaloniki. My idiot brothers want me back next week, unfortunately. But I could use a night out before I go."

Edo claps his hands. "Yay! Party time. Too bad Jalousie only caters to the most chauvinistic mafia pigs you can imagine."

"I thought you said they were hotties?!"

"They are," Edo says. "But they might be assholes."

Now he tells me. Edo would have said anything to get me out of my damn apartment. I hope I don't regret it.

"Watch it," Cass cautions, an impish smile on her face. "Those chauvinistic mafia pigs are my cousins and brothers."

Edo shrugs. "Fine. Fine. But I need dick too. Gay rights."

Cass swats his shoulder.

"Edo, why don't you let me take her for the night? There's no one at Jalousie for you, and you can go meet up with Klaus or... that other one."

Edo suddenly straightens his back and reminds both of us that just because he's gay doesn't mean he's given up on old world chivalry.

"I can't send Jodi off with a stranger," he says.

I appreciate the sentiment, but I don't know if Edo would do much damage against... any man who weighed more than his slight 108 lb frame.

"I'm fine," I tell him. "Seriously."

"I'm armed anyway," Cass says. I think she's joking, but neither of them laughs. Is she serious? She doesn't look armed, and she looks more like a model than someone who knows how to use a weapon.

I could use a female friend in my life over here. I've got plenty of female friends back home, but they all want to talk about Kyle and my "healing journey". They don't want to hear that I'm still lost after all these months.

Edo shrugs. "If you insist."

"I insist," I tell him. "You've done enough taking care of me. Plus, I'll get to know my new friend... Cass."

"Exactly," Cass says. "Jodi... I think we can become wonderful friends. We can swap stories about Edo."

"There are no stories about Edo," he chimes in. "Because Edo is an incredible friend and a better bartender."

"Shoo," Cass says. "I can handle things from here."

Edo doesn't quite walk off, but he checks his phone and begins texting furiously to plan his next move.

"It's the last time they have DJ Fat Camel playing here. We'll dance, drink and later, I'll take you home, yes?"

"That sounds good to me."

"Well, you have my number if Cass abandons you on the top of a Ferris wheel," Edo says as he swipes four times quickly across his screen and then shoves his phone into his pocket.

Cass rolls her eyes. "I have done nothing of the sort. Get out of here, you big drama queen."

"Ciao!"

Cass and I say "Ciao!"

Edo walks down the cobblestone streets and lights a cigarette before disappearing around the corner. Cass breathes a sigh of relief and turns to me.

"I just think you're perfect," she says.

Weird comment to make, but I mumble a gracious thank you, assuming something got lost in translation.

"Do you have friends with you?" Cass asks, taking out a hand mirror and fixing her bright red lipstick.

"No. I'm here solo tripping. Had a quarter life crisis and... here I am."

"Do you like Italy?" she asks genuinely. Her eyes are so intense.

"It's beautiful."

"Not as pretty as Greece," Cass says. "But I agree. Shall we go in?"

"We should head to the back of the line," I say, my stomach knotting as I see the line stretched around the block. I hope we can even get into the club.

Cass grins, unperturbed by the growing line outside Jalousie.

"My cousin owns the place. Come on, we go in through the back."

Before I can protest, she takes my hand and we walk around a back alley that smells like trash, vomit and again — cigarettes. Cass drags me over to a door and surveys me once before touching the handle.

"Very proper outfit. Excellent. Let's go. Ready to dance?"

I nod, even if I'm nervous. Sure, I'm trying to have an adventure tonight, but I just met this chick. How do I know she isn't crazy? Well, she has Edo's backing, so at least she'll be a good time. Edo definitely knows how to have fun if his clubbing stories are even 55% true.

Cass punches in a six-digit code and the back door to the club opens. I can smell the club before I hear the music and Cass drags me in through the back before I can second guess myself. What am I really doing? I don't know this chick at all and I agreed to go clubbing with her? Is Edo's word really enough?

Once we're in the back door, a man appears. He's tall, with dark brown slicked back hair, tattoos all over his arms and grey eyes. He has broad shoulders, but is otherwise lean and very muscular. He's handsome, but it's too bad he smokes. I can smell the cigarettes from a distance.

"Cass? What the fuck are you doing here?" he asks, seeming genuinely upset.

"Shut the fuck up, Enzo," Cass snaps, her expression changing suddenly into a disapproving scowl. "I have business here."

The man smirks. He's around Cass' height, but he looks… greasy.

"Is that her?"

"Mind your fucking business."

Cass pushes him hard so we can get past him. The grey-eyed man's eyes land on me and he runs his hand over his jawline before snickering.

"He's going to kill you."

"Shut up," Cass snarls. Enzo laughs and raises his hands in defeat.

"Enjoy your night," he says to me in a sing-song voice. For the first time, I feel real hesitation. But Cass grabs my hand and drags me inside of the club.

Cass drags me all the way to the tables and chairs surrounding the dance floor, chatting excitedly and peppering me with questions about America. I struggle to understand her accent at first, but then I get into the rhythm of her voice and it's easier for us to communicate.

I have to listen in so hard that I barely scan the room we enter. At least the nightclub has a nice interior, and it doesn't seem like any ghetto shit might pop off. Another Edo exaggeration, it seems. I relax as Cass sets me up at a small, two-person table.

"I'll get you a drink. Wait here. If anyone comes to talk to you, tell them you are with Cass Pagonis. That will shut them up."

Before I can protest, or offer to come with her, Cass disappears. Shit. I guess I have to wait here. I already have five texts from Edo about the hotties he met at the club a few doors over. Damn, he moves quick. I've been here for weeks already and I still haven't met a heterosexual male who hasn't been an incredibly old and excessively horny man offering for me to be his 'African prostitute' — offers I have obviously declined.

Cass returns quickly, before I have any time to worry with two shots, each one with some blue flavoring at the bottom.

"Okay, Jodi. This is to a long and beautiful friendship between us, starting with one crazy night, yeah?"

I nod. "Hell yeah. I've never done anything like this before."

I blurt out the last part nervously, but Cass has a way of soothing me. She just smiles and nods. "Don't be scared! I'm a good Greek girl. Now come on… we'll take the shots together."

She counts us down.

"1… 2… 3…"

I take the shot — and it's the last thing I remember about that night.

Click here to keep reading:
https://bit.ly/amalficoast1

Extremely Important Links

ALL BOOKS BY JAMILA JASPER
https://linktr.ee/JamilaJasper
SIGN UP FOR EMAIL UPDATES
Bit.ly/jamilajasperromance
SOCIAL MEDIA LINKS
https://www.jamilajasperromance.com/
GET MERCH
https://www.redbubble.com/people/jamilajasper/shop
GET FREEBIE (VIA TEXT)
https://slkt.io/qMk8
READ SERIAL (NEW CHAPTERS WEEKLY)
www.patreon.com/jamilajasper

JAMILA JASPER

Diverse Romance For Black Women

More Jamila Jasper Romance

<u>Pick your poison…</u>

Delicious interracial romance novels for all tastes. Long novels, short stories, audiobooks and more.

Hit the link to experience my full catalog.

FULL CATALOG BY JAMILA JASPER:
https://linktr.ee/JamilaJasper

Thank You Kindly

Thank you to all my readers, new and old for your support with this new year.

I look forward to making 2022 an INCREDIBLE year for interracial romance novels. I want to thank you all for joining along on the journey.

Thank you to my most supportive readers:

Cortney, Yolanda S., MonaGirl, Dianna, Mary, Nysha, Fayola, Ty, Shyra, Andi-Mariee, Keisha, Jennett, Fredericka, Candece, Lydia, Sabrina, JM, Jackie, Mo, Ashaunte, Tolu, Lori, Dionne, ZLB, Nicol, Elbert, Jesi, Brenda, Desiree, LaShan, Only1ToniD, Debbie, Tiffanie, Shawnte, Lisema, Christine, Trinity, Monica, Juliette, Letetia, Margaret, Dash, Maxine, Sheron, Javonda, Pearl, Kiana, Shyan, Jacklyn, Amy, Julia, Colleen, Natasha, Yvonne, Brittany, June, Ashleigh, Nene, Nene, Deborah, Nikki, DeShaunda, Latoya, Shelite, Arlene, Judith, Mary, Shanida, Rachel,Damzel, Ahnjala, Kenya, Momo, BJ, Akeshia, Melissa, Tiffany, Sherbear, Nini, Curtresa, Regina, Ashley, Mia, Sydney, Sharon, Charlotte, Assiatu, Regina, Romanda, Catherine, Gaynor, BF, Tasha, Henri, Sara, skkent, Rosalyn, Danielle, Deborah, Kirsten, Ana, Taylor, Charlene Louanna, Michelle, Tamika, Lauren, RoHyde, Natasha, Shekynah, Cassie, Dreama, Nick, Gennifer, Rayna, Jaleda, Kimvodkna, Jatonn, Anoushka, Audrey, Valeria, Courtney, Donna, Jenetha, Ayana, Kristy, FreyaJo, Grace, Kisha, Stephanie E., Amber, Denice, Marty, LaKisha, Latoya, Natasha, Monifa, Alisa, Daveena, Desiree, Gerry,

Kimberly, Stephanie M., Tarah, Yolanda, Kristy, Gary, Janet, Kathy, Phyllis, Susan

<u>Join the Patreon Community.</u>
www.patreon.com/jamilajasper

Patreon

Instantly access all six seasons of *Unfuckable* (Ben & Libby's story) with 375 chapters.

For a small monthly fee, you get exclusive access to my all this & my recently completed serial Despicable (275 chapters)

www.patreon.com/jamilajasper

Patreon has more than the ongoing serial and previous serial releases…

⚡ INSTANT ACCESS ⚡

- NEW merchandise tiers with **t-shirts, totes, mugs,** stickers and MORE!
- **FREE paperback** with all new tiers
- **FREE short story audiobooks** and audiobook samples when they're ready
- #FirstDraftLeaks of Prologues and first chapters **weeks** before I hit publish
- Behind the scenes notes
- Polls and story contribution
- Comments & LIVELY community discussion with likeminded interracial romance readers.

**LEARN MORE ABOUT SUPPORTING A
DIVERSE ROMANCE AUTHOR**
www.patreon.com/jamilajasper

www.ingramcontent.com/pod-product-compliance
Lightning Source LLC
Chambersburg PA
CBHW070505160726

48003CB00004B/1434